Possessed BY YOU

BY

J.M. WALKER

Possessed by You
Copyright 2014, J.M. Walker

ISBN-10: 1499730055
ISBN-13: 978-1499730050

Dedication

This book is dedicated to a very special person who shone a light on my life for many years. She was my go to person for when I needed to brainstorm. She always listened, even if she had no idea what I was talking about. Brenda Smith Travis, you will forever be missed. This book is for you and for your love of Brett MacLean. You helped me shape him. I will never forget the day you told me that he didn't have a tattoo. You were adamant and refused for him to have ink on his body. You would be the only person, besides Evvie Neal, that he would listen to. Thank you for all that you did for me and for your constant support and encouragement. I will never forget you. Miss you Mama Hen. xx

Possessed by You

To everyone out there who just needed that extra push when it came to loving...deep.

Possessed by You

Acknowledgements

First off, I wouldn't be where I am today without the support from all of you. You're my rock, my light, my constant encouragement to keep going and trudging on. Thank you to everyone for your support and never ending encouragement. Words cannot describe how much you all mean to me.

Thank you to my family and friends for constantly supporting me in my journey of writing. I wouldn't be where I am without each and every one of you.

My husband, Michael, for always being there for me and for giving me that extra push and for challenging me. I love you.

To my book club, you all are amazing and special to me. I'm so thankful to have gotten to know you throughout the years.

Chrissy (C.A. Szarek), thank you for the fantastic blurbs and for the constant support, bestie. I love you!

My team of awesomeness:

My girls. My Jems. You know who you are and your constant support is appreciated and I have no words to describe how much you mean to me.

My beta readers, Amee and Karen. I love you girls like sisters. Thank you for being honest with my work and for helping me make it better.

My CP, Susie, you freaking rock my socks. Thank YOU for telling me straight up how it is and for helping me make this story better.

Brenda Wright, my very patient editor. Thank you for everything!! And thank you for helping me with "your" Brett. ;)

To all the blogs out there. There are just too many to name but I love each and every one of you. You all have helped me in your own way and for that, I thank you.

Twinsie Talk Book Reviews, you girls are my sisters and I couldn't do this or the pimpage without you. Thank you for everything for always hosting my tours and for just being you.

Once Upon a Time Covers: Thank you again for the beautiful and sexy cover!

To my readers! Thank you so much for your patience and for joining me on this journey. I hope you enjoy this book as much as much as I enjoyed writing it. I love each and every one of you. Without you, this would not be possible.

Possessed by You Playlist

Here is a list of songs that reminded me of Brett and Evvie, either together or apart. I hope you enjoy them as much as I do. Even if you don't like the music, the words are what captured me and brought me into their world.

A deep and powerful love is never quiet, never dormant but loud and fierce. ~ J.M. Walker

Bound to You – Christina Aguilera, Burlesque Soundtrack
Radioactive – Imagine Dragons
Unconditionally – Katy Perry
This is the Best – USS
Pour Some Sugar On Me – Deaf Leppard
Stay – Rihanna ft. Mikky Ekko
What Now – Rihanna
Adore You – Miley Cyrus
Wrecking Ball – Miley Cyrus
Loving Me 4 Me – Christina Aguilera
Give Me a Reason – Pink ft. Nate Ruess
Try – Pink
I Am – Christina Aguilera
Mirrors – Justin Timberlake
Demons – Imagine Dragons
Say Something – A Great Big World ft. Christina Aguilera

Possessed by You

Warning
Due to the graphic and adult content, this book is not suitable for a younger reading audience

Possessed by You

One

"WHAT THE hell do you think you're doing here, Evvie?"

My back stiffened as I turned to the familiar but harsh deep voice of my best friend and roommate. Kane Stohl glared at me, his pale eyes hardening as they lowered to the bottles in my arms before meeting my gaze.

I shook my head. "What?"

"Why are you here?" He took the crate from my grasp.

I sighed. "I told you I was looking for a job and this place needed a bartender so here I am."

Kane narrowed his eyes and placed his hands on his hips. "What the hell do you know about bartending?"

A giggle escaped my lips. He didn't look so big and tough when he stood in that prissy stance.

He glared.

I bit back a smile and calmed myself before I burst. "I used to make drinks at the parties in college, remember? It's not that hard."

His blue eyes softened, his broad shoulders relaxing. "Does your father know that you're working here?"

My gaze snapped to his and I swallowed hard. "No and he's not going to find out now is he?"

Kane rolled his eyes and scrubbed a hand down his face. "Who hired you?"

I moved to the counter and continued putting bottles away and shrugged. He was not ruining this for me. "What does it matter?"

"Evvie, who hired you?" he pressed.

I sighed and rose to my full height. "Jake. He was very nice. Said the owner needed some extra help around here now that business has picked up."

Kane raised an eyebrow. "Did you actually meet the owner?"

I frowned. "No. He's on vacation or something."

"Brett doesn't take vacations," Kane laughed.

"I dunno. I haven't met him yet though," I huffed.

"I'm going to have to talk to Jake," he mumbled.

I turned to him and placed a hand on his arm. "Kane, don't you dare mess this up for me. I need this job."

"Darlin', there are a million other jobs—"

"What's wrong with this one?" I asked, placing my hands on my hips. "My father won't know I work here."

"What about your brothers?"

My stomach churned. The overprotective men in my life didn't need to know my every waking move.

"You don't know the kind of douches that come in here..."

My heart swelled and I wrapped my arms around his middle. "Kane, you're my best friend and I love you like a brother but sometimes you're a pain in the ass."

"Who the hell are *you*?"

We jumped apart at the hard voice as I saw a tall man approaching us with ease. The air around us became thick as confidence bled from the guy's pores.

His light brown hair was cut short. My fingers twitched, wanting to run them through the no doubt soft strands.

Our gazes locked and he smirked, making my stomach flip. Oh this guy was dangerous and I had no idea who the hell he was.

He crossed his arms under his chest and glared at me with deep blue eyes. God, he was gorgeous.

"I asked you a question."

My heart stuttered and I frowned. "I…I'm…"

Kane cleared his throat but the guy ignored him and took a step closer to us.

"Speak up," he snapped.

Wow...okay... I lifted my chin and took a deep breath. "I'm Evvie Neal. The new bartender."

The guy's gaze flicked to Kane's and he shrugged. *Thanks a lot, bestie.*

"Who the fuck hired you?" the man asked.

My blood boiled at the tone this guy was taking with me. Who the hell did he think he was? "I don't know what your problem is asshole but—"

"Welcome to *The Red Love,* baby." The guy smirked and with that he walked away.

14

I gaped. "Who—" My mouth opened and closed and I couldn't form the words on my tongue.

Kane clapped a hand on my shoulder. "Ignore him."

"Who the hell was that?"

Kane looked away. "That, darlin', was Brett MacLean."

My eyes widened. Brett's tailored suit hugged curves of a hard body. My stomach twisted at the unexpected flush that ran over me completely. "The owner?" I whispered.

Kane nodded.

I had heard that he had become an asshole but had no idea that he was that bad. Maybe my choice of working there was not a good thing after all.

***

AS I wiped the bar down, the hairs on the back of my neck tingled. I knew Brett was watching me. I had been working at *The Red Love* for weeks, not talking to him again really since the first time we had met. I tried to stay clear of him, which was hard to do since he was the boss. He got under my skin and he damn well knew it too.

The way he studied me and his dominating air, left me shaking with need. I tried to deny it but a deep rooted part of myself wanted him. A darker part. A part that had laid dormant. It left me breathless that a man could actually make me feel this way even when they were being a dick.

I wanted to experience what a night with Brett MacLean would be like. Women paraded in and out of his office on a revolving door. Beautiful models that were slender with silky legs that stretched well over my five-foot-nothing head.

He ran his business like he did his women. With control.

My body hummed and I wanted him to appease the ache that had slowly formed in my belly but I wouldn't let *him* know it. He was dangerous and he would probably break my heart without even thinking twice about it.

"Evvie," Brett barked.

I took a deep breath and turned around, leaning against the counter. "What?"

His blue eyes darkened, boring into mine. "My office. Now."

I ignored the way my heart fluttered at the demand in his deep voice and rolled my eyes before turning my back to him. "I'm busy."

"It wasn't a request," he snapped. "Jake take over."

I gaped at Brett over my shoulder as I watched him walk away. His black tailored suit fitting the hard contours of a body that I would love to sink my teeth—

"Evvie."

The sound of Jake's deep voice behind me made me jump and I took a breath, easing my racing heart. I smiled up at him. His perfectly arched brows furrowing as his eyes darted around the room.

"Don't keep him waiting," he said, chewing his bottom lip.

I looked into Jake's warm brown gaze and sighed. He was probably right. I patted his arm reassuringly. "I'll go see what the *Master* wants."

I walked through the dance floor and down the long hall. I had learned very quickly that most people who came back from Brett's office, unless they were one of his whores, didn't come back happy. He was a hard ass who loved his job. It was a part of him. Anyone with a pair of eyes and a brain could see that.

Once reaching his office, I took a deep breath and knocked, my nerves kicking into overdrive.

"Come in."

My skin tingled unexpectedly and I opened the door. Two black leather couches sat in the middle of the office with a table in the center.

The door shut behind me making me startle and I leaned against it. My gaze instantly meeting Brett's, my stomach flipped at the heated stare behind his blue eyes.

His big body sat behind an even larger cherry oak desk. He leaned forward and rubbed his chin, his dark navy eyes boring into mine. He motioned to the chair in front of his desk. "Sit."

"Brett, why—"

"Sit."

16

I huffed and crossed my arms under my chest but didn't move. I wasn't his pawn to do with as he pleased. "Not until you tell me what you want."

The corners of his mouth turned up as he sat back in his chair. "We'll get to that."

My body heated under his scrutiny. Suddenly feeling exposed in the tiny uniform, I tried covering the cleavage that sported from the vee of my shirt. The red and black plaid skirt barely covered my ass. Curvy girls like me were doomed in these stick-like uniforms.

"Look, if you're not going to tell me what you want, then I should get back to work," I croaked.

"I want to talk to you about your job performance."

"My job performance?" I frowned.

He raised an eye brow. "Are you going to sit?"

"No."

He smirked, making my heart skip a beat. "Didn't think so."

"What the hell's wrong with my job performance?" I cringed. *He's your boss, Evvie. Be nice.*

He rose to his feet and walked around the large desk and leaned against it, mirroring my pose. He nodded at the chair. "Sit."

Finally giving in, I huffed and pushed off the door, walking to the chair. I slumped down on the arm and crossed my legs, sighing loudly. "Will you please tell me what you want?"

His eyes roamed down my body, stopping at my feet. The corners of his lips lifted.

I followed his gaze and looked back up at him. "What?" My red flats weren't standard uniform attire but they were easier to walk in than the fuck-me shoes the other girls wore.

He smiled. An actual smile on Brett McLean's face. I would have made a smart ass remark about it too if I didn't feel like I was sitting in the hot seat.

"Now Evvie, I don't think those shoes are appropriate work attire," he chided.

My back stiffened. "Have you tried walking back and forth behind the bar in six inch stilettos?"

He didn't respond. Just continued to stare at me. God, he was infuriating.

17

I let out an exasperated breath while twitching in the chair. "Fine. I'll get new ones. Are we done?"

His jaw tensed. "No, we're not."

It was my turn to raise an eyebrow. "Brett, you obviously didn't bring me here to talk about my shoes. What's wrong with my job performance?"

"Nothing."

I shook my head. "Then why—"

"I have a proposition for you," his voice lowered.

"Um…what kind of proposition?" My palms went clammy as my heart thumped hard.

He smirked. "I think you know."

I shook my head.

He closed the distance between us and wrapped his hands around my wrists, pinning them to the arms of the chair.

My mouth went dry and my core clenched at being restrained by him. *Oh God, this was not good.*

Brett leaned in, his hot breath scorching my neck. The scent of musky cologne invaded my nostrils, making my mouth water.

His lips grazed my ear before he bit down gently. "I want to fuck you, Evvie."

Two

I GASPED. He wanted...*oh God.*

My mouth opened and closed but words wouldn't form on my tongue. I was frozen, captivated by his smug stare as he continued to breathe hard against my neck.

I licked my lips. "Me?"

He grinned and ran his hands up my arms, sending goose bumps along my skin. His fingers, although gentle, were strong, letting me know that there was no way I was leaving anytime soon.

He brushed his nose along my neck, inhaling deep. "You've never had a man tell you they want to fuck you, Evvie?"

I swallowed. "Not...like that."

He grazed his teeth along my jaw line making my lips tingle. God, I wanted him to kiss me, to devour my mouth until I couldn't breathe.

"Evvie?" He lifted his head and looked down at me, his beautiful eyes filling with a level of lust I had never seen before. No man had ever straight out told me what he wanted from me. The honesty from Brett, although overwhelming, was kind of refreshing also.

"Why?"

He frowned. "I want to show you what it's like to be with a real man."

I bit my bottom lip. "I...I've been with men."

He smiled, looking down at my mouth. "Did they make you scream their name?"

My breath caught. "Um..."

He leaned back down to my neck and licked over my ear lobe. "Give you orgasm after orgasm, Evvie?"

"Brett," I breathed.

"Did they?" Brett gripped the back of the chair and looked down at me.

"Does it matter?" I whispered.

"It does. Every woman should experience hours of raw passion at least once in their life."

My eyes searched his face and my breath caught.

He smiled.

My skin tingled, every muscle tensing at holding back from diving into his arms. I wasn't experienced when it came to sex but I knew that Brett could teach me things. Unleash a part of myself that I had never seen.

His gaze roamed down my body, the short skirt barely stopping mid-thigh. The tight black V-neck t-shirt sporting cleavage making him lick his lips like he wanted to ravish me.

Brett ran his thumb up the side of my neck, sending a shiver down my body. "Are you single?"

I frowned. "Brett."

"Answer me," he demanded.

I swallowed. "Why?"

He smirked and leaned towards me, his mouth mere inches from mine. "I need to know what's stopping me before I fuck you, Evvie."

"Who says you can, even if I am single?"

His eyes darkened and he ran a thumb over my bottom lip, sending a jolt of electricity straight to my groin. "Answer. Me."

I looked down at his mouth and met his gaze. "I'm single."

He trailed a finger along my jaw. "Good. Then I don't see what the problem is."

"I'm not going to be one of your sluts, Brett."

His jaw tensed and he pinched my chin before looking down at my mouth. "I don't want you to be one of my sluts. But after one night with me, I guarantee that you'll be begging me for more."

A laugh escaped my lips. "Confident much, aren't you?"

He breathed against my mouth. Even though we weren't touching yet, the air crackled between us. The current so strong, it took my breath away.

"I know what I want, Evvie."

I crossed my arms under my chest and lifted my chin. "Yeah and what's that?"

In a quick move he grabbed my hands, lifting me to my feet. He held my wrists in one hand and pushed me up against the desk.

20

My breath came out in short gasps as he pressed his erection between my legs. He ran a hand up the back of my leg, reaching under my skirt and squeezed my ass. I moaned at the rough touch of his hands on me. *More.*

"I want *you*, Evvie," he growled.

I panted and pulled my hands from his grip before placing them on his chest. "Brett."

He brushed his lips along my jaw to my chin. "And I *will* have you."

"Like hell you will," I said, pushing him. I didn't want him to stop but he was my boss. *Get your head together, Evvie.*

Brett lifted his head, his deep blue eyes boring into mine. "You playing hard to get?"

I scoffed and tried shoving out of his grip. "No. But you're my boss, Brett."

His hold on me tightened as he ground his hips into mine. "I know you want me."

Did I ever. My body burned with a need so strong, it took control of me. "You're a smug…"

"I'm a smug what, Evvie?" He ran his nose up the side of my neck and inhaled.

My eyes fluttered as he ground his hips against me. A soft moan escaped my lips before I pushed out of his grasp and walked around him.

I continued walking away from him and shook myself, needing to get ahead of my raging hormones. "I don't think it's a good—"

I gasped when I was tackled from behind and landed on the couch with an oof. Warm hands rolled me onto my back when a heavy body covered mine.

I stared up into the darkest ocean blue depths that I had ever seen.

Brett's eyes flashed with hunger and ran his hand up my thigh, leaning down to my ear. "I enjoy the way your muscles jump under my touch."

I grabbed onto his shirt and gasped when he pushed his pelvis into mine. The bulge in his pants pressed into my core and I involuntarily spread my legs wider for him. *My traitorous, needy hips.*

A smug grin formed on his handsome face as he ground into me. "Do you feel how much I want you, Evvie?"

Oh God. I moaned. "Brett."

Brett nipped gently along my jaw to my chin. "Tell me to stop and I will."

I didn't want him to stop. I bit back a gasp as his lower body continued torturing me. The way my skin hummed for him while wearing clothes made me want to find out what it would be like with no barriers. No clothes. Just skin against skin. I wanted to dive into him, wrap myself around him and fuck him until we were both exhausted, spent and sore.

Liquid heat pooled in my panties as a fire burned through my body. God, this man was dangerous. One touch from him and I threw all caution to the wind.

I took a deep breath and cupped his face. A flutter of hesitation soared through my belly and before I could let it stop me, knowing that this was it and there was no turning back, I pulled his mouth over mine. As soon as our lips touched, it was like an explosion went off inside of me.

A deep guttural growl erupted from his chest as his lips pressed hard against mine.

I opened to him. Inhaling his hot breath as it soared deep into my lungs.

The taste of liquor mixed with the velvety softness of his tongue, travelled through me, sending my senses into overdrive. I curled my hands around his nape and pulled him to me, deepening the kiss.

He groaned, making my stomach flip.

I grabbed his shirt, undoing the buttons as fast as my fumbling fingers would allow. I needed to feel him. To feel if his body was as hard as the rest of him.

I pulled the tails out of his pants and ran my hands inside his shirt. His hard smooth muscles twitched under my touch as I brushed my fingers down his chiselled torso.

Brett released my mouth and grabbed the hem of my shirt. I lifted my arms as he pulled it over my head. His eyes roamed over the full mounds of my breasts, his kiss-swollen lips parting.

My chest rose and fell as I watched him trail a finger from my belly button up to between my breasts. With a flick of his

22

fingers, he unclasped my red lace bra, leaving me exposed before him.

Brett licked his lips as he ran a thumb over my dark pink nipple.

I arched under him, the soft caress sending jolts of electricity to my groin.

He leaned down and sucked my bottom lip and pinched the peak.

I cried out, my pussy pulsing unexpectedly at the delicious pain that soon morphed into pleasure.

Brett licked back into my mouth, sucking my tongue. Massaging. Kneading. *Owning.*

I grabbed onto his shoulders and moaned as his hands roamed over my naked torso.

He nipped my tongue gently before releasing me, trailing kisses down my neck to my collar bone.

My pale breast was the color of milk compared to his darker hand, tanned and forceful.

He looked up at me and a wicked smile spread on his face. He revealed his teeth and grazed them over my nipple making me jump.

An unexpected tingle ran straight to my clit making me hiss. I never thought that I would be making out with him. In his office. On his couch. To have his hands all over me was satisfying. But knowing that he wanted me as bad as I wanted him wasn't enough.

He covered the nipple completely, pulling it into his mouth as he flicked the nub with his tongue.

Our gazes locked as he licked the hard peak. My groin throbbed at the rough impact and my body arched under him as he sucked harder. Brett released me with a pop and rubbed his thumb over the darkened areola.

I panted, my skin buzzing at the soft caress.

He leaned down to my ear. "You have perfect tits, Evvie."

I turned my head, giving him access to my neck as he breathed against my skin.

"Perfect enough to fuck."

My eyes widened at his words. Images of him thrusting his cock between my breasts made my mouth salivate.

"Would you like that, Evvie?" he purred against my neck.

"I…" No man had ever suggested such a thing. "I don't know."

"I think you would." He covered my mouth again and drove his tongue between my lips.

I moaned as they danced and dueled, fighting for control. I jumped when his fingers brushed my inner thigh and inched higher. My core throbbed. Never needing sex so bad in my life, I lifted my hips. Hinting. I wanted him. Right then.

His finger pushed under the fabric of my thin lace panties and grazed over my opening. It caressed, teased before diving deeper.

I gasped when his finger thrust into me. My thoughts were scattered as he continued pleasuring my lower body. My hips moved in tune with his hand when a second finger entered my core, stretching me. "Brett."

My body hummed, begging for him to go faster when he removed his hand from between my legs. I whimpered.

He released my mouth and stuck his fingers between his lips, licking them.

My breath hitched at the sight.

His eyes darkened as he swallowed before looking down at me. "I will definitely enjoy eating your pussy."

My heart raced at the erotic image.

He grinned. "So how about that proposition?"

I licked my lips and looked down at the large bulge in his pants. I smiled. "Maybe I should proposition you instead."

He smirked and ran his hands up my hips. "I bet before the week is out, I'll have you begging me for my cock."

I brushed a finger down his insanely hard six-pack. I wanted to nip and lick every single inch of him but I wouldn't beg. "Well, I—"

A heavy knock on the door sounded around the room.

Brett grabbed my hand from his chest, kissed my knuckles and placed our joined hands between us. "Come in."

My eyes widened.

Brett winked at me and looked over the back of the couch. "What's up?"

"Sorry, boss. That dick, Mathis is here to see you again."

24

My stomach dropped. *Kane. Oh please don't see me.*

Brett nodded. "Thanks. Give me a few."

"Take all the time you need, my man."

My cheeks heated at the amusement in my best friend's voice. If he knew it was me that Brett was with, he wouldn't have taken it so well.

Brett looked down at me, his eyes blazing. He ran a thumb over my kiss swollen lips. "Oh, I plan on it."

My throat went dry.

The sound of the door closing brought me back to reality. I couldn't believe I almost had sex with my boss. *Nice move, Evvie.*

I snapped my bra back into place and sat up. "Brett, I don't think this should happen again."

Brett rose from between my legs and casually walked back to the desk while buttoning up his shirt. "You can think that all you want."

I huffed, sat on the edge of the couch and pulled my shirt back on. "This can't go any further."

"Yes it can." Brett placed his cell phone in his pocket and looked up at me. "And it will."

"I—"

"If Kane wouldn't have interrupted us, would you have let me fuck you?" He took a step towards me.

My heart thudded at his question. I swallowed hard. Yes, I would have but that was before my best friend walked in. I stood up from the couch and smoothed down my skirt.

He smirked, rolling up the sleeves of his white dress shirt to his elbows. "I will have you, Evvie Neal. Beneath me. Shaking. Screaming my name."

I backed up until I hit the door as he closed the distance between us. "I am not having sex with you."

Brett placed his hands on either side of my head and captured my mouth in his. He slowly licked between my lips, igniting a moan from the back of my throat. All too soon he released me and ran his thumb over my lips. "I like seeing your lips swollen by me."

"Brett," I breathed.

He smirked and pinched my chin, tilting my head. "By the end of the week, Evvie, you *will* beg me."

"I—"

He pushed me up against the door, his erection pressing into my lower belly. "And your hot pussy will be mine."

Three

AFTER LEAVING Brett's office, my body shook, aching with a need that took over my very being. My core throbbed, pulsing for him. Needing to feel his fingers inside of me again. *More.*

The dominating way he took control of my body set my skin on fire. I was drawn to him. He was dark, dangerous, everything my father and brothers told me not to date. And that made me want him even more. But I wasn't going to be used. It would be on *my* terms.

No matter how controlling Brett was, if I did give in, it would be only after I made him work for it.

I neared the end of the hall and took a breath. As I walked back to the bar, I glanced around me. Could anyone notice that I just had the life kissed out of me?

The hairs on the back of my neck tingled and I looked up, watching Brett talk to Kane.

Brett looked at me and even though the lights were dim, I could see the twinkle in his eyes. The hunger and lust for more.

The magnetic pull that I felt from him made my heart skip a beat every time.

"Hey Ev. You okay?"

I looked up at Jake as he finished serving a customer a drink and nodded. "Yup."

"What did he want?" he asked, grabbing a bottle of beer.

"Just to talk about my job performance." And to kiss the hell out of me. *You kissed him first, Evvie.* My stomach twisted. Oh God, I did.

Jake frowned. "What about it?"

I sighed and patted his arm when a large man stepped into my view.

His tall demeanor was overpowering as his cold gray eyes bored into me. His black tailored suit fitted to his lean but no doubt hard body gave off a dominating air. "Miss? Come with me."

I scoffed. "Yeah. Right."

The man didn't say anything, his dark eyes boring into mine.

I swallowed, the tiny hairs on my body tingling and my stomach clenching under his scrutiny.

"Evvie?" Jake grabbed my arm, holding it tight as the man continued to stare at me.

My back stiffened and I noticed Brett look our way, frowning. A man was sitting with him in one of the private booths at the back of the club. Even though they were several feet away, I could sense an uncomfortable moment between the two.

I looked back at the large man in front of me. "What do you want?"

"My boss," he indicated the guy sitting with Brett. "wants a word with you."

I removed my arm from Jake's grasp and smiled up at him reassuringly. "It's fine, Jake." I frowned at the man and headed towards Brett. He had moved to get up, noticed me and then looked back at the other guy.

I glowered at the man sitting across from him. His dark hair slicked back perfectly, his groomed brows narrowing over dark eyes that stared into me.

As I approached him, he sat back, making room for me.

"Sit," the other man demanded.

I raised an eyebrow and crossed my arms under my chest. "Are you going to order drinks?"

The man smirked and rubbed his chin. "I said, sit."

I huffed. "If you're not going to order drinks, then I'm heading back to work." I turned around and bumped into the larger man from before.

His brown eyes darkened and he motioned for me to turn around. *Shit.*

I glared at him and slid into the booth beside Brett. I took a breath and tilted my chin. "What the hell is going on?"

The guy smirked. "What's your name, beautiful?"

My back bristled at the underlying tone of smugness coming from this guy. "Why?"

He looked between the two of us, his gray eyes darkening in warning.

28

Brett sighed. "Answer the question."

I huffed. Like hell. "Who are *you*?"

"Mathis Verlinden. At your service of *any* needs."

I shifted in the seat, swallowing hard when a rumble erupted from Brett. *Did he just growl?*

"Now. *Your* name."

"Evvie Neal," I whispered.

"Evvie Neal." His accent rolling over my name, made my stomach cringe.

Mathis sat forward. "Daughter to retired cop, Edward Neal. Sister to Evan, Everett and Ethan. Your mother, Sara Neal, passed away, didn't she, Evvie?

I bit back a gasp, ringing my hands together in my lap. "Why bother asking my name if you already know who I am?"

Mathis smirked. "Am I right?"

Brett grabbed my hand, my heart racing at the small contact and the revelation of Mathis' words and what he knew. Words froze on my tongue and all I could do was nod.

"Your daddy has been a bad boy, though, hasn't he?"

My breath hitched. "He had a hard life. He had four kids to take care of." I didn't know why I was explaining myself to him but no matter what poor choices my father made, I loved him. Everything I had was because of him.

Mathis nodded. "He was desperate."

My body tensed. "What the hell do you want and how do you know so much about me?"

He made a point of lowering his gaze to my chest before looking back up at my eyes. "I've done my research."

"Mathis," Brett grumbled.

Mathis raised an eyebrow at Brett and looked back at me. "Your mother passed away from a stroke when you were twelve."

"Who—"

"Am I right?"

Tears burned my eyes at the memories of losing my mom to such a horrible disease. Slow healing wounds being torn open by a man who I knew nothing about.

I looked down at Brett rubbing his thumb over the back of my hand, that small touch sending strength into my body to deal with the asshole across the table.

Mathis smirked. "You live with a man."

Brett stiffened beside me and Mathis caught his movement. He winked before looking back at me. "But you're single."

I shook my head, not understanding why any of this information was important. "Do you get off on trying to make people uncomfortable, or is it merely a hobby?"

Mathis' eyes darkened and then a grin broke out on his face. His strong jaw relaxing. "I can tell that you've lived with just men most of your life. You've got balls, beautiful."

I rolled my eyes. "I need to get back to work."

"Oh darling. You will learn very quickly that things get done on my time." Mathis handed Brett a business card. "How would your daddy feel about you working in a place like this wearing a uniform like that?"

My stomach sunk. "Like you give a shit what my father thinks. Or of my reputation."

Mathis laughed. "You're gorgeous but you're not a good liar." He looked at Brett. "You *will* contact me."

Brett glared at him. "Fuck. You."

Mathis smiled. "Sorry, I only like pussy."

"Listen you motherfu—"

"No," Mathis landed a heavy fist on the table, making the glass ash tray jump. "You listen to me, Brett. You *will* contact me."

"How the hell do you know that?"

He sneered. "Money talks." Mathis rose from his spot in the booth and followed his large beast of a bodyguard out of the club.

Brett scrubbed a hand down his face and turned to me. "Are you alright?"

I looked up at him and sighed. "Three brothers and an overprotective father. It takes a lot more than that for a man to scare me."

Brett smiled and rubbed his thumb over the back of my hand. "But?"

I chewed my bottom lip, watching his thumb. That small touch sending an electric shiver down my spine. The need to touch him grew as each second passed. "Who the hell was that guy?"

"Don't you watch the news?"

I scoffed. "I live with a guy remember? All I watch is sports."

Brett frowned. "Who's the guy?"

"My roommate. Why do you care, Brett?" I moved to get out of the booth when he grabbed my arm, pulling me against him.

My breath caught as he held me tight, running his thumbs up and down my soft skin. The spicy scent of cologne mixed with the fresh smell of soap, filled my nostrils making my body stir. God, he smelled good. "Brett, people can see us."

Brett smiled. He reached up and pressed a button on the wall, the red satin curtains closing half way.

My eyes widened as the small area darkened. "Brett, what do you think you're doing?"

He ran a finger down my arm and brushed his nose along my nape, inhaling deep.

My eyes fluttered closed. "I need to get back to work."

"You will, Evvie."

"Why are you doing this?" I arched against him as he kissed my neck.

"I told you."

I huffed. "I'm not having sex with you here."

Brett looked around the small booth and cleared his throat.

I looked up at him and frowned. "You were thinking about it, weren't you?"

He cupped the back of my neck and brushed his lips along mine.

My lips parted, spreading for him.

His body tensed, holding back as he brushed a thumb over my bottom lip. He smiled and leaned down to my ear. "When I fuck you, Evvie, it will be in private." He nipped my ear lobe. "The first time at least."

My breath hitched. The thought of having sex with Brett in a bed, let alone in public, made my inhibitions fly out the window. Almost. "As much as I would love to take you up on that offer," I patted his arm. "I'm not interested."

His eyes flashed with hunger. "You know, Mathis was right about two things."

I raised an eyebrow. This should be good. "Oh?"

He grabbed my wrist and in a quick move, pulled me onto his lap. "You are beautiful."

I gasped as the heavy bulge in his pants pressed against my core sending a thrill down my back. "Brett."

He ran a finger down my neck to the vee in my shirt. "But you fucking suck at lying."

I glared at him and tried pushing out of his grasp. "I have to get back to work."

His hold tightened, restraining me. My core clenched at not being able to move. *Oh dear God.* "You won't get in trouble. I'm the boss, remember?"

I grabbed his hand from between my breasts. "People might get suspicious."

"So?" Brett placed his hands on my legs and ran them up under my skirt.

I huffed and stopped his hands from going any higher, my skin tingling from his rough caress. "Stop. I'm not having sex—"

Brett reached around me and gripped my pony tail, pulling my head back. I gasped at the sharp tug, my sex pulsing.

"We are not having sex here," he growled in my ear.

"Brett," I placed my hands on his shoulders, gripping them tight as he brushed his mouth along my jawline. My self-control was slowly dwindling as the seconds ticked by. Every time he touched me, I became more and more attracted to him.

"As much as I want to rip off those sexy as hell panties and dive into that hot cunt of yours," he bit my chin making me yelp. "you *will* beg first."

My core throbbed at words no man had ever said to me. My ex-lovers, if you even wanted to call them that, were selfish but the dirty talk they used were not as erotic as Brett's.

I swallowed, licking my dry lips. "I'm not begging."

"Maybe not now."

I jumped as his hand moved to my center, cupping my mound. "I can feel the heat coming off of you, Evvie."

I panted, curling my fingers at his nape. "I…"

He smirked, smoothing small circles over my clit. "What?"

The words were on my lips but I couldn't say them. I didn't want to admit defeat but my body ached in a way I never experienced before. I needed him on a level I never thought was possible. A dark part of me wanted everything I could get from him. "Brett, I want—"

Brett covered my mouth, diving his tongue between my lips.

My stomach fluttered, my lips tingling at the rough impact. I tugged his head back, deepening the kiss.

Brett growled and cupped my ass, lifting me to my knees. He massaged and kneaded my flesh, running his hands under my panties.

I moaned, pushing against his lips. I felt the sense of control being pulled from me as his tongue penetrated my mouth and his hands caressed my lower body.

His fingers moved to my hips and I felt a tug as the laced fabric was ripped off of me.

I released his mouth, my chest rising and falling. I looked down at the fabric in his hand and watched as he lifted the red lace to his nose. He inhaled, his eyes darkening.

My pussy pulsed at the sight.

Brett placed the panties in his pocket and smirked. "I can smell how much your body wants me."

Oh God. "My body doesn't know what it's thinking."

He chuckled and hooked a hand in the vee of my shirt, pulling me against him. He ran a hand up my inner thigh.

I closed my eyes, biting my bottom lip, as I waited.

"Look at me," he demanded.

My gaze met his. A shiver ran down my spine as he caressed the soft skin between my thigh and center.

"One night."

"I really don't think…"

His finger grazed over my opening, making me whimper.

"Stop thinking. Just feel. I know you're curious."

I shook my head. "I've had sex before. I have no reason to be curious." I gasped when he thrust a finger into me and stopped. My body quaked around him, begging him to move.

"You haven't had sex with me, Evvie," his voice lowered on a growl.

No, I haven't. "Brett, I don't think…" I moaned as he started pumping his finger in me.

"You think too much, Evvie. I just want one night. That's it. No rules. No commitments."

I panted. My skin humming as he continued thrusting his finger into me at a painfully slow rate.

"One night of pure, raw, hot, messy…" he purred each word, making my body heat like the words were caressing my skin themselves.

"…sex," he breathed in my ear.

"If…if I say no?"

"Evvie," he pulled my head back and thrust two fingers into me at a quick rough pace.

I cried out as a tingle spread through my center.

"You won't say no."

I licked my lips and moved my hips in time with his fingers. "How…how can you be so sure?"

A smug grin spread on his gorgeous face as he pushed his fingers into me as deep as they would go.

A breathless gasp escaped my lips. Oh…wow. My body burned, throbbing as he continued to finger me in the booth. No man had ever made me feel so good from just his fingers.

Brett lowered me to the bench and covered my mouth with his as he slowly pumped his fingers into me.

I moved my hips in tune with his hand as it sped up at a frantic rate. The beat of the music flew around us, making my heart jump. We were in public. One swipe of the curtain and people would see us making out in the booth.

The thought of getting caught sent a thrill down my spine as he continued pleasing my lower body.

The deep thrusts of his fingers drove into me with a fervor I never felt before. This man was losing control. He acted all cool. Calm. Collected. But he was as desperate for me as I was for him.

Brett released my mouth and trailed kissed down to my ear. "Your pussy is nice and slick, Evvie."

I panted, rocking my hips back and forth.

34

"You wanna come?"

My stomach flipped. "Oh God, yes. Please."

Brett growled and ran his thumb over my clit, pressing the hardened nub.

I whimpered as electricity shot through my body at the soft contact.

"You like that?" he purred, flicking the erect peak.

I panted and nodded. "Brett."

"Feel my fingers fuck you, Evvie," he breathed against my neck.

My core clenched, needing more than his fingers. I bit my bottom lip as the pad of his thumb pushed against my clit, sending a tremor of ecstasy exploding through me. I cried out, my body shaking through the release.

His fingers slowed before removing from me completely, my body whimpering at the loss. *More.*

The tingle that was spreading through me, simmered to a dull roar as I panted at the unexpected emptiness.

A smug smile formed on Brett's face as he licked his fingers free of my juices. He looked down at my lap. "I cannot wait to smother my face between those milky white thighs of yours."

My stomach flipped. The way he talked about sex so casually left me breathless. Maybe I was in over my head but God did I ever want him. I wanted him to teach me. Show me what he liked. I wanted...sex. "Brett?"

He smirked. "What's wrong, Evvie?"

My body buzzed as blood rang in my ears. "I...you..."

His eyes twinkled with mischief. "What?"

He was going to make me beg. The realization hit me, my jaw clenching. I sat up and crossed my arms under my chest. "You're an asshole."

A deep booming laugh erupted from him as he brushed the hair off my nape and ran a hand up my inner thigh. "I told you. By the end of the week, you will beg me."

I smiled and took a breath, reaching into his lap. My gaze locked with his as I cupped the bulge in his pants, squeezing the thick length. My mouth watered at the feel of him through the fabric. I bit back the feeling of losing control. He wanted to play, I was game.

His eyes darkened as I rose to my knees, rubbing the heavy bulge in his black dress pants. "Do you like the feel of my cock beneath your hand, Evvie?"

I licked his bottom lip. "By the end of the week, *you* will be begging me, Brett."

He cupped my ass, pulling me against him. "I enjoy the confidence you have, Evvie, but I don't beg. For anything. Especially not sex."

I ran my thumb over the tip of his rigid penis, smirking when he bucked under me. "No?"

Brett's features hardened, a malicious smile forming on his face. "Oh Evvie, I am so going to enjoy making you beg to be fucked."

My breath hitched at the rough edge of his voice. "How do you know I'll beg?"

He winked. "You just begged me to let you come."

My heart fluttered. He was right. *Shit.*

He grabbed the vee of my shirt, making my stomach jump as he tugged me against him. He licked up my ear lobe, sending tingles racing down my back at the soft contact. "You will beg."

"I don't beg for anything. Especially not sex," I smirked.

Brett chuckled, his hot breath scorching my skin.

"Boss?"

I jumped at the unexpected deep voice and pulled out of Brett's embrace when the curtain opened, revealing Kane.

Kane's pale blue eyes widened. "Sorry. I didn't realize you weren't alone."

Brett grabbed my hand. "No worries, my man."

Kane looked between the both of us, his gaze landing on mine. "You all right, Ev?"

I smiled. I just had the best orgasm of my life. "Yes."

The hard lines in his face relaxed at my admission and he nodded once, before closing the curtain.

I breathed a sigh of relief and pulled my hand out of Brett's hold.

"He cares for you."

"He's my best friend."

36

"He wants more."

I rolled my eyes and turned to him. "He's like one of my brothers. And just as overprotective."

Brett cupped the back of my neck, running his thumb up and down the side, sending shivers over my skin. "Oh, I know."

I huffed. "Did he threaten you?"

Brett smiled. "He tried to."

My belly churned. What was it with the men in my life trying to control my every move? "I swear...wait. Does he know about..." I motioned between us.

Brett's eyes twinkled. "Does he know about what, Evvie?"

I swallowed as his voice lowered. "Us?"

His blue gaze bored into mine as he ran a thumb over my bottom lip. "Is there an *us*?"

"Well I didn't think so, but..."

Brett trailed a finger down my arm. "But what?"

Goose bumps spread on my skin as he reached for my hand. "I refuse to be one of your whores, Brett."

"You won't be, but I want you for one night. No commitments, Evvie."

I bit my bottom lip. "Just one night?"

He winked. "For now."

I watched as he curled his hand in mine, linking our fingers together. "Take me on a date first." I regretted the words as soon as they left my lips when Brett stiffened beside me. I pulled out of his grasp and moved to leave the booth when a heavy arm wrapped around my middle.

"You want to go on a date with me, Evvie?"

My eyes fluttered closed as his hot breath warmed my neck. "Do you want to sleep with me, Brett?"

"No."

My eyes shot open. "You said—"

His grip on my arm tightened. "I want to fuck you, Evvie. All night. There will be no sleep."

I looked up at him. "Then go on a date with me."

"People will see us," he said, a teasing lilt to his voice.

I licked my lips. "Does that bother you?"

Brett ran his thumb over my mouth. "Does it bother *you*?"

I grabbed his hand and nibbled his thumb as it passed over my lips. I smirked as his nostrils flared. "Friday night. Pick me up at eight."

Four

BRETT MACLEAN didn't do dates. I didn't know what had happened but rumors were that he got hurt and sworn off relationships altogether.

He curled his hand around the back of my neck. "Evvie," he purred.

My lips parted, my pink tongue peeking out. I licked my bottom lip as I let out a breath. With a shaky hand, I cupped his cheek, running my thumb over his bottom lip. Just that soft caress made my blood hum.

His dark eyes bored into mine, watching me. In a quick move, he covered my mouth in a bruising kiss, diving deep inside me. A growl erupted from the back of his throat as he devoured my mouth.

"Does it make you wet?" he asked, placing a hand on my knee. He inched it under my skirt, making my breath catch.

"Does what make me wet?" I breathed.

He bit my chin. "Does it make you wet knowing that soon I'll be spending the night between your legs?"

My heart jumped and a moan escaped my lips as he licked his way back into my mouth. God, I couldn't get enough of the sweet velvet of his tongue. I pushed against his, rubbing, devouring as I tried to take control. My stomach flipped. I would never been in control.

He squeezed my inner thigh and placed a soft kiss on my lips before releasing me.

I sighed. My eyes were heavy from unadulterated lust for the man sitting beside me.

"You're so beautiful."

My cheeks heated. "I should go."

He nodded and brought my hand up to his lips, placing a soft kiss on my knuckles. "I'll text you."

I watched his mouth caress my skin. "You don't have my number."

"It's in your work file," he replied, brushing a thumb over the back of my hand.

I smiled. "Checking up on me?"

Brett smirked, wrapped a hand around my wrist, and leaned down to my ear. "I like knowing who calls me an asshole," he breathed against my neck.

I laughed.

He lifted my hand to his lips. "Until Friday night, Evvie."

My mouth parted as he placed another soft kiss on my knuckles, before releasing me once again. As soon as he let me go, my body hummed, needing to touch him again.

Brett frowned and cleared his throat.

"Bye Brett," I husked and pulled the curtains open. My back stiffened when I saw my brother standing in front of me.

I stared up into big blue eyes that matched our father's. Big, blue and surrounded by long blonde lashes.

Evan's strong jaw twitched as he looked over my shoulder. "What the hell are you doing here, Evvie?"

I rose to my full height and looked up at my oldest brother's cold stare. "I work here."

His eyes snapped to mine. "Does Dad know?"

I scoffed. Our father wasn't around. I loved him but he never made time for his kids anymore so he wouldn't even notice if I joined a nunnery. "He won't care."

Evan raised a blonde eyebrow. "He's been asking about you."

I sighed and smoothed a hand over my skirt. "I'll go see him soon."

"Everything alright here?" Brett asked from behind me.

The back of my neck prickled as his smooth voice relaxed my tense shoulders.

"Who the hell are you?" Evan glared.

"He's my boss. Be nice." I said, smacking his arm.

My brother ignored me and took a step towards Brett. "Fraternizing with the staff, Brett MacLean?"

I gaped at him as Brett came up beside me. He placed a hand at the small of my back, the light touch sending shivers down my body. My stomach flipped. I didn't know Brett that well but I knew that he wouldn't want whatever the thing was between us to be public. Him touching me in front of people, seemed odd for him.

A smug smile formed on his handsome face. "You know who I am."

Evan's brows narrowed. "And I know your reputation."

I frowned. "Evan, stop."

Brett chuckled. "Enjoy yourself, Evan. Drinks are on me."

Evan rolled his eyes. "What are you doing in one of your private booths with my sister?"

My cheeks heated and I took a step towards Evan, placing a hand on his arm. "Come to the bar. I'll make you a drink."

He shoved out of my grip. "Answer the question, Brett."

I huffed. "Evan—"

Brett crossed his arms under his chest. "Nothing she didn't consent to."

The next moment happened fast as Evan charged past me. A fist flew across Brett's jaw, bringing a snarling Kane around the corner.

"Evan, stop." I grabbed his arm and pushed him. "What the hell do you think you're doing?"

The veins in Evan's neck jutted out as he took another step towards Brett.

"Evan." Kane hooked an arm around his shoulder, stopping him.

I shook my head at my brother's aggravating protection that I didn't need. I looked up at Brett.

He was rubbing his jaw, a slight smile on his face.

I rolled my eyes.

Men.

Five

"EVAN, I can handle myself," I huffed, storming down the hall to the storage room.

"Evvie, do you know anything about the man you work for?" he asked, pushing the door marked *Storage* open for me. He rubbed his red knuckles.

I rolled my eyes and headed into the cool room. "I don't care as long as he signs my checks." I did care. I wanted to learn more. I wanted to find out everything about him and that scared the shit out of me.

Yeah, Brett had women come and go but one night with him might do me some good. Satisfy the hunger that had set up permanent residence in my belly since being hired at *The Red Love* weeks ago. Or make the ache worse.

After Evan clocked him one, Brett had the kitchen make him whatever he wanted. Even if it wasn't on the menu, he demanded his cook to please Evan's appetite. If only mine could be pleased. My body heated at the thought that only one man could please that desire. The fast orgasm he'd given me was not enough.

Knowing Brett's short temper, I was surprised he didn't kick Evan out.

"Evvie."

I cleared my throat and looked over my shoulder at Evan, ignoring the heat that had crawled up the back of my neck. I carried the crate of beer bottles to the back of the room and turned to my brother. "What?"

"Are you sleeping with him?"

My eyes widened, my blood boiling at his accusation. "Not that it's any of your damn business who I sleep with, Evan, but no." Not yet at least.

He sighed and shoved a hand through his short blonde hair. "I'm just looking out for you. With Dad..."

I closed the distance between us and wrapped my arms around his middle. He returned the embrace, running a hand over my head.

"I'm sorry, Evvie. I know it's none of my business but I know guys like Brett—"

"Stop." I pulled out of his grip. "What I do on my own time is my business."

"Just be careful."

I rolled my eyes and pushed him out of the small room. "Evan, I am always careful."

"Good. I'd hate to have to kick your boss' ass if anything were to happen. Or better yet, I'll have Ethan kick his ass."

My stomach dropped. "You wouldn't dare."

Evan shrugged and leaned against the wall. He rubbed his chin, his blue eyes boring into mine.

I searched his face for signs that he was bluffing. Being in a family of men, I was taught at a young age how to deceive one's father but my brothers were so good at it, that I couldn't even tell if they were joking. "Evan."

He grinned and pushed off the wall, taking a step towards me. "I just want you happy, sis. If that means that we have to bash in a few guys' heads, so be it."

I huffed, biting back a grin. "I hate you."

He chuckled and pulled me into an embrace.

I sighed and wrapped my arms around his middle. After a moment, the hairs on my body tingled. I looked up, my gaze instantly meeting Brett's. His eyes warmed, the corners of his lips turning up.

My nerves tingled as Evan released me.

"You free this weekend?"

"Hmm?"

Brett smirked and walked away making me wish that I could follow him. The way my body reacted to him was a shock. No man had ever made me feel the way he did from just one touch.

"Evvie?"

I looked up at my brother, my cheeks heating. "Sorry. What?"

His eyebrow rose. "You seem distracted."

I bit back a scoff. Distracted wasn't the word I would have chosen.

Possessed by You

***

THE CROWD cheered as I threw the martini shaker into the air and caught it behind my back. Jake laughed, shaking his head as he lit a drink on fire. Blue flames erupted from the small tumbler before he covered it with another tumbler and handed it to a customer.

"I think we have too much time on our hands," I yelled over the music.

Jake's dark eyes twinkled as he poured beer into a mug. "Maybe but keep going. Your man is watching you."

I frowned and looked over my shoulder to find Tatiana and Brett standing at the end of the hall to his office.

The little hairs on my body tingled as Brett's gaze bored into mine. Even though we were several feet apart, I could feel him touching me. Caressing me with his rough needy hands like he was desperate for me. Friday could not get here soon enough.

Tatiana smiled and gave a little wave before heading towards us. My phone vibrated in my pocket and I pulled it out.

I love watching you move those hips to the beat of the music. B

My stomach flipped and I looked up. Brett was gone. I glanced around the vast room but couldn't find him anywhere when my phone vibrated again.

Looking for me, lover?

I was. My body heated at the new nickname from him. My thumb flashed across the pads on my phone. *I'm not your lover.*

You will be.

I wanted to be. For more than one night though? I wasn't sure. I couldn't compete with all of the other women in his life. His whores.

My phone vibrated and I looked down.

Stop thinking so much.

I smiled.

That's better.

I laughed and shook my head, putting my phone back in my pocket.

"What's so funny, Ev?"

I looked up at Jake, my cheeks heating. "Nothing."

44

He grinned. "Ready for round two?" he asked, handing me a martini shaker.

I nodded and took a step back when the hairs on my nape tingled. I looked behind me and found Brett standing against the wall a few feet away. He rubbed his mouth making me instantly look at his lips. Lips that had been on mine only an hour before.

Friday couldn't come quick enough.

Six

THE ALLURING red dress hugged my curves. I smoothed the soft satin down the front of my body as I stood in front of the mirror.

It was Friday night. I couldn't believe how fast the last two days had come and gone.

I didn't see Brett at all since I caught him watching Jake and I do our fancy tricks with the drinks. The tips poured in that night thanks to Jake's obsession with a prominent actor who'd played a bartender in a movie.

I smiled to myself. This was it. It was date night with Brett. Brett MacLean. A world class ass at times. The only time he had ever shown an inkling of a sweet side was when he walked in on my embrace with my brother. I hoped tonight would show more sweet sides of Brett.

I puckered my mouth and ran the pale gloss over my lips. My blonde hair was pulled into a low messy bun and my makeup was minimal. I didn't want Brett thinking I was trying too hard. Not doing this for him, I was going to go and have a good time, hopefully enjoy some good company and see where things took us. If I happened to end up in his bed…my skin bloomed.

Oh God, what the hell is wrong with me?

A ding sounded from my phone, making me jump. My heart gave a start and I huffed, picking up the phone.

Wear red and no panties. B.

My stomach fluttered. *And if I don't?* I smiled and pressed send. My phone buzzed a moment later.

Don't test me, lover.

I laughed. I placed my phone on my dresser and turned in the mirror. The snug blood red dress hugged my curves, enhancing my figure. The built in bra lifted my breasts, showcasing cleavage that would hopefully distract my date. He may have thought he was in control but the bag was mine this time. I reached under my dress and pulled off the black lace thong, a shiver running down my back. No panties in public for the first time.

My phone dinged again as I threw the panties in the hamper. *Meet me downstairs.*

I frowned. *Why?*

We'll never leave your apartment if I come up there.

My heart thumped and I took a deep breath, placing my phone on my dresser. I touched up my lips and left the apartment, grateful that Kane was nowhere around to interrogate me. I got that enough from Evan.

I took the elevator to the main floor and ran my hands down my dress. Maybe it was too much? I should have grabbed a cardigan.

When the doors opened, I took a deep breath and walked right into a hard body. I gasped, my hands landing on a chiseled chest covered by a black suit. I looked up into the dark blue depths that had invaded my thoughts for the past couple of nights.

Brett smirked and pushed me into the elevator as the doors closed. He pressed a button on the panel before pushing me up against the wall.

My breath caught as he pressed his pelvis against me. A hot shiver ran down my back as he cupped my ass. "Brett."

He leaned down, grazing my neck with his nose and inhaled. "You fucking smell good, lover."

The scent of musk and man invaded my nostrils making my core clench with need. I grabbed onto his suit jacket, pulling him against me. "Y-you smell good, too."

Brett ran his hand up under my dress, squeezing my flesh. "It makes me hard knowing that you listened to me," he breathed against my neck.

With shaky hands, I brushed my fingers down his chest and tilted my head, exposing my neck.

He took the hint and nibbled under my ear, pushing his hips against me. The slow tortuous movements made me pant. My heart thumped hard. Too many clothes. I wanted to feel him. Forget dinner. I wanted him now.

My pussy throbbed at the thick bulge pressing against my lower belly. I did that. I caused him to feel that way. A desire burned deep in my belly. I wanted to fuck him wild, leaving us sweaty and spent with passion.

47

Brett lifted his head, his deep sapphire eyes boring into mine, filling with a dark hunger I had never seen before.

Kiss me.

He smirked and ran his thumb over my bottom lips before placing a kiss on my forehead.

I sighed at the soft contact when the door dinged. Brett moved behind me as an elderly couple made their way into the enclosed space.

My heart pounded as we rode the elevator to the parking garage.

The older woman looked at me over her shoulder and winked before turning back around.

My cheeks heated.

Brett chuckled, his hot breath caressing my neck. He ran a hand down my arm, linking our fingers together as the doors opened.

The cool air wrapped around me, making me shiver. It eased the ache that had set up since I had kissed him a couple of nights before but it wasn't enough. *More.*

We walked up to a sleek black sedan and I frowned.

"What's wrong?"

I looked up at him. "I was expecting you to have a red sports car."

He smiled and winked at me while opening the passenger door. "I do have a sports car but it's not red."

"Oh," I said, stepping up beside him.

"Why?" Amusement danced in his eyes.

"You seem to like the color red."

His gaze roamed down my body, making my cheeks heat. "I do like the color red." He grabbed my chin and brushed his mouth along mine before placing a soft peck on my lips.

My heart fluttered.

He smirked and released me completely.

I sighed and slid into the passenger seat as Brett closed the door behind me. The scent of musk and a new car smell invaded my nostrils, making my nervous muscles relax.

I wiped my clammy hands on the skirt of my dress and tried pulling it down. I wished I would have chosen a longer dress. Maybe I should have worn pants or a snowsuit. Or at least a

48

cardigan. I sighed, swallowing past the dryness in my throat as Brett slid into the driver's seat.

I looked out the window and my heart gave a start when a warm hand landed on my inner thigh. "Nervous?"

I turned to him and scoffed. "No."

Brett leaned down to my ear. "You should be."

My eyes widened. *Oh Evvie, you are getting in way over your head.*

He squeezed my leg in reassurance. "Relax, Evvie. I don't bite," he said, winking.

I cleared my throat, the back of my neck heating. Images of him nibbling my skin rained full force in my mind. "I'm trying to relax."

"Do *I* make you nervous?" he asked, rubbing his thumb back and forth over my thigh.

I took a deep breath. "Yes."

He chuckled.

I smiled. "You weren't expecting me to answer honestly, were you?"

He looked down at me, his blue eyes twinkling. "No. Why do I make you nervous?" he purred.

My stomach flipped. "Your confidence is intimidating."

A smug smile formed on his face but he didn't respond.

I trailed a finger over the back of his hand. In the moonlight glow, I could make out his tanned skin against my pale form. He gripped my thigh like he was taking possession of me. My heart fluttered. Did I want him to?

Seven

"DID YOUR roommate ask who you were going out with tonight?"

I turned to Brett and leaned my head against the back of the seat. "No. He wasn't home."

Brett smiled. "That's because he's working."

My brows narrowed. "You knew all along that I lived with Kane, didn't you?"

He winked. "You two have the same address on your employee files."

"Jealous?" The moment the question left my lips, I bit my bottom lip.

His gaze met mine, heating with hunger. "Should I be?"

My tongue peaked out, licking my lips as my eyes bored into his. His hand on my thigh slid under my dress to my mound. I gasped, grabbing a hold of his wrist when he pushed a finger through my folds.

"Would it make you wet if I was jealous?" he husked.

I whimpered as he thrust a finger into me. Oh God, his fingers felt good. I closed my eyes and held his hand, spreading my legs.

"Beg."

I bit my bottom lip, spreading my legs wider.

Warmth radiated through my body as he leaned over to my ear. I opened my eyes, realizing that we were parked by the restaurant.

"Say. It." He pressed the pad of his thumb against my clit, making me cry out.

I moved my hips against his hand, biting back a whimper. I wouldn't beg. Not yet.

"I can feel your pussy clenching around my fingers, begging me for a release."

Oh God. I inhaled a gasp as he pushed his fingers deeper. "I'm begging now. Please."

A growl escaped his lips as he covered my mouth, plunging his tongue between my lips at the same time as he pumped two fingers into me.

I moaned, moving my hips against his hand.

The minty scent of his breath washed over me. I cupped the back of his neck and pulled him against me, turning my body towards his.

A deep growl erupted from the back of his throat as he fingered me at a frantic pace. Forget dinner. I didn't need a bed. The back seat of the car would do.

He pushed his fingers into me deep, making me buck against him. He released my mouth and looked down at me before glancing into the back seat.

"Please."

He looked back at me and pinched my chin before cupping the back of my neck. He tilted my head, holding it in place as he licked his way back into my mouth. Our tongues crashed and danced together. Each kiss getting hotter and more desperate.

I wasn't sure if we would make it to his place. Give me a wall or a floor and he could take me any way he wanted. My stomach clenched, those thoughts momentarily throwing me off.

His thumb rubbed over my clit, igniting a spark from within. I came fast and he devoured my cries of ecstasy.

His fingers slowed down and he released me, sitting back in his seat. Our gazes met as he stuck his fingers in his mouth, licking the juices clean.

My breath caught as he swallowed. "Brett?" I panted.

He turned to me and grabbed my hand before placing it on the bulge in his pants. My eyes widened. His long thick erection growing under my touch.

He leaned down to my ear and inhaled. "The next time you come, it'll be around my cock, lover."

I took a breath and squeezed him.

"And when I come," he grazed his thumb over my bottom lip. "it'll be between those plump lips of yours or," he looked down. "in that sweet pussy."

A moan escaped my mouth making him buck under my hand. "Brett," I breathed.

"Would you like that, Evvie?"

"Yes."

He kissed the corner of my lips and trailed the soft touches down my jaw. "I can't wait to wrap you around me, making you tremble beneath me as I take you hard."

His words caressed me like silk, touching my skin like they were made just for me. "Oh…God…"

He took a deep breath and kissed my forehead. "Let's go."

I frowned. "Brett."

"You need to eat."

"I'm not hungry."

He smirked and pinched my chin, placing a hard kiss on my lips. "I need you to have energy for the things I want to do to you."

***

I SLID into the booth of the small French restaurant as Brett sat beside me. The dim lighting gave off a warm romantic feeling. The glow of a candle on the table, flickered.

The view of the restaurant was hidden by the privacy of the booth.

Without even looking, he placed his hand on my knee like he was claiming me.

My heart stuttered. *Mine.*

"I need you to have energy for the things I want to do to you."

My skin buzzed and I placed a hand on top of his. I liked the look of his tanned skin against my pale form.

I let out a breath and sat back, scanning the vast area. Waiters milled about, serving customers.

A large crystal chandelier hung from the middle of the ceiling, glowing in the dim light of the restaurant.

"Here you go, *monsieur*." The waiter handed a wine menu to Brett and smiled at me. His brown eyes brightened as Brett scanned the items on the list.

I looked over his shoulder and frowned. Everything was written in French. I hoped Brett knew—

"Nous aimerions que votre meilleure bouteille de Vin rouge."

My eyes widened as the fluent French rolled off of Brett's tongue like it was second nature.

The waiter's eyes widened. *"Ah, vous parlez Française."*

Brett smiled. *"Juste un petit peu."*

The waiter nodded.

I looked back and forth between the two, not having any idea what they were talking about. Just listening to Brett communicate in another language made my stomach flip. Who knew it would be such a turn on? The way his deep voice rolled over the R's and enunciated every word and syllable, set my heart fluttering wildly.

"Suffisamment pour bien vous faire comprendre?"

Brett nodded. *"Oui."*

My body warmed at the conversation going on in front of me between Brett and the waiter. He was a man of many surprises and I had a feeling that I was going to learn more as the night went on.

"Elle est très jolie."

I looked up as the waiter glanced at me.

Brett turned to me and squeezed my thigh. He winked. *"Oui, elle l'est."*

"What did he say?" I whispered.

Brett pinched my chin. "He said that you're beautiful and I agreed."

My heart gave a start at his compliment. He had said that I was beautiful before but hearing him say it again while on our date, speaking the language of love, made me hopeful for more dates with him. *Oh shit.*

Brett's eyes twinkled and turned back to the waiter.

"C'est votre première sortie?"

Brett nodded. *"Oui."*

"Je vous amère votre bouteille de vin rouge, monsieur."

"Merci." Brett placed the menu in his hand.

The waiter smiled and walked away.

"Okay, really?"

Brett looked down at me and raised an eyebrow. "What?"

I shook my head. "You speak French?"

He caressed his fingers down my cheek before pinching my chin. "I speak enough to get by."

"Really?"

He smiled, his eyes glancing down at my lips. "Did you like that, lover?"

"It was sexy as hell," I blurted, my cheeks heating at my admission.

A cheesy grin spread on his face. It was so unnatural for him that it took my breath away. In that moment, he wasn't the uptight controlling Brett that I had come to know but laid back and relaxed. Was it me that did that to him?

He cleared his throat and looked away as the waiter approached the table, holding a bottle of wine.

Something had shifted between us as the minutes ticked by. A strong current of lust and mutual attraction soared in the air, crackling the more we spent time together.

The waiter poured a small amount of wine into a glass and handed it to him. *"Votre Vin, monsieur."*

Brett smiled and took a sip.

I watched as his strong jaw worked the wine around in his mouth before swallowing.

"Parfait."

The waiter's shoulders relaxed.

Brett turned to me. "Are you allergic to anything, Evvie?"

I shook my head.

He smiled and ordered our dinner.

I could listen to him speak for hours. His tongue rolling perfectly over the words. A tongue that had been in my mouth and on parts of my skin. *More.*

I shifted in my seat as my pussy clenched. A couple of hours from now and we would be at his apartment. Spending the night together. A part of me couldn't believe I had actually agreed. But a darker part of me wanted to experience Brett in every way possible. I wanted to find out what made him tick. What turned him on? I wanted him to teach me the ways of his body and my own. In the short amount of time together, I had already learned so much about myself, it was a little overwhelming.

"Lover?"

I met Brett's gaze. "Hmm?"

His eyes twinkled. "Thinking about me?"

54

My stomach flipped at his smugness. I cleared my throat and shrugged. Needing to distract myself, I grabbed a roll and broke it into pieces.

Brett poured some wine into my glass.

I took a breath and grabbed the glass of red liquid and brought it to my lips when it was gently snatched from my hand.

I frowned and watched him take a sip. His full lips turning up at the corners. I raised an eyebrow as he placed the glass back on the table and cupped my chin. His eyes darkened as he lowered his mouth to mine.

His soft lips electrified my brain, and then the warm fruity liquid flowed into my mouth. Followed by his sweet tongue massaging mine. I moaned and deepened the kiss.

His velvety tongue danced with mine as the taste of wine and man flooded my senses.

I grabbed onto his suit jacket and pulled him closer to me, my fingers itching to touch his skin.

The kiss ended all too soon when he pulled away, leaving me panting beside him.

Brett ran his thumb over my swollen lips and leaned down, licking my neck. "If you fuck as good as you kiss, lover…" he covered my mouth again, igniting a groan from us both.

The way he kissed, it was like he was making love to my mouth. No, Brett didn't make love. He fucked and I couldn't wait.

Eight

THE FOOD was delicious, but not nearly as mouth-watering as Brett.

This was it. Dinner was over and we were heading to his apartment.

My heart fluttered as a large building came into view. I couldn't believe the area of town that he lived in. Fancy boutiques lined the streets as the setting sun kissed the businesses before us.

Brett had done quite well for himself since buying *The Red Love*. From what I heard, he had made a name for himself all on his own.

After the very intense and hot kiss, we finished off our meal with friendly conversation. I had never seen that side of Brett. He wasn't a man of many words but he listened to me. I rambled on and on about my family and not once did he look bored. I had never been out with a man where he actually looked interested in what I was saying.

A cold shiver ran down my spine at the way my skin buzzed. *Don't get attached, Evvie.*

I sighed and wrapped his suit jacket tighter around myself. Brett's thumb moved slowly back and forth on my thigh. Something tugged at my heart. He had kept his hand on my leg the whole evening, even when supper arrived.

My stomach knotted. Maybe I was in over my head. Brett was a man who got what he wanted when he wanted it. Was I stupid that I gave in? *It's just sex, Evvie.*

The sound of the door opening and shutting made me jump. I looked around us and realized we were in a parking garage. I didn't even notice that we had parked. I huffed, needing to get my act together.

I turned and saw Brett walking around the car before casually leaning against it, waiting. For me. He crossed his arms under his chest, the white dress shirt stretching over a broad back. His black slacks hugged a perfect ass that I couldn't wait to see bare. He was gorgeous and distracting. An air of confidence oozed off of him, taking my breath away.

I swallowed. He was giving me an out. I wanted this. Just as bad as him, if not more.

I stepped out of the vehicle.

Brett shut the door and cupped the back of my neck, brushing his lips across my mouth. "After tonight, Evvie, you will beg me for more."

"You think so?" I teased.

His eyes flashed, the corners of his lips turning up as he leaned down to my ear. "What's your number?"

I swallowed. "My number?"

He kissed under my ear. "How many men have you had sex with?"

"Why do you want to know?"

He lifted his head and smirked. "Everything you think you know about sex, forget it."

My heart sped up, racing against my rib cage. "Okay…"

"I'm going to show you how a real man pleases his woman."

"I'm not yours," I mumbled.

In a quick move, he wrapped his hand around my neck and pushed me up against the car before leaning his face into mine. A hint of annoyance flashed in his gaze as they heated. "Tonight you are, lover."

My skin hummed and if we weren't in a parking garage, I would rip off his clothes and wrap myself around him until we were sweaty and spent from exhaustion.

I cleared my throat and stepped out of his embrace, needing some distance between us. The hairs on my body stood on end as Brett followed me to the elevator. Confusion coursed through me. I was his. For the night only.

I leaned against the wall as Brett pushed the button, the doors closing behind him.

He turned to me and mirrored my pose against the opposite wall. "How did you like the wine?" he asked with a smirk.

My cheeks heated and I licked my lips.

His eyes heated as they followed the movement.

My throat went dry at the casual but dominating way he leaned against the wall. A gleam passed through his eyes as they bored into mine.

We rode the elevator to the top floor in silence, little glances passing between us every so often.

The doors dinged a moment later, opening out into a large foyer. Brett grabbed my hand and kissed my knuckles before throwing an arm over my shoulder.

The musky scent of man and cologne filled my nostrils, making my loins quiver. With shaky hands, I wrapped the jacket tighter around me as we walked down the hall to his apartment.

By the time we reached the door at the end of the long hallway, my blood was ringing in my ears. Brett was a different level of man. Even when he was relaxed, he was controlling. Dominating.

He unlocked the door and moved behind me. "After you, lover," he whispered in my ear.

I let out a breath as I stepped into the open space of his apartment. He lived at the top of one of the most prestigious high-rises in the city.

A light flicked on, revealing black leather furniture circling a large dark wood coffee table that sat on a white shag rug. The place was modern but homey. A light cinnamon scent wafted into my nostrils, easing my tense body. Two orgasms from the sexiest man alive and I was addicted. Worse than a drug addict needing their fix.

My heels clicked as I walked into the foyer. My footsteps being the only sound. I looked over my shoulder and saw Brett standing still, watching me take in his home.

I pulled off my shoes, the ache in my feet seizing when I stepped onto the cool tiled floor.

The hairs on the back of my neck stood on end as I made my way into the vast living room. The large patio windows revealed the twinkling lights from the city below. The shine of the moon spread over the expanse of the room, drawing me forth.

A click sounded around me, making my heart jump. I took a deep breath and tugged off Brett's jacket, placing it on a black high backed chair as I walked up to the window.

My skin tingled as warm arms wrapped around my middle. My breath caught when a large bulge pressed against my ass.

Brett brushed the hair off my nape and kissed my neck, slowly easing the strap of my dress off my shoulder. "I've wanted you since the first day I saw you, lover."

My heart raced at the low husk of arousal in his voice. "I thought you were an asshole."

He chuckled and brushed his fingers over the full mounds of my breasts, pushing the second strap off my other shoulder. "You're so beautiful."

My heart caught in my throat and I pushed back against him. I could never get used to the feeling of him touching me, no matter how small the movement. He touched me like he was staking his claim. He didn't own me but I wanted him to own my body for the night.

Brett ran his hands down my arms and kissed my neck.

My stomach fluttered, the sexual tension rolling off of them in waves. I had never wanted a man as bad as I wanted Brett.

I took a deep breath and stepped out of his grasp, turning before him.

His eyebrow rose, his gaze roaming over my body.

My cheeks heated and before I could change my mind, I pushed the dress down to my hips, keeping my eyes locked with Brett's.

His nostrils flared as I pushed the dress down the rest of the way to my ankles, before kicking it to the side.

A cold draft circled me while I stood naked in front of him. My nipples peaked, goose bumps rising on my flesh. The way he was looking me over like he wanted to devour every inch of me, made me feel like the only thing that mattered was me.

Something flashed in his eyes and before I could even process what he was thinking, he was on me. Our mouths crashed, hands massaged and kneaded. Suddenly, I was pressed up against the cool glass window with Brett's hips grinding against mine. He lifted me, wrapping my legs around his hips as he circled his pelvis over my core.

Our tongues danced, dueled, fighting for control as I gripped his shirt. With a tug, I pulled it open, the buttons flying everywhere, pinging off the window before hitting the floor. He growled and pushed into me, making me gasp.

It was highly erotic the way he was fully clothed when I didn't have on an ounce.

He squeezed my ass and released my mouth, panting. "I intended to go slow."

I shook my head and started unbuckling his belt. "I need you fast."

Brett snarled and wrapped a hand around my neck, plunging his tongue between my lips. "I'm gonna fuck you good, lover."

I moaned at the way he took possession of my mouth while I struggled with getting his pants undone. My core clenched, aching for him. The thought that he would be inside of me at any moment set my skin on fire.

Brett reached between us and ripped open his fly, the sound of a tinfoil wrapper erupting around us.

I wrapped my hands around his nape, pulling him towards me, deepening the kiss when he lowered me onto him in a smooth move. I gasped, panting at the full feeling deep in my womb. He was finally inside of me. After all of this time.

Brett groaned before pulling out of me and slammed back into my waiting heat. "You're so tight, lover."

I whimpered, his hard cock reaching a spot inside of me that no man had ever been able to reach. His long thick length filled me, stretching me to the max. God, he was huge. The sharp pain quickly turned into pleasure as his thrusts lengthened and picked up speed.

"Brett...oh God."

He growled and licked into my mouth, the movements in tune with his hips. He reached under my knees, bringing them to my chest and pushed into me as deep as he could go.

I gasped, my body humming with the need for release when he stopped. I released his mouth and looked up into his heated gaze.

A wicked smile formed on his face.

I swallowed hard and ran my hands inside his shirt. His chiselled torso flexed and tensed with every thrust, so tantalizing I couldn't wait to nibble on his abs. "Please."

He licked my bottom lip. "Tell me."

Maybe it was the wine swirling around in my belly, making my mind fuzzy or the intoxicating way he was taking me. Either way I didn't want him to hold back. No holds barred. I wanted to experience *him*.

I grabbed his neck and pulled his head down, my mouth grazing his ear. "Fuck me hard, Brett. Don't hold back."

His hips sped up, slamming into me in hard deep thrusts as his mouth crashed to mine.

Whimpering and mewling sounds came from my lips as he fucked me against the patio doors.

He said he had wanted to take it slow but the tension that had built over the past few days made us snap.

Brett released my mouth, trailing kisses down my jaw. "I want to hear you come. To hear the sounds of passion escape your lips as I fuck an orgasm out of you."

"Oh. My. God." I scratched my nails into his shoulders as his thrusts turned harder, deeper.

He smirked. "Nah, it's just me, lover."

I would have giggled if I could've caught my breath.

He nibbled my neck, breathing hard against my skin as he drove deep between my thighs. He groaned as I clenched around him, my breathing picking up.

"That's it, lover. Come for me."

"Brett," I moaned.

"Scream loud." Brett pulled out and thrust back in hard at the same time as he bit my shoulder.

I screamed, shaking around him as his hips picked up speed. "Oh God."

He covered my mouth, swallowing the rest of my cries as my body shattered.

I looked up at him, my mouth parting with small bursts of air.

He smirked, gripping my waist. "Watch me."

I followed his gaze, watching his thick length move in and out of me, the juices from my center coating him.

"Watch my dick fuck your sweet pussy, lover." His length slid in and out of me in smooth moves, sending shivers down my body.

"Brett."

He pushed into me deep, making me gasp and slam my head back against the window.

A smug smile formed on his face. "Feel me."

I panted. "Oh God, I do. I feel you all through me."

He smirked and pulled out, driving back into me hard. "I've been waiting for this."

I wrapped my arms around his neck. "You have?"

He leaned down to my ear. "Yes, lover. The feel of your tight cunt wrapped around me has invaded my thoughts for weeks now."

My pussy pulsed. "Y-you thought of me?"

"Yes, Evvie," he responded as his hips sped up, driving slow and deep. He gripped my waist and brought us to the chaise, laying me gently on it.

The cool leather caressed my skin. My hands curled around his neck as he covered my mouth. He pulled out and slammed back into my core making me gasp. "Oh…my…"

"That's it, lover." His hips pumped faster, pushing me to the edge of the chaise.

I planted my feet on either side of him and lifted my ass, meeting him thrust for thrust.

Brett groaned, pushing into me deep.

My eyes rolled back into my head, a small moan escaping my lips.

He sat back on his heels and removed his shirt, throwing it on the floor.

I looked up at him and licked my lips, my eyes roaming over his torso.

He reached for my hands and pulled me to a sitting position, cupping the flesh of my ass in his hands.

I gasped, throwing my head back and circled my hips. The change in positions made my body open to him, taking him deeper. "Brett."

He gripped my hips and lifted me up and down on his cock, powering into me hard as I rode him. "Come for me, lover."

I groaned, digging my nails into his shoulders.

"That's it. Come around my cock, Evvie." He pumped into me as my pussy tightened, squeezing him.

I gasped, shaking against him.

62

"Scream. I want to hear my name between your lips." He drove into me, his hips speeding up, lengthening the cry of pleasure that left my lips.

"Oh God. Brett."

"Louder."

His name left my lips a second time as he pumped into me.

"My favorite sound." He groaned and crashed his lips to mine.

I smiled, opening my mouth to his, our tongues fighting for control. The sweet taste of the wine flowed into my senses, setting my skin on fire.

Brett released my mouth and trailed kisses down my neck to my breasts. The image of him pumping his cock between the two mounds, made my body hum.

He opened his mouth and took a hard nipple between his lips, flicking his tongue back and forth over the peak.

I moaned, gripping his shoulders tight.

He lifted me off of him and placed me on the chaise, rolling me onto my stomach. I looked up at him as he trailed a hand down the skin of my back. The soft touch made me realize I didn't want to leave in the morning. I wanted more than one night.

Shit.

Nine

BRETT HAD me pinned beneath him and in a smooth move, thrust back into me hard, knocking my breath away. "Take me, Evvie."

I moaned, arching my hips to the deep rough strokes of his cock. The extreme heat flowing through my blood set my skin on fire as he pounded into me.

He grunted, filling me completely.

"Brett."

He gripped the chaise and trailed kisses across my shoulder blades.

I held onto his wrist, spreading my legs. "Please."

He groaned, pushing into me as deep as he could, setting off an unexpected explosion deep inside my core.

I screamed and came undone around him, shaking through my release.

The long hard thrusts of his cock bottomed out deep inside of me. His thick length rubbed the bundle of nerves making me gasp. "I can't…no more."

"You can and you will." Brett bit my shoulder setting off a wave of ecstasy that slammed into me like a tidal wave.

His hips slowed and he covered my body with his own, his long cock twitching inside of me.

I sighed as he pulled out of me. "Brett?"

He rose from the chaise and pulled me to my feet, placing a hard kiss on my lips. "What's wrong?"

I stood on shaky legs and wrapped a hand around his rock hard cock, stroking it slowly.

He bucked against me, his breath leaving his lips on a gasp. "*Fuck.*"

I grinned and squeezed him making his gaze shoot to mine. I swallowed hard at the mischievous glint in them before he grabbed my neck.

"What do you think you're doing?" he asked, thrusting his cock in my hand.

I licked my lips. "Making you come."

He smirked and licked my bottom lip. "I don't fucking think so."

"Why not?"

He leaned down and bit my earlobe. "Because I'm going to come in your mouth."

A breath left me on a whoosh as he pulled out of my grasp.

Brett ran a thumb over my bottom lip, gripping my hair tight in his hand. "Have you given head before?"

I looked down at his large erection and shook my head.

He pinched my chin and placed a soft kiss on my lips. "I'm going to be your first."

My stomach flipped, my mouth watering at the image of him pumping between my lips.

Brett took a step back and removed the condom, throwing it in a wastebasket by the bookshelf. He slowly turned to me, his eyes darkening. "Kneel."

I swallowed at the hard dominating tone of his voice and lowered to my knees. My pussy, although satiated, clenched with desire for him.

I reached out to him and wrapped a hand around his thick length, squeezing lightly from base to tip. The soft pink head of his cock, glistened as pre-cum coated the pad of my thumb. My tongue peaked out, licking my bottom lip.

Brett held onto my head, fisting my hair as I lowered onto him. I opened my mouth wide, taking him in.

"Suck my cock, lover."

I closed my lips over the tip and with smooth, even strokes, I took him in. It was like taking shots of tequila as he reached the back of my throat.

"Fuck, lover. Your mouth feels good."

My heart leapt as I picked up speed with the strokes of my mouth and hand. Releasing him with a pop, I licked up the veiny ridge of the length before taking him back between my lips.

"I'm going to fuck your mouth, Evvie. Slap the chaise if it gets to be too much. If you don't, I'm going to go as fast and hard as I want. Understand?"

My stomach flipped and I nodded. I took a deep breath as the thrusts of his cock plunged into my mouth. My lips burned at being opened wide and when I looked into the blue eyes of Brett's heated gaze, my body relaxed, taking him deeper.

"Shit," he groaned as his grip on my hair tightened. "Evvie." My name left his lips on a growl when his cock pulsed in my mouth.

Salty cream coated my tongue, running down my throat as I swallowed his orgasm. I moaned around him, lapping up his release.

"Fuck. Me."

I released him and smiled, rising to my knees. I licked my lips, the essence of him making my taste buds hum.

Brett pinched my chin and placed a hard kiss on my swollen lips. "Every time I see your mouth, I'm going to picture fucking it."

I grinned and grabbed onto the waist band of his open pants. His semi hard cock jumped as I lightly brushed my fingers over it.

Our gazes locked and Brett smirked before kissing my forehead. "My little vixen."

My cheeks heated and I looked away.

"What's wrong, lover?" he teased.

I cleared my throat. "Nothing."

Brett ran a hand down my arm and brought my hand up to his mouth, lightly kissing my knuckles.

I met his gaze, my stomach flipping at the warmth. As we stood there staring at each other, the air crackled around us.

He backed away, releasing me and shoved a hand through his hair before walking down the hall.

I sighed at the strength of the walls that he put up around him, not letting anyone in if it made him vulnerable.

I watched him walk away. The hard contours of his back dipped into a tight ass hidden by his pants that I'd love to sink my nails into as he fucked me.

"Checking me out, lover?"

My chest tightened as he looked at me over his shoulder. I turned away and stretched out on the chaise, sighing as my muscles jumped and twitched under the small movements.

"No sleeping."

I jumped at the deep snarl in my ear. "I wasn't."

66

Brett chuckled. The sound of a crinkling tin foil wrapper erupted around us before he covered me with his body. He knelt between my legs, spreading them as his cock rested against my hip. "Yes you were, lover."

The tiny hairs on my skin hummed, my heart pounding in my ears at the feel of his growing erection. I couldn't believe he was ready to go again so soon.

"Did I wear you out?" he whispered, running a hand down the side of my body.

"No," I breathed.

He kissed my shoulder and lifted my hips before sliding back inside me.

I gasped, my throbbing pussy gripping around him. "Brett."

He nipped my ear, sending a hot jolt straight to my clit. "I told you that I was going to spend the night fucking you."

My core clenched, my skin blooming at his stamina. "I…" I licked my lips, panting as his thrusts turned slow, deep, heating me from the inside out.

"What, lover?" he asked, grabbing hold of my hands.

"I wasn't expecting it all night."

"You thought I would let you sleep after one time?" he teased.

"Yes."

"You feel how hard I am for you?" he asked, lifting my hips after a hard thrust.

I inhaled on a gasp and nodded.

He bit my shoulder blade. "I've wanted this for too long to let you go to sleep right now."

I moaned, spreading my legs wide, taking him deeper.

Brett drove into me fast, his pelvis hitting my ass after each rough impact. "Fuck, Evvie."

I smiled as his breathing picked up, sweat coating our skin.

"Get ready, lover."

I panted and licked my lips. "For what?"

"You're going to feel me for days."

***

MY BODY stirred and I groaned, my muscles sore as I moved. After the many times we had sex during the night, we both passed out from exhaustion. Our bodies entwined on Brett's large chaise gave me one of the best sleeps I ever had.

I lifted my head and my gaze landed on Brett. He was sitting on the couch, wearing red plaid pajama bottoms and nothing else.

"Good morning, lover," he purred.

The room around us glowed in the sunlight that streamed through the curtains. I smiled. "Morning."

His deep ocean blue eyes roamed down my naked body, heating my skin as if he were touching me himself.

"Something you want, Evvie?"

I licked my lips and shrugged. "Nah, I'm good."

His eyes twinkled. "Is that so?"

Brett rose to his feet and moved to the edge of the chaise, kneeling in front of it. My eyes widened when he grabbed my ankles.

I looked at him over my shoulder. "What are you doing?"

He rubbed small circles over the soles of my feet making me giggle. He smiled.

His gaze roamed down my naked body. He licked his lips.

My heart fluttered at his intense stare. Like he wanted to devour me completely.

He flipped me onto my back and leaned down, kissing my lower belly.

"Brett?" I breathed.

"I want to taste you," he said, kissing my hip bone.

My breath hitched. "I've never...no man has..."

Brett paused and looked up at me. "No man has ever gone down on you?"

My cheeks heated and I shook my head.

"I promise you'll enjoy this."

I chewed my bottom lip and nodded.

Brett smirked and trailed kisses over the top of my mound. He gripped my hips and pulled my ass to the edge of the chaise.

He rose to his knees and spread my legs, revealing me to him.

Our gazes locked and he kissed my inner thigh. "You have a beautiful pussy, Evvie."

My core clenched.

A smug smile formed on his lips.

"Brett?" My tongue peaked out and I licked my bottom lip. My brows furrowed.

"Relax and enjoy, lover," he bit out. He ran his thumbs over my folds and kissed the spot above my clit, inhaling deep.

My body hummed. "Don't hold back."

His eyes searched my face. "Are you sure?"

"Yes." I tilted my hips.

At that point, everything shifted. He growled and dove between my legs, covering my pussy with his mouth.

I cried out at the rough impact as he thrust his tongue into me.

Brett's eyes rolled into the back of his head.

He released me and spread the folds of my sex, revealing the dark pink nub of my clit. He flattened his tongue and ran it over the hard peak.

I whimpered and bucked against his face. In a quick move, he flicked it back and forth until I was writhing and shaking under him. I moaned.

He smiled and covered my clit between his lips, sucking and pulling as hard as he could.

"Oh...please."

He thrust two fingers into my heat, my core clenching around him. I cried out as he rubbed my G-spot, moving my hips with the licks of his tongue. "Oh. My. Brett."

He chuckled and grazed his teeth over my clit making me scream. His name left my lips as I came hard around him. The pleasure of ecstasy erupted in me so fast, spots danced in my vision.

In a quick move, he rose to his feet and pushed between my legs, thrusting his cock into me. He grunted, lengthening my orgasm as he plowed into me at a speed we both craved.

Brett grabbed under my knees, driving into me hard.

I tilted my head back and panted, clenching his shoulders. My pussy squeezed him in a tight grip as he set off another explosion inside of me.

I moaned under him, scratching my nails down his back as he covered my mouth. The sweet taste of the juices from my body coated my tongue making my body heat.

Brett pulled out of me and thrust back in hard, making me gasp. He smirked, our tongues dancing as we continued to move as one.

"Brett," I breathed.

"Come again for me, lover."

"I…" I panted when he pushed into me as deep as he could go. "I can't."

"Yes, you can and you will."

"Please."

Brett grabbed under my knees and pushed them up under my chest, his hips speeding up. He groaned. "I can feel your hot pussy squeezing around me."

I moaned. "God, you feel good."

A smug grin formed on his face. "Tell me."

I frowned. "What?"

He smirked and slowed his hips. "What do you want?"

"You."

He leaned down and sucked my bottom lip, igniting a groan from the back of my throat. "What else? I'll stop if you don't tell me."

I glared and dug my fingers into his arms. "You wouldn't."

He bit my chin. "Try me."

"Please."

"Tell. Me," he snarled in my ear.

"Make me come."

He growled and thrust his tongue between my lips at the same time as he pumped his cock into me hard.

"Brett," I screamed.

"Come for me."

I met him thrust for thrust as he drove home with a desperate need I felt to my soul.

Ten

BRETT'S BODY tensed. "Shit."

I frowned as he covered me with his warm, slick body. My racing heart slowed after the intense orgasm and I ran my hands down his strong back. "What's wrong?"

"I...fuck..." he breathed against my neck. His body continued to release into me as he cursed up a storm.

What the hell was his problem? I lifted his head but he pulled away, shutting his emotions down before my very eyes. "Brett."

He huffed, his cold gaze meeting mine. "I forgot a condom."

I swallowed hard. I hadn't even noticed. "I'm on the pill."

He shook his head. "Doesn't matter."

"Hey, it's not a big deal."

"It won't happen again," he bit out.

My heart ached. I wasn't sure if he meant the sex or the no condom as he rose from the chaise.

I sat up and watched him head down the hall, the sound of the door to the bathroom slamming shut behind him. He blamed me. My chest constricted, my body going numb.

My chin trembled unexpectedly, my knees weak with shame as I picked up my dress. My mind reeled with the possibility of what could come out of us having sex with no condom. It was every bit my fault as it was his. I was clean but did he use condoms with the other women he slept with?

After having the most amazing night with a guy I met a couple of weeks ago, my boss even and when I thought he was finally opening up, he closed off instantly.

I pulled on the dress, groaning when my muscles protested at the small movements. My body ached in places that hadn't been used in what felt like years and definitely not in a way like last night.

I trudged to the door and grabbed my shoes, stopping to look back at the vast bright living room.

I reached into my clutch for my cell when I realized I had left it at home. "Shit." I'd have to call Kane.

My gaze landed on Brett's cell that laid on the table. My stomach felt heavy with lead as I dialed my roommate's number and waited. *Stupid stupid stupid.*

"Boss, do you have any fucking idea what time it is?"

I cringed. Of course he would think Brett was calling him. "Brett?"

I swallowed hard. "Um…it's not Brett."

There was a pause. "Evvie?"

"Yeah," I croaked.

"What the hell are you doing at Brett's?"

I frowned and opened my mouth to respond when Brett came around the corner. His hair was slicked back and he wore a white t-shirt fitted to his hard torso. Light blue jeans hung low on his hips making my mouth water. God, he was even more gorgeous when he dressed casual.

"Evvie," Kane snapped in my ear.

"What?"

"What are you doing?"

"Having tea. What do you think, Kane?" I bit out. God, he was worse than my brothers.

"Shit, Ev, you have no idea what you're getting yourself into."

My heart lifted at the concern in his voice but I was a big girl. I could deal with men like Brett. He was an asshole. A smooth talker. Knew what he wanted and would do anything to get it and even though it went against my moral code, I gave in. Willingly.

I watched as Brett took a step towards me. His demeanor was still off, like he was pissed at me for the whole condom incident.

Brett grabbed the phone out of my hand and placed it to his ear. "Yup." He waited. "I'll drive her home."

My heart sped up as his deep blue eyes bored into mine. I reached for the phone but he took a step back.

"Give me the phone," I demanded.

"Don't worry, Kane." He winked. "She's in very good hands."

72

I huffed and punched him in the stomach playfully, forcing him to bend over. I yanked the phone out of his hand and placed it to my ear. "Pick me up, Kane." I disconnected the call and pulled open the door when a heavy hand slapped it shut.

My heart jumped as the scent of soap and man invaded my nostrils. Images of water running down his hard body, eased into my mind. What I wouldn't give to take a shower with him and lick off those droplets of liquid.

Hot breath landed on my neck as Brett brushed his nose up the side and inhaled. "I enjoy the smell of me on you, lover."

My jaw clenched. "Could have fooled me."

Brett ran a hand down my arm, sending goose bumps along with it. He pushed me up against the wall, digging his fingers into my shoulders. "I've never fucked a woman without a condom before."

I frowned. "So…"

He brushed a finger down the length of my jaw before placing his hands on either side of my head. He leaned down, his mouth mere inches from mine, his minty breath running over my lips. "The taste of you made me lose control."

I swallowed, frozen in place as his deep voice caressed my skin. "That's not my fault."

His eyes searched my face, his mouth grim.

"I should go," I whispered.

"Do you want to go?" he breathed against my lips. The electric current surrounding us was so strong that even though we weren't touching, the air crackled and buzzed as if we were.

"No."

A smug smile spread on his face. "What do you want to do?"

I took a breath, letting my gaze roam down the length of his body. Skin I had been all over the night before. One evening with him and I was doing new things. He tested me. Took me to the highest limits of pleasure I never knew existed. I wanted him in every way possible.

"Evvie?" His eyes twinkled.

"I want last night to happen again," I said on a quick breath.

He smirked. "I know."

I looked up at him and waited. The electric current in the air grew. It was like the universe had pulled us together, taking us both to places we had never been before.

"Lover."

I licked my lips, small bursts of air leaving my mouth. My fingers twitched, my core clenching, needing him inside of me again.

"I'll see you at work, Evvie."

I frowned. "I—"

"Kane will be here soon." He backed away without so much as a kiss.

"Fine." I huffed and left his apartment abruptly. Once reaching the elevators, I looked down the hall. Disappointment fluttered through me when Brett didn't come after me.

Knowing our time together was obviously over, I should have been grateful. I got him out of my system.

My blood boiled as frustration settled deep within me. As livid as I was with him, I had a feeling that our time together had only just begun.

Eleven

I MOVED my hips to the beat of the fast techno music that sounded around the vast expanse of the club. The sound flowed through me as I made drinks for waiting customers.

After leaving Brett's apartment a week before, I was tempted to call in sick to work each night but he would know that I was only doing it to avoid him.

I caught him watching me as he stood against the wall beside Kane. I was still frustrated from the way we had left things so I bent over, making sure he would see my panties.

My blood pumped through me knowing I would hear it from Brett later about my little show that I gave him. Feeling a need to tease him, letting him know that I was in just as much control as he was, bending over in front of him seemed like a good idea. For the moment.

When I had lifted to my full height, Brett was headed towards me. His powerful walk gave off an air of ownership.

A few regulars at the bar laughed and I put on my brightest smile before turning to them. Their eyes were dark, hungry as they roamed over me. My skin crawled but I put on a brave face.

"What's your name, gorgeous?" the blond slurred.

I smiled and opened my mouth to reply when I saw Brett nearing us. Chewing my bottom lip, my body heated under his intense scrutiny.

It had been a week since our night together and I had been avoiding him ever since. Except for the times that I would tease him, make him jealous but the cold look he always gave me let me know that he hardly noticed.

As Brett closed the distance between us, he licked his bottom lip, his heated gaze watching me. His jaw clenched and unclenched. Okay, maybe he did notice my little show.

My gaze followed his movement, my core clenching at the sight. I cleared my throat, taking a breath and crossed my arms under my chest.

Brett's gaze lowered to my full breasts and back up to meet my gaze.

My eyebrow rose.

He smirked and clapped his hands on the back of the necks of the guys. "My bartender treating you good?" he asked, not taking his gaze away from mine.

"Yes, we were asking what time she gets off," the blond answered.

Brett's jaw clenched. "Why don't you guys go enjoy your drinks elsewhere?"

The blond shoved out of his grip. "I don't fucking think so. Not when the view is so appealing."

I watched him lean down to the guy's ear, his gaze darkening.

"Let's go, Adam," his friend said, rising from the stool.

The blond huffed. "Bye Evvie."

"Bye," I bit out, glaring in Brett's direction.

The guys left and Brett sat in front of me, placing his elbows on the counter.

"You just shooed away my next big tip."

Brett shrugged. "I have no idea what you're talking about."

I scoffed and turned around, roughly putting bottles away.

"You enjoy dancing?"

My back stiffened and I looked at him over my shoulder. The music flowed through me, begging me to dance to it.

"Hey Ev." Tatiana placed her tray on the counter. "Can I get a beer please?"

I nodded and poured a beer from the tap.

She winked. "So, you two fuck yet?"

I coughed, my cheeks heating.

"Wouldn't you like to know?" Brett grinned.

Tatiana licked her lips and made a point of looking him up and down. "Would I ever."

"Here's your beer," I growled and slammed the bottle on the tray.

Brett chuckled. "Something wrong, Evvie?"

I huffed. "No."

Tatiana blew me a kiss before turning to him. She cupped his cheek and leaned down to his ear, whispering something to him. She brushed her thumb along his bottom lip.

Brett smirked.

76

My nostrils flared as I glared daggers at the back of Tatiana's head. Right in front of me? Really?

Tatiana kissed his cheek.

He smiled and shook his head. He watched her walk away before turning back to me.

I leaned against the counter, my heart thudding hard.

He tapped the bar top. "Are you going to make me a drink?"

My jaw clenched. "Make it yourself."

Brett rose from the stool and pulled off his jacket. He rolled up his sleeves and walked behind the bar. He smirked and met my gaze. "You don't think I can handle making my own drink?"

I huffed and placed my hands on my hips. "This is *my* bar."

He took a step towards me. "Is it now?"

"Evvie, can I get a drink, babe?" another customer asked me.

I spun on my heel and smiled brightly at the man, thankful for the interruption. "Sure thing, hun. The usual?"

The guy nodded.

I turned around and grabbed a bottle off the back shelf.

"What's your problem, asshole?" the guy slurred.

Brett growled. "You."

I turned around and grabbed Brett's arm, placing a tumbler on the counter in front of the guy. "Enjoy," I said sweetly.

The man's gaze landed on my chest and smiled. "Oh, I will."

A snarl escaped Brett's lips as I pushed him back. "Stop."

His body tensed as he leaned against the counter. He scrubbed a hand down his face.

"Hey."

He looked down into my eyes. My body throbbed, needing to wrap myself around him again. The thought of another woman touching him, made me sick to my stomach.

He stared into the depths of my gaze, the fury that had burned in them a moment before, simmering to a dull roar as the seconds ticked by.

I took a breath. "What the hell is your problem?"

He glanced down at my lips. "I don't have a problem."

"Brett." I punched him in the arm making him meet my gaze. I raised an eyebrow. "You look like you want to gut every guy that talks to me."

Brett took a breath. "You looked like you wanted to claw Tatiana's face off."

My mouth opened and closed before I scowled. I turned and continued serving customers.

Brett leaned against the counter.

My body buzzed as I felt Brett's eyes on me. As I walked by him, the hairs on the back of my neck twitched, tingling like he was touching me himself. I was attuned to him, attracted to him on a level that left me breathless. He was controlling. Domineering, but I wanted more.

The club slowly emptied at closing time. Customers waved at me as they walked by, most of them regulars.

My heart jumped as a warm body stepped up behind me. Fingers brushed the hair off of my nape, sending shivers down my spine. He infuriated me but I missed the feel of his touch. Watching Tatiana hit on him made me want to drive the woman's face into my knee. I took a deep breath. I liked Tatiana but this jealousy thing was new for me.

"Tatiana wasn't hitting on me."

I rolled my eyes. "Sure looked that way."

Brett brushed his thumb up and down the side of my neck. "She was trying to make you jealous."

I cleared my throat and grabbed a cloth, wiping down the counter.

"Did it work, lover?" he asked, wrapping a hand around my wrist.

Yes. "No."

He chuckled. "You are such a bad liar."

I clenched my jaw and turned around, leaning against the counter beside him. "You think you're funny, don't you?"

He placed an arm around me and kissed my shoulder. A shiver ran down my spine as his lips lingered on my skin. His gaze met mine, twinkling with lust and mischief.

"Brett?"

He smirked. "Yes, lover?"

My body inched closer to him, unaware of the inner turmoil going on inside my head. *I want him. I don't want him. He's dangerous but gorgeous. Oh God.*

I took a breath and glanced down at his mouth. Full lips that had been all over me a week before. My core clenched at the memories of him inside me, taking me rough. I wondered what he would be like gentle. Sensual even. Did he want me so bad that he couldn't control himself? Was he always a dominating lover?

Words lost on my tongue, I continued to stare into the hunger filled depths of his gaze.

He smiled and lowered his mouth to my ear. "How many days after I fucked you did it take for you to stop feeling me, lover?"

My heart jumped at the way he talked about sex like the weather. "Brett."

He grinned. "I felt you for days. I still feel you." He kissed my shoulder again. "Riding me. Sucking my cock."

My body heated, my skin vibrating at the erotic images his words put into my head.

He reached up and brushed a thumb across my bottom lip. "How are you getting home?"

"Kane," I whispered.

"Not tonight." Brett released me and walked away.

I watched him mingle with some of the remaining customers.

Every so often he would glance my way and even though we were several feet apart, I could feel the magnetic pull.

"Evvie?"

I jumped and turned to Tatiana, my stomach clenching at images of the woman having her hands all over Brett a moment before. "Hey T," I bit out.

The spunky shooter girl smiled. "What's wrong?"

"Nothing." I continued wiping up the counter, ignoring the scrutiny from the other woman.

"I wanted you to know that I'm not interested in Brett in any way. He's a good guy but not my type."

I shrugged and grabbed a cloth. "You can have him," I swallowed hard. "If you want."

Tatiana laughed. "You're gorgeous, but you suck at lying."

I sighed. I was getting sick of being told that. "I don't care what or who Brett does."

"Yes, you do."

"Look T, I—"

Tatiana grinned. "Ev, I would be more interested in you than him."

I frowned. "What does that mean?"

Tatiana raised an eyebrow and made a point of checking me out.

My eyes widened. "Oh."

"Now, if I was straight," she looked away.

I followed her gaze. My stomach flipped when Brett met my stare and rubbed his mouth. My gaze instantly dropped to his lips, sending my heart fluttering.

"Damn. I would love to take a bite out of that."

My cheeks heated.

"But, I'll just live vicariously through you, beautiful."

I leaned against the counter, watching Tatiana make a drink. "So you're not interested in him?"

She winked. "Nope. He's all yours, baby."

I scoffed. "He's not mine."

"Then why do you care how I feel about him?"

"Um…"

Tatiana chuckled and poured us both a shot of golden liquid. She lifted the glass to her lips and grinned. "Now that he's had you, Evvie, you belong to him."

Twelve

THERE WAS no way that I belonged to Brett. No way at all.

My stomach fluttered, an image of his deep blue eyes boring into mine as he took me hard. The way he had controlled my body and the things he did, left me quivering for more. *Oh God.*

I huffed and cleaned up the same spot on the counter that I had been working on for the past ten minutes.

Brett didn't want me. Not me completely. It was too soon. He was dominating. Demanding things of me that I didn't even know I was capable of. And the sex? My loins throbbed. What the hell was wrong with me?

"Bye, darlin'," Kane called out as he walked by me.

I startled and looked up. "Wait, you're not driving me home?"

He winked. "Nope."

"Why not?" I gaped after him.

"Because I'm driving you home."

I jumped at the smooth voice in my ear.

Kane winked.

"I hate you," I mumbled.

Brett chuckled and wrapped a hand around my wrist, rubbing his thumb up and down my pulse point.

My heart raced, the scent of his spicy cologne invading my nostrils, sending my heartbeat into overdrive.

"Kane?" I called out. Why was he so keen on the idea of Brett and me all of a sudden?

He smiled. "I'll see you later, Ev."

I let out a breath as my best friend walked down the hall, leaving me alone with the dark brooding man behind me. "I'm surprised he left me alone with you."

Brett stiffened behind me, tightening his hold on my wrist. "You don't trust me?"

My stomach clenched at the hurt in his voice but I wasn't going to lie. I didn't trust him. At all. He would rip my heart out and not think twice before sleeping with the next woman. I knew how men like him worked. I saw my mom go through it with my dad before she died. As much as I missed her, my mother was probably better off.

"Evvie." His hot breath scorched my neck. "Do you trust me?"

I swallowed. "I trust that you'll make me feel good."

His lips caressed the soft spot under my ear as he gripped my hip.

My eyes fluttered closed at the warmth radiating off of his body. I needed to feel him. All over me. I wanted another night of pure, raw, messy sex. Last time was amazing but tonight, was on my terms.

"We're alone, lover," he purred.

I smiled and slowly opened my eyes. The room had emptied as the night wore on. Last call being two hours ago, only the regulars stayed until the very end.

I looked up at Brett, our mouths only inches apart. His blue eyes bored into mine, heating my skin on fire like he was looking deep inside of me. Learning all of my secrets, my wants and my needs.

I shook my head, ridding myself of those thoughts and turned to the back counter. I lined up a row of shot glasses and grabbed a bottle of my daddy's favorite liquor, tequila. I twisted the cap off, pouring the amber liquid into the small tumbler. I took a breath and brought one up to my lips and slammed it back, letting the burn of the spicy liquid coat my throat. I repeated the movements, taking two more shots before a hard body leaned against me.

"What are you doing?" Brett asked, trailing a finger down my arm.

My head spun at the deep velvet of his voice as it washed over me. I pushed back against him. "Getting drunk."

"I see that," he said, grabbing my glass.

I watched him lift it to his mouth before he winked and swallowed the golden tequila. He coughed and placed the cup upside down on the counter.

"Can't handle your liquor, Brett?" I teased, taking another shot.

Brett's eyes twinkled as he poured another glass. "Careful, lover."

I grabbed the bottle of golden liquid and turned around to face him. I held it up to my lips and smiled. "Or else what, lover boy? You going to bend me over your knee and spank me?"

His eyes darkened as he closed the distance between us, pinning me against the counter. "Would you like it if my hands were on your ass, marking that pale skin?"

My body buzzed at the deep husk of his voice and I tilted my chin. My core clenched, throbbing with need for him. "Brett, I am so wet, you could bend me over right now and fuck the shit out of me and I wouldn't stop you."

His nostrils flared as he ran the pad of his thumb over my mouth. "I enjoy the liquid courage pouring from those delicious lips of yours."

My heart fluttered at the soft contact. "I know."

He smirked. He leaned down and licked up the side of my neck, sending a ripple of shivers racing down my back.

The burning sensation from the alcohol and the scent of his cologne made my body hunger for him. Crave him on a deeper level.

Brett cupped my ass and pushed his lower body into me.

I grabbed onto his dress shirt and pulled him closer, needing to feel his lips on my skin. It didn't matter where.

He grabbed my wrists and held them in one hand behind my back before grinding his hips against mine.

My mouth parted on a small gasp. I couldn't move. Liquid heat seeped into my panties at being restrained by his hard body.

His thick erection pressed into my lower belly, sending a new understanding through my body. My pussy clenched, needing him inside of me at that very moment but I needed to wait. I was in control tonight but maybe a little taste wouldn't hurt.

I looked up at him and licked my bottom lip in a slow smooth stroke.

His eyes darkened as he captured my mouth in a bruising kiss.

I opened to him, letting him in while his hips continued grinding against me.

He kissed me like he fucked. Hard, dominating. *Erotic.*

Brett devoured my mouth like he was desperate for me. Like he needed me as bad as I needed him.

I parted my legs and released his mouth as his hand travelled up under my skirt before squeezing my ass.

He let go of my wrists and grabbed my hips, lifting me onto the counter.

I wrapped my thighs around him, bringing his mouth back down to mine. I sucked his bottom lip, igniting a deep rumble from his chest.

He plunged his tongue into my mouth, rubbing it hard against mine as he pushed his way between my legs.

My body buzzed, my head swirling from the alcohol.

His hands travelled up the thighs to my hips and gripped my panties. With a rough tug, he ripped them off.

My heart thumped as his fingers massaged and kneaded my flesh.

He released my mouth and wrapped a hand around my neck, tilting my head back. His fingers curled around my nape with a squeeze.

I bit back a gasp and ran my hands through his hair, pulling hard.

His eyes flashed and a wicked smile formed on his face making my breath catch.

The alcohol rippled through my body like it was a part of me, controlling my actions. He thought he was in charge. I smirked and pushed him away.

He raised an eyebrow.

I took the last shot before grabbing the bottle off the shelf. My belly burned with the acidic force of the tequila, my head spinning but I felt good. Light as a feather as I walked out from the behind the bar.

"Lover?"

I spun on my heel, almost losing my balance as I met Brett's heated gaze. I let my eyes roam down his body.

My skin hummed at the bulge in his black dress pants.

I licked my lips and took a swig from the bottle. "I'm getting drunk with or without you lover boy."

He looked between me and the shelf of bottles before letting out a sigh. He grabbed a bottle of rum and took a step towards me.

"That's the spirit," I shouted, making my way to the dance floor. I pulled a chair to the middle of the wooden area and waited for Brett. I pointed to the chair. "Sit."

Brett raised an eye brow and took a swig of the dark brown liquid. "Why?"

I made my way to the DJ booth, sashaying my hips. "You asked me if I like to dance." I looked up when he didn't respond.

He sat in the chair and placed the bottle on the floor, running his hands down the legs of his pants.

I grinned and turned on the sound board, slowly spinning up the volume to a hard sensual beat that got my heart pumping. Or maybe it was the liquor. It could also be the gorgeous man sitting in the chair waiting for me. My body was so hot for him. Controlling the urge not to let him take me when we were behind the bar, surprised even me. I had no idea what the hell I was doing but I wanted one night of not feeling anything except skin.

"Lover, I think you've had too much to drink."

I grabbed the bottle and took a couple of steps towards him before stopping. "I'm only getting started, Brett."

"Are you now?"

"Yes. I won't stop until I get fucking shit faced." I took a breath and pounded back another swig from the bottle before I met his gaze. "I want to lose control."

His eyes darkened. "What else?"

I licked my lips and slowly closed the distance between us. "I want to do things I wouldn't dare do sober."

Brett's nostrils flared, his heated gaze taking me in as I stood a foot away. "You already have."

I shrugged. "Maybe so." I stepped between his legs and leaned down, my mouth mere inches from his. "But I want more."

Keeping our eyes locked, I took a step back, slowly moving my hips to the beat of the deep music that flowed around us. I kicked off my shoes and made my way back to him.

Blood pounded in my ears as I turned and circled my ass above the crotch of his pants. Even though I was drunk, my body

85

moved in an erotic way to the slow drum of the bass of the techno beat.

He held back. Not touching me at all. Being in control sent a thrill down my spine and knowing it wouldn't last for long, I reveled in it.

I placed my hands on his knees and ground my ass against him feeling him harden under me. "Lover boy?"

He grabbed my hips, pulling me down harder onto his lap and fisted my hair in his hand.

I gasped when he tugged my head back, a slow smile spreading on my face as I continued rubbing myself against him. "My ass makes your cock hard."

Brett grabbed the bottle of rum beside his chair and held it to my lips.

I grinned before covering the opening, allowing him to give me a taste. I swallowed and moaned, pushing back against his lap harder.

He brought the bottle to his mouth, taking big gulps before placing it back on the ground.

My mind buzzed, the hairs on my skin jumping as I continued moving my hips over him to the beat of the music. "Brett, I'm gonna fuck you so hard, you'll always remember me."

A deep chuckle sounded behind me when I was lifted off of his lap. Before I even knew what was happening, I was bent over the bench in the booth.

I gripped the cushion and gasped as my skirt was hiked up to my hips. Cool air washed over my naked ass when a hard swat landed on my skin. I yelped, the tingling fire of pain soaring through me. Another swat landed on the other cheek of my rear and my pussy clenched. I bit back a moan.

Brett fisted my hair, pressing my head against the bench and leaned over me. "You thought you were in control, didn't you, lover?" he whispered in my ear.

I chewed my bottom lip and dug my nails into the plush leather as his deep voice washed over me.

He grazed his teeth over the back of my neck. "I let you play your game but now it's my turn."

I panted, waiting. Anticipation built as the heat from his hard body soared into mine. All of our senses mixed with the alcohol increased the passion that flowed through us. The power of lust and hunger seeped through my blood as he continued teasing me.

"I'm going to take you how I want you. You won't stop me, will you, lover?"

My sex clenched at his words and I shook my head. I was his. I wasn't sure if it was the alcohol or the dangerous attraction that I felt towards him but I submitted. Completely and utterly. I was his.

Thirteen

HIS TONGUE grazed over my ear sending a hot tingle down my back. "I'm going to fuck you hard.

I smiled. "Get on it then."

Brett caressed my ass and squeezed.

Delicious pleasure soared through my body as the sting jolted to my clit. Whenever an ex of mine had tried to spank me during sex, I'd cringe. But with Brett…oh God, I wanted to do anything with him. Give myself completely to him.

My heart sped up, the alcohol swirling in my belly.

"You sure have become demanding in the last week."

I swallowed and took a breath, letting the intoxicating tequila take over. Whatever I said, it would be blamed on the alcohol. Not like Brett would think I was serious anyways. It was just sex. "Not demanding enough apparently."

Brett grabbed my hands, holding my wrists behind my back. With the other, he turned my head and covered my mouth in an agonizingly slow kiss.

The hold on my hair loosened and I jumped when he ran the tip of his cock over my center, trailing the juices from my body down to my clit. Hot tremors ran through me as I inhaled a gasp.

"Your cunt's nice and wet for me, lover," Brett said against my lips, brushing his rigid length from the hard nub to the area between my ass cheeks.

A shiver slid down my back at the unexpected contact. I spread my legs and arched my hips, hinting. I needed him. My core ached, throbbing. Begging for a release.

"Beg me."

I latched onto his bottom lip and pulled, gently biting down.

He growled, pushing his cock against the tight opening in my rear.

I gasped, my body shaking. I was drunk but not that drunk. "Brett," I groaned. But God, did it ever feel good. Just when I thought he was going to go further, he slammed his cock into my waiting heat.

"Fuck, lover. I've missed your tight pussy." He shivered above me, slowly pumping in and out. Torturing me.

"Faster." I couldn't take it anymore. "Oh God, fuck me hard," I cried. Words left my lips that I would never even dream of saying sober but the alcohol and the desire for him to fulfill my every waking need took full control.

Brett released my wrists and gripped my hip, brushing his thumb over the puckered hole in my rear. He pulled out and paused. "Are you ready for me to give you what you want?"

I licked my lips and nodded. "Plea—"

He drove back in at the same time as he pushed his thumb into the tiny dark hole.

I gasped, my body shaking around him as he filled me everywhere. The burning pain soon erupted into pleasure as he plunged into me at a pace that left me breathless.

I gripped the cushion, the cool leather soon turning hot from my heated skin.

His thumb slid all the way in and I clenched around him.

I looked over my shoulder, our gazes colliding. I licked my lips and pushed back.

A smug smile formed on his face as he lifted my hips.

I crawled onto the bench, releasing myself from his grasp when my feet were pulled out from under me.

He wrapped a hand around my throat and towered over me, breathing hard in my ear. "Trying to get away so soon?"

A shiver ran down my back as he slid back into me, making me moan. "If you don't make me come soon, I'll do it myself," I panted.

Brett covered me with his body and grabbed my wrists, holding them above my head. "As much as I'd love to see that, Evvie, you're going to come around my dick. And you're going to come hard."

His words travelled over me, heating my skin. I looked up at him and licked my bottom lip slowly. "Then fuck me, lover boy."

His nostrils flared. "Spread those milky white thighs for me."

I did as he said, placing my left foot on the floor, opening myself to him. I needed him. More than I ever thought was possible.

Our gazes locked as he pulled out and slammed back into my pussy.

I whimpered.

He smirked and did it again.

I cried out at the tight full feeling of him deep inside me but I couldn't take my eyes away from his. They were captivating. Drawing me in as he fucked me hard.

He pulled out when a wicked smile spread on his face.

My heart beat fast as he thrust into me so hard, my hips rose from the bench. I screamed, clenching around him as the sensation of him hitting the bundle of nerves deep inside of me set off and explosion. Pure white-hot ecstasy travelled through my body and I screamed his name.

"Louder."

"Oh God. You're so hard," I cried out as he pounded into my pulsing core.

He grinned and kissed the back of my neck, his hot breath scorching my skin. "Feel me, lover."

"I do," I whimpered.

"Good. I want you sore."

He held my wrists with one hand and pushed my knee up to my chest before continuing his deep thrusts.

I moaned, my skin tingling from post orgasmic bliss. His cock lengthened inside of me as his breathing quickened. He groaned, pushing into me as deep as he could go before he shook.

His hot release spurted into me as he came on a roar. "Oh fuck, Evvie," he growled.

I tugged my hand from his grasp and cupped the back of his neck, pulling his mouth down to mine. I licked between his lips, swallowing his moan. Our tongues dueled, danced as we both fought for control.

Brett released my mouth, nipping my bottom lip before lifting himself off of me. The warmth of his semen ran down my inner thighs.

I turned onto my back and bit back a groan as my core pulsed from the rough way he had taken me.

With his body still above mine, he wrapped his hand around his cock, stroking slowly.

I licked my lips as he continued to come onto my lower stomach and mound. Coating me. Marking me. *Mine.*

My stomach twisted and I pushed those thoughts to the back of my mind. I kept my gaze locked with his and brushed a thumb over his bottom lip while reaching between us. I swiped my finger through the white liquid and brought it to my lips, licking the taste of him off of me.

His eyes darkened and with a quick move, he wrapped a hand around my throat, squeezing lightly.

I gasped, my eyes widening at the rough hold.

"Do you like the taste of me?"

I nodded, swallowing hard at the husk in his voice.

He smirked.

I whimpered when his finger thrust into me.

Removing it a moment later, he brought it to my mouth, the juices from my body coating it. "Open."

My lips parted.

He brushed his finger along my tongue before pushing its way deeper. I closed my lips, sucking the acidic juices from both of our bodies off of it. I moaned, swallowing the salty liquid. The heady scent swirled through my senses, setting my skin on fire.

He removed his finger with a pop. His grip on my neck tightened as he tilted my head back before he covered my mouth, devouring me.

The sweet taste of sex mixed when our tongues collided.

I wrapped my hands around his neck, brushing my fingers through the hair at his nape. Tilting my hips, I ran my center over his hardening length, needing him again. My pussy throbbed, dripping with desire.

I reached between us and wrapped a hand around his slick cock.

He groaned into my mouth and pushed against me, deepening the kiss.

I squeezed him, needing him inside me again even though I was sore. I smiled against his lips.

Brett lifted his head, his breathing hard. "What's so funny?"

"I'm sore just like you wanted."

A smug grin formed on his face as he crashed his lips to mine at the same time he thrust back into my waiting heat.

I whimpered.

His movements were slow, sensual, not rough like a moment ago. I wasn't sure if it was the alcohol but something switched between us. A pull grew deep in my belly.

His lower stomach rubbed against my clit sending a jolt of electricity through me.

"Fuck, Evvie. Your body was made for me," he breathed against my lips as he pumped into me at a slow pace.

I cried out as an explosion of ecstasy crashed into me like a tidal wave.

The sweet heady scent of sex flowed around us as we moved as one.

His length pulsed, erupting inside of me as he came hard. His body covered mine as he continued to shake through his release, filling me with his warmth.

My core throbbed, clenching around him.

He sat back on his hunches and ran a thumb over my kiss-swollen mouth. His eyes were glassy from the alcohol but warm with affection.

My heart fluttered.

Brett cleared his throat and rose from the booth, righting his pants.

I sat up, pulling my skirt down and bit back a moan as the remnants from the hot sex ran down my inner thighs. "Brett?"

He walked back to the chair in the middle of the dance floor and grabbed the bottle of liquor off the floor. He turned back to me and winked, taking a large chug from the golden liquid.

My stomach twisted as a chill ran down my back. The warmth in his gaze from a moment ago disappeared as he stalked towards me.

He took hold of my hand and pulled me to my feet before cupping my ass.

I groaned, loving the feel of his hands on me. My fingers ran down his chest of their own accord, tingling, wanting more.

He tilted the bottle to my lips.

I opened, swallowing the burning rum as it warmed my body. My head reeled, fuzzy from passion and liquor.

The heated look in Brett's deep blue gaze made me realize that there was no way this night was even close to being over.

***

MY BODY stirred, my head pounding with agony as I attempted to open my eyes. I groaned, my muscles jumping and twitching under the added strain. God, what the hell did I do last night?

My skin heated. Oh yeah. A small smile splayed on my face at the memories of the night came crashing into my mind.

Brett all over me. Inside me. Over and over again. We finished the bottle of tequila and then some, passing out hours later.

A deep moan sounded beside me as a heavy arm wrapped around me, pulling me against a hard body.

My heart fluttered when I realized Brett's hand was cupping my breast, his thumb casually running back and forth over my nipple.

I lifted my head and pinched the bridge of my nose as a sharp pain erupted behind my eyes. "Shit."

A husky chuckle sounded in my ear and I turned to Brett.

His blue eyes were captivating as they took me in. "Mornin'."

I swallowed, my mouth as dry as a desert. "Morning."

His hand stayed on my chest, holding me tight like he was claiming me. We continued to stare at each other and I couldn't help but feel as though he was starting to have feelings for me. Was it all in my head? I had feelings for him but I wasn't sure if it was just lust or something more.

My stomach churned, the alcohol clouding my thoughts. I took deep cleansing breaths, swallowing past the nausea.

"How are you feeling?"

I stood up and looked around us. We had passed out in his office, empty bottles still beside us. My head spun, my body aching from sleeping on the floor. "Like hell." I looked down at Brett. "You?"

He rose to his feet and handed me his dress shirt. "I'm getting too old for this shit."

I laughed and pulled on the white shirt. The scent of cologne invaded my nostrils as the soft material caressed my skin making my body stir.

"Do you remember everything from last night?"

My cheeks heated as I did up the buttons. "I think so." I frowned. "Did we use condoms?"

He thought a moment. "No."

"You didn't freak out this time."

His gaze searched my face. "I enjoy the feel of you wrapped around me. No barriers."

My body flushed. "Do you remember everything from last night?"

He made a point of letting his gaze roam down my body, his dress shirt barely covering my ass. "I do."

"I'm..." I swallowed. "I'm sorry if I hurt you."

He closed the distance between us and brushed a thumb over my bottom lip. "You didn't hurt me."

I grabbed his hand, linking our fingers and sighed. "Well I was a little rough." Words from the night before rained into my mind.

Fuck me hard, Brett. Give it to me. Take me.

And damn, did he ever. My pussy throbbed with every movement, every step.

Brett pulled me into his arms and brushed my hair off my forehead. "I like it rough, lover." He kissed my nose. "You know that."

I sighed.

Waking up hung over as hell was quickly replaced with desire as I leaned my head against his chest. It felt normal, familiar. The fact that we hadn't been together in a week mixed with the alcohol, brought out a sense of passion in us both that left me breathless and sore. Brett was rough during sex but last night, I was just as bad. I remembered everything, the things I had said to him, the things he'd said to me...my pussy throbbed, images of the many times we had sex during the night raining full force in my foggy mind.

"Do you have plans today?"

I lifted my head and looked up at Brett. "Coffee and a shower. Sleep too, would be good. You?"

Brett kissed my knuckles and released me before pulling on his jacket. "I need to figure out what the hell Mathis wants," he mumbled.

I nodded and looked around the dim office. "Where are my clothes?"

Brett chuckled. "Uh…I cut them off of you."

My eyes widened. "You did what?"

He smirked and ran a hand through his hair. "After fucking you in the booth, we came in here and you pushed me onto the couch, demanding me to cut your clothes off." His eyes darkened. "Hottest fucking thing a woman has ever said to me."

I shook my head, vaguely remembering handing him a pair of scissors. Him cutting my clothes off because he was desperate for me was hot as hell. I remembered the dark look of lust in his heated gaze as he cut through the fabric before tearing the rest with his hands. My pussy pulsed and I cleared my throat. "Well I guess I need a new uniform then."

"I was going to get you a new one anyways."

I frowned. "Why?"

"The beginning of the night, you bent over, showing me your panties, remember?"

The sound of his deep husky voice washing over me as it filled with anger, set my heart thumping. I had forgotten I did that. "I was frustrated with you."

"Oh, I know," he grumbled. "That's why I'm getting you pants to wear."

"Excuse me?"

His gaze met mine before he took a step towards me. "The skirt is too short."

I narrowed my eyes and placed my hands on my hips. "You can't tell me what to wear."

A smug smile formed on Brett's face. "Yes. I can."

I huffed. "Just because you're jealous of every man that looks at me doesn't mean you can control what I wear. What do

95

you expect me to do? Wear a snow suit to work? Or a garbage bag, Brett?"

Brett closed the distance between us and cupped the back of my neck, tilting my head. "Whatever works, lover."

I pushed him and glared. "You don't own me."

His jaw clenched, his mouth set in a firm line as he met my glare head on. "Are you fucking anyone else?"

My mouth fell open. "What the hell does that have to do with anything?"

"Answer the question," he growled.

"No. Are you?"

He shook his head. "No. Do you remember the things you said to me last night?"

My cheeks heated. "Yes."

Brett grinned and took a step towards me as I backed up to the wall. He placed a hand on either side of my head and leaned down. "*You* started dancing. For *me*. *You* begged me. *You* demanded me to fuck you hard."

"I was drunk."

Brett brushed his lips along the side of my neck and inhaled. "You still smell like me," his voice lowering.

My heart thumped hard. "Brett."

"You weren't drunk a week ago."

"No, I wasn't."

Brett lifted his head, his dark blue eyes boring into mine. "So what are you telling me?"

"I'm telling you that you don't own me."

He smirked. "Oh lover, I own you more than you think."

"Like hell you do."

Brett wrapped a hand around my throat and pushed me up against the wall.

I gasped.

"Has a man ever made you wet just from words?" he asked, grazing his teeth along the length of my jaw.

I chewed my bottom lip, biting back a moan. "No."

He smirked. "Didn't think so."

I pushed him and frowned. "You're way too smug for your own good."

Brett winked and grabbed my hand, placing a light kiss on my knuckles. "If I didn't feel like ass, I'd bend you over right now and fuck the shit out of you, showing you how much I own you."

I gasped, my core clenching at that image. "Just because you make me feel good doesn't mean you own me."

"Right, Evvie. Keep telling yourself that," Brett said as he opened the door.

"What does that mean?"

"Forget it," he mumbled.

I grimaced and grabbed his arm. "Brett, what's your issue?"

Brett's back stiffened and cleared his throat. He tugged me behind him as we walked down the hall to the exit. "I don't have a fucking issue."

"Brett."

He stopped in his steps and spun on me, his gaze roaming down my scantily clad body. "We need coffee, a shower and sleep." He licked his lips. "After all of that..." he cupped my ass and pulled me against him. "I'm going to make you smell like me again."

Fourteen

THE LIGHT of the early morning sun forced its way into my head making my skull pound. My stomach churned when the car drove over potholes, making it jerk and jump. I groaned and took a deep breath, inhaling through my nose, breathing past the nausea.

Brett chuckled and placed a hand on my knee. "I know the feeling, Evvie."

I smiled and covered his hand with mine. "A shot gun would be the only thing that would make me feel better," I mumbled, pinching the bridge of my nose. When Brett didn't say anything I looked up at him.

The muscles in his strong jaw tensed, his eyes hidden by dark aviator sunglasses. He turned to me and smirked. "Checking me out, lover?"

My cheeks heated and I looked away. "Even hung over, you're sexy as hell."

He grinned and ran his hand up my thigh. "I enjoy your honesty."

"When I'm not feeling well, I usually say exactly what's on my mind," I said on a laugh.

"And when you're drunk."

A flush crept up my body at the memories from the night before. My body ached and throbbed in all the right places.

I looked out the window as Brett turned into the underground parking lot of my apartment.

As he parked the vehicle, I debated asking him to come up to my apartment. I didn't care if Kane was home.

The sound of a door closing made me jump. I sighed and opened the door when Brett stuck out his hand, helping me out of the vehicle. I smiled, my heart lifting at the thoughtful gesture.

When I looked up at him, my heart stopped. His deep blue eyes went cold as they bored into mine.

I swallowed. "Brett?"

He slammed the door shut and pushed me up against the side of the car, letting his hands roam up the side of my hips.

My stomach flipped, my blood pounding hard in my ears as he ground his hips into mine. "What are you doing?"

He leaned down, breathing hard against my neck. "I can't stop touching you."

I gripped his jacket, biting back a moan as he pressed his pelvis against my core. "Then why do you seem pissed?"

He nipped the soft skin under my ear, squeezing my ass at the same time. "Because. I can't stop touching you."

I panted as he ground into me, setting my skin ablaze. "Brett."

He pushed off me and cleared his throat, grabbing my hand roughly. "Come on."

I sighed and rushed to keep up with him. We made our way into the elevator and I jabbed the button leading to my floor. My skin tingled under his scrutiny. I could feel him on me and he was several feet away.

His heated gaze lit my world on fire.

His strong features relaxed and he opened his mouth to say something when the elevator doors dinged.

I left the confines of the small space and headed down the hall with Brett on my heels.

A warm hand wrapped around mine, linking our fingers together.

"Kane will be pissed that I'm here," Brett mumbled.

"Right now, I don't give a shit what he thinks." I unlocked the door and threw my keys on the table. A mixture of fashion and car magazines covered the dark cherry wood.

The scent of lemons invaded my nostrils as I walked into the kitchen. My eyes drifted to the fridge and I noticed a yellow sticky note on the white door.

Gone out.

Kane

My shoulders relaxed. I wasn't in the mood to face the wrath and lectures of my best friend. I turned to Brett. "He's not home."

A wicked glint filled his heated gaze as he looked around the small apartment. "Do you want me to leave?" he asked.

"No." And that was the truth. I wanted him to stay over. I wanted more. More than sex. But I didn't want to scare him off.

My heart jumped in anticipation as I walked past him and the small kitchen island that was cluttered with empty beer bottles. I didn't need to look up at him to know that a smug smile had spread across his face. As much as I wanted him, I needed a shower first.

Once reaching my bedroom, my feet stepped onto the plush beige carpet. My only light came from the slit in the mauve curtains that covered the window.

I grabbed pajamas out of my dresser and headed into the bathroom. I turned on the water when a hard body shoved me into the stand-up shower.

I gasped, the hot water raining down over us, soaking the white shirt completely.

A hand fisted my hair, pulling my head back as teeth grazed the side of my neck. A growl sounded from Brett's throat as he pushed his hips against me.

I panted at the hard erection pressing against my ass. God, he was gorgeous and the way he made my body feel alive with indescribable amounts of pleasure, left me needing more.

"Brett?" I pushed back against him until we hit the wall, my chest rising and falling with ragged breath.

His free hand roamed up my hips, rough and needy. His hot breath against my neck made my heart race and my blood soar. He was desperate for me.

"Seeing you in just my shirt makes it hard to be in control, lover," he breathed against my neck.

I swallowed and licked my lips. "That's not my fault."

Brett wrapped a hand around my throat. "Why would you think it is?"

"It's the way you look at me."

He turned me around and pushed me up against the glass wall, placing both hands on either side of my head. "You don't like the way I look at you?"

100

My fingers grazed down his chest to his now soaked pants. The droplets of water running over his torso made my pussy clench with desire. "Not when you're pissed, no."

Brett's jaw clenched. He unbuckled his belt and pulled down his soaked pants, leaving him naked.

My gaze roamed down his hard muscular body, tanned and defined in ways I had only seen in my dreams. I had seen him naked before but standing there, in the shower, was different. More intimate.

"Strip."

I looked up at Brett's deep voice, my stomach flipping at the hard edge in his eyes. With shaky fingers, I undid the shirt and pulled it off, dropping it on the floor.

He grabbed my hand and pulled me in front of him, letting the water rain over us. "I'm never pissed with you, Evvie," he whispered.

My breath caught as his hands roamed down my arms, his fingers lightly grazing the sides of my breasts. Words lost on my tongue, I waited for him to continue.

"Waking up this morning with you in my arms made me realize something." He kissed my shoulder.

"What did you realize?" I asked. When he didn't respond, I turned in his arms and looked up at his handsome face. "Brett?" I cupped his cheek, rubbing a thumb over his bottom lip.

He didn't meet my gaze but the tightness in his shoulders and the firm press of his lips made me realize something. He was scared.

When Brett's gaze finally met mine, I gasped.

His eyes were dark, stormy, the look of fear replaced by lust as he pushed me up face first against the cool glass wall of the shower.

"Make love to me," I blurted. The words left my lips before I could stop myself.

He growled behind me as he wrapped a hand around my neck, fisting my hair with the other.

I whimpered as he tugged my head back.

"I don't make love, Evvie," he snarled in my ear.

I leaned my head against his shoulder and whimpered as he thrust into me so hard, my body was lifted into the air.

"I fuck and I fuck hard."

I moaned, slapping my hands against the wall.

Brett released my throat and lowered my feet to the floor. He bent me over at the middle and ran a hand down my back, sending shivers along with it. He gripped my hip and his other hand held my hair as he impaled me slow and deep.

My core clenched around him as he gave long even strokes, his pelvis hitting my ass after each rough impact.

I tilted my hips, taking him as far as my body would allow. "Harder."

He grunted, lifting my waist after each thrust.

I moaned, a slow simmer of ecstasy building deep in the pit of my belly.

"Come for me, lover," he growled.

His command set me off as an explosion erupted through me. I screamed and came around him, shaking through my release.

His hips sped up, his cock pumping into me at a fervor that left me panting and aching for more. "Fuck, Evvie. Your cunt's nice and tight."

I panted and pushed back, my hands sliding down the glass as I met him thrust for thrust. His rigid length rubbed inside of me, filling me. It swelled and pulsed but before I knew it, he pulled out and released me.

I frowned, turning around.

He turned off the water and left the shower before wrapping a white towel around his hips.

A cold chill ran down my spine as he left the bathroom. I quickly threw a towel around me and followed him to my bedroom. "Brett, talk to me."

His back stiffened as he reached my room and scrubbed a hand down his face.

I shut the door behind me, clicking the lock into place and leaned against it.

Brett sat on the edge of the bed and ran his fingers through his hair, drops of water falling on his shoulders.

I watched the rivulets run down his back, my lips tingling, wanting to lick every drop.

Frustration settled in the pit of my belly but I took a breath, needing to crack his walls. To let me in. Even if it was only piece by piece. I knew there was a mutual attraction. He could deny it all he wanted but there was something there.

I crawled onto the bed, moving behind him and pulled off my towel. I threw it on the floor in front of him, smiling when his breath hitched.

I rubbed the tension out of his shoulders and kissed his nape making him jump. I inhaled, the scent of man invading my nostrils making my core clench with desire for him.

"Evvie," he breathed.

I trailed kisses along his upper back and leaned my naked chest against him. His head rested against my shoulder as I brushed my fingers down his torso. His muscles twitched, rippling under my touch. The hard contours of his abs made my mouth water and want to nibble every inch of him.

I pushed my hand under the towel, grazing my fingers over the soft skin on his lower stomach before delving deeper.

His body was silky smooth, no hair covering his hard torso at all except for a thin line of brown hair. It lead from his belly button to a part of him that had pleased me in more ways than one. But this was for him. The straining erection in his lap must have been painful as it pitched a tent under the towel.

I kissed his nape. "Why did you stop in the shower?" My hand brushed the base of his long cock. It jerked under the towel as I cupped the heavy sac, massaging, kneading.

"Lover," he said through gritted teeth. "I don't know why I stopped."

My heart skipped a beat as I rose to my knees and wrapped my free hand around his jaw. I kissed the side of his neck, licking the droplets of water off of his skin.

My fingers closed around the base of him and slowly moved up the shaft to the tip. I ran my thumb over the swollen head, his pre-cum coating my finger. "Well I'll give you the release your body craves," I whispered in his ear.

A soft growl left Brett's lips as his hips started slowly moving to the strokes of my hand. "I...*fuck*."

I grazed my teeth over the soft skin under his ear, making his body shake against mine.

103

He swelled under my touch, the rigid length of him filling my hand.

Brett slapped his hands on the edge of the bed, gripping the mattress tight. "I need. Inside. You."

"No. I want to watch you." My hand moved up the length of him, squeezing harder as I brought it down to the base.

He turned his head to mine, his blue eyes darkening with lust. "You want me to break?"

I brushed my mouth along his, igniting a spark between us. "I want to make you think of just me."

"I do," he whispered.

My heart gave a start, not sure if I heard him properly.

He squeezed his eyes shut, small bursts of air leaving his full lips. "Faster."

My arm muscles burned as I gave him what he wanted. What he needed.

Brett moved his hips in tune with my even strokes. Sweat coated his brow and his breathing picked up. "Harder, Evvie," he demanded.

My eyes widened when he ripped off the towel and covered my hand with his. His fingers curled around mine, squeezing as we stroked him together. Teaching me. Showing me what he wanted

My breath quickened as his cock jerked in my fingers, the warm essence of his release coating our joined hands.

"Evvie," he said on a growl as he came hard, spurting his semen onto his lower belly.

I kissed his neck. Slowing my strokes, I brought my fingers up to my lips and licked the saltiness of him off of them. I moaned, my core throbbing with the need for him.

Brett's chest rose and fell, his nostrils flaring as he watched me. His eyes darkened with an animalistic hunger before he grabbed my hand.

My breath caught when he pushed me back onto the bed. My body hummed, spreading my legs wide for him as he crawled between my knees.

He leaned down, brushing his nose along my neck and inhaled. "*Mine*."

104

Fifteen

MY BODY buzzed as I stared up into Brett's deep blue gaze. I panted, brushing my thumb along his lip before covering his mouth. He groaned, opening for me. I was hungry for him.

I wrapped my hands around his neck, pulling him against me, deepening the kiss as he sank his cock into me.

A gasp escaped my lips as he pushed into me, diving deep before pulling out slowly. A shiver ran down my back, rocking me to the very core. I was lost to him.

The sound of a door slamming shut made my heart jump.

He released my mouth and looked down at me. A wicked glint flashed in his passion filled gaze.

He pulled out and leaned down to my ear. "Think you can be quiet, lover?"

I panted and whimpered when he lowered into me in a hard thrust.

He covered my mouth with his hand and kissed my jaw. "Shhh, lover."

I moaned as he brought my knee up to my chest, pushing into me deep. Oh God, Kane was home and I had to be quiet. *Not good. Not good at all, Evvie.*

My fingers gripped the mattress as Brett's hips sped up, pumping into me hard. I cried out around his hand, squeezing my eyes shut, forcing myself to be quiet.

"Every time I'm near you," he breathed against my neck. "I need to have you."

I panted, spreading my legs, opening to him.

His thrusts sped up, plowing into me with a fervor that was desperate. "It's a need so strong, it possesses me."

I moaned, my core clenching around him as he thrust into me hard. His words washed over me like a blanket of silk.

He replaced his hand with his mouth, devouring me. His hands roamed down my body, kneading in their paths as his body tensed above me.

"Brett?" I said against his lips.

He lifted his head and brushed his fingers down my cheek before kissing my mouth. Slow and tender as he licked his way between my lips.

I deepened the kiss, pouring everything I felt for him as I lifted my hips.

"Shit." He lifted his head and shuddered as he came on a growl, filling me with his semen.

I pulled his mouth down to mine, swallowing his groan.

He pushed into me one last time that set off a tremor of pure raw bliss. I shook around him, coming undone as my body heated from ecstasy.

I rained kisses on his face and wrapped my arms around him, pulling him tighter against me. The scent of him coated us as the remnants from his earlier release meshed between our bodies.

"I enjoy when you smell like me," he said against my mouth.

"Brett, I think we should—"

A soft knock on the door made me jump.

"Brett, phone," Kane said, his voice muffled by the closed door.

Brett lifted his head and looked down at me, grinning.

My cheeks heated at being caught and I chewed my bottom lip.

He kissed me fully on the mouth, pulling my lip from the onslaught of my teeth. "Never been caught with a man in your bed before, lover?"

I huffed and pushed him off of me.

He chuckled and rested his head on his arm, pulling the thin sheet over him.

I took a breath and met his gaze. The way he casually laid back in my bed like nothing had happened and that we weren't just caught by my very large best friend made me frown. Why was he so calm?

I rose from the bed and pulled on a robe. Taking a deep breath, I opened the door. "Hi, Kane."

Kane eyes narrowed. "Brett's damn phone has been ringing for half an hour."

"Thanks man," Brett mumbled from my bed.

"No problem, boss. And Evvie?"

I looked up at him.

"I'm not cleaning the bathroom," he said on a laugh.

I scowled and slammed the door shut, heat creeping up the back of my neck.

"Red looks good on you, lover," Brett teased.

I glared and slapped the phone in his hand, crawling onto the bed beside him.

He chuckled and lifted the sheet.

I pulled off the robe and spread myself over his body, resting my head against his arm.

His hand rubbed small circles on my upper back as he checked his phone.

"Shit."

My stomach twisted and I looked up at Brett as he threw his phone on the bed. He scrubbed a hand down his face and huffed, his shoulders tensing.

"Is everything okay?"

His jaw clenched and he gently pushed me off of him before rising from the bed. He picked the towel up off the floor and wrapped it around his waist.

"What's wrong?" I asked, hopping off the bed.

He looked around the room. "My clothes are wet," he mumbled.

"I'll put them in the dryer." I closed the distance between us and placed a hand on his arm. "Brett?"

He let out a heavy sigh, his gaze finally meeting mine. "I have to go."

My stomach sunk. "You have no clothes to wear."

"I know that," he snapped.

I glared. "What the hell is your problem, Brett?"

Brett met my stare head on and raised his eyebrow before he sighed and turned away. "I'm sorry...I..."

My body felt heavy as I threw on my house coat and left the confines of the bedroom. I didn't know who was trying to get a hold of Brett but it made my stomach clench, knowing that it pissed him off.

I grabbed his clothes and threw them in the dryer when a shadow crossed my path. I rose and met Kane's hard stare. "What's up?" I asked, casually.

"Be careful," was all he said as he left the doorway.

My mouth hung open and I shook myself. I quickly headed to the washroom, cleaned myself up and went back to my room. I braced myself before opening the door.

"I can't see you anymore," Brett said as I shut the door.

My stomach dropped to my feet and I opened my mouth to reply when I saw him holding a phone to his ear. A breath of relief left me making my heart flutter.

"No. I told you that we're through…no…I don't care…Claire, dammit, listen to me. It's over."

The hackles rose on the back of my neck. He was talking to a woman. A woman who clearly still had her claws into him. A woman that had affected him and got under his skin.

"I'm not discussing this with you. Whatever we had is over. Yes, there is…that's none of your fucking business."

I wanted to go to him. Comfort him but the intense air of rage seeping from his pores stopped me.

"What do you want me to tell you, Claire? That I loved you? Because it's not fucking true. Fine…yes…you better not…shit." Brett lifted the phone from his ear and huffed. "How much did you hear?"

I startled and cleared my throat. "Enough."

He nodded and rose to his feet. He pulled back the covers and met my gaze. "Get in."

I raised an eyebrow. "Who's Claire?"

"Don't worry about it."

My jaw tensed as his eyes went cold. "Brett."

"Get. In."

My back stiffened and I ripped off the housecoat.

His gaze travelled down my naked body as I took a step towards him. "Evvie," he husked.

I placed a hand on his chest, slowly grazing my fingers down his torso. "An ex-girlfriend?"

He grabbed my wrist, his eyes darkening in warning. "I don't have ex-girlfriends."

I pulled out of his grip. "A fuck-buddy?"

108

Brett wrapped a hand around my throat and pushed me onto the bed, covering my body with his. "I don't want to talk about her," he snarled.

I gasped, struggling against his hold when his grip on me only tightened. "Brett."

He leaned into my face, his mouth mere inches from mine. "Jealous, lover?"

I glared and grabbed his wrist as he tilted my head back. "Let go of me."

He brushed his lips along mine sending a flutter of pleasure racing down my back. "Does it turn you on?"

My stomach clenched and I shoved out of his grip. I pushed him and sat up when he grabbed my wrists, pinning me under him. My chest rose and fell at the added force as we stared at each other. "You're an asshole."

He smirked, his hold on my wrists tightening as he lowered his head to my neck. He licked and sucked my skin, breathing deep while pushing his pelvis against mine.

I bit back a moan, my body tensing that no matter how much of a prick he was being, I would always want him.

"You are so fucking hot, lover. I know it pisses you off that you give in so easily to me."

My eyes widened and I pushed him off of me. "You don't know shit."

He chuckled, letting me up.

I glared. A cold chill ran down my back mixing with the desire that curled in my belly. It set my blood racing on overdrive. I sat up and scrubbed a hand down my face and looked at him.

A smug smile spread on his face as he laid there casually with an arm under his head, his dark gaze boring into mine.

I ground my teeth together, my muscles quivering as my eyes roamed down his towel clad body. The back of my neck heated, my core throbbing.

I shook my head and rose from the bed. Being there with him, without an ounce of clothing on, left me feeling exposed. He saw all of me. Took me to new levels of ecstasy I only dreamt about but I wasn't one of his whores.

I stomped to my dresser and pulled clothes out of the drawer.

A phone rang, startling me when I realized it was my own. I quickly pulled on a t-shirt and picked up the cell. I sighed before meeting Brett's gaze. "Hey Evan."

"Evvie," he said, breathing heavy.

I frowned. "What's wrong?"

"Shit…" A loud bang sounded through the phone making me jump. "Sorry, Ev. Hold on," he called out. "You there?"

"What's going on?" I asked, leaning against the dresser.

"Dropped my damn phone."

"Evan, what happened?" I watched Brett leave the room and come back a moment later with his clothes in his arms.

"Evvie, Ethan's in jail."

A breath left me on a whoosh as I crumpled to the floor. Not again. "What? Why?"

Brett closed the distance between us and grabbed my free hand, rubbing his thumb over my palm. My heart stuttered, pulling the strength from him into me.

Evan sighed. "Wrong place, wrong time. Same shit with that fucker."

"How long is he in jail for?" I asked, curling my fingers in Brett's.

"I don't know yet. I just found out that he was picked up a week ago."

"Does Dad know?" I whispered.

"Not yet, as far as I know. This is gonna fuck everything up. Dad's supposed to be getting out any day now. He's going to lose his shit once he finds out Ethan's back in jail."

My stomach sunk. "What do you need from me?"

"Go to Ethan. Tell him I'm contacting our lawyer and to stay out of fucking trouble."

"Okay. I'm headed there now."

"Evvie?"

"Yeah?" I said, rising to my feet.

"Be careful."

I sighed. "I will. I can handle him."

"I know."

I hung up the phone and tossed it on my desk. My heart raced as I took deep breaths, gripping the edge of the dresser. "Shit, Ethan." What the hell was he thinking?

"Evvie?" Brett cupped the back of my neck, rubbing his thumb up and down the side.

I sighed and turned to him, wrapping my arms around his middle. The scent of fresh dried laundry invaded my nostrils, easing my racing heart.

He ran a hand in small circles over my back, holding me against him. "Talk to me, lover."

I bit back a scoff. He wanted me to talk to him when he wouldn't talk to me. "You want me to talk to you, when you're all tight-lipped with me?"

His body stiffened.

I sighed and squeezed my eyes shut, snuggling into his chest. "My dumbass brother got himself locked up again."

"Again?"

I let out a deep breath and pulled out of his grasp. "Since my mom died, he's been in and out of jail. Hung out with the wrong kids."

"What was he charged with?"

"I don't know." My chest ached, my head pounding as thoughts of my messed up family rained full force in my head. My mom would be so pissed if she were alive right now.

A lump formed in my throat as I stepped out of Brett's grasp. I pulled off my clothes and threw on a black lace bra and panty set. My heart stuttered when he did up the snaps at my back and kissed my shoulder. Our gazes locked in the mirror, the gentle touch making my body heat.

Only knowing Brett for a couple of weeks, I felt bare, stripped completely like he could see inside my soul. Vulnerable. He touched me like he owned me but it was always in private. If we ever made our relationship official, would he become more possessive?

I almost laughed at myself. What relationship? *It's just sex, Evvie.*

I stepped around him, clearing my throat and headed to the closet. I wanted more than sex. I wanted him. Always and completely but I didn't know how to even begin telling him that.

"Where's your father?"

My back stiffened as I pulled on a red blouse and did up the buttons, leaving the top four undone. "In jail but Evan said he's supposed to be out soon. He could even be out now."

"Shit, Evvie."

I smiled lightly and wiggled into a black high wasted skirt, tucking in the ends of the shirt. "My whole young life, my brother and father have been in and out of jail. My middle brother, Everett was the smart one and left the country." I turned to Brett and leaned against the wall. "Evan took care of Ethan and I. Because of him…" My eyes burned with unshed tears. "I'm sorry. I don't know why I'm telling you this." My cheeks heated.

Brett stepped up to me and pinched my chin. He brushed his mouth along mine, sending my heart a flutter. "I like it when you talk to me."

My stomach jumped at the soft kiss on my lips. "I like that you listen to me," I whispered.

He smiled and kissed my nose. "You don't seem too upset about your brother."

I scoffed. "It's the same shit, different day. I'm used to it." I turned to my mirror and frowned, the buttons on my shirt were done up all the way. I looked back at Brett. "Brett?"

He met my gaze, staring at me head on. His dark eyes challenged me to argue about the buttons. "Need a ride, lover?"

My jaw clenched. "Please."

***

I COULD feel Brett glance at me every so often as I stared out the window. A brother and father that were both in jail. God, I could kill Ethan for doing this again.

His hand cupped my inner thigh, comforting me. Claiming me as his. *Mine.*

When Brett had said that I was his earlier, I couldn't even begin to comprehend what he was saying as the passion tore through me. Was I his? I sure as hell wanted to be. But could my family accept him? Could he deal with the men in my life?

He was jealous, possessive and we were only having sex. Confusion soared through my body. What the hell did it all mean?

My phone rang and I paused before answering. "Hey Evan."

"You headed to see Ethan?"

"Yes, I'm on my way now," I answered, cupping Brett's hand.

"How are you getting there?"

"Brett's driving—"

"Evvie."

"This is not the time for that shit," I snapped.

Evan huffed. "I don't want you seeing him."

My back stiffened. "You have no right saying that to me."

"You don't even fucking know him."

"I know him enough. At least he's not being a jack ass right now."

"Evvie."

"No. I'm sick of all of you trying to control *my* life. I can see whoever I want, when I want."

Brett squeezed my thigh reassuringly.

"Evan, I love you but you're being an asshole. Brett has nothing to do with this. He's here for *me*." I sighed.

"I'm sorry, sis. I'm just worried for Ethan but if Dad finds out about Brett..."

I rolled my eyes. "Daddy is not going to do anything. I'm not scared of him like the rest of you."

Evan chuckled and let out a deep breath. "Call me after you see Ethan."

"I will." I hung up and squeezed Brett's hand, holding onto him. I needed him. I couldn't deal with this shit on my own.

Brett pulled into the parking lot of the large brick building. The local jail was older, a chain linked fence surrounded the yard, sporting guards at each entrance. The only thing new about this place were the cameras mounted on the wall every 20 or 30 feet. "When was the last time you were here?" he asked, looking down at me.

I stared straight ahead as memories invaded my thoughts. "A year ago."

"Father or brother?"

113

I looked up at him. "Both."

We sat there staring at each other for what felt like an eternity. Unsaid feelings soared around us as I fell into the depths of his gaze. My heart fluttered, my stomach flipped and I realized at that very point that I was falling in love with him. It was too soon for those words to leave my lips. Distracting my thoughts, I grabbed his hand and kissed his palm. "I should go. Get this shit done and over with."

He nodded, and sighed.

I took a deep breath and unbuttoned the top four buttons of my red blouse.

A growl escaped Brett's lips at the show of cleavage threatening to escape my shirt.

I looked up at him and narrowed my eyes. "Don't."

"Evvie," he bit out.

"Brett, stop. It gets me longer visits with my brother." I shrugged. I was the only person Ethan had that could get through to him. I learned at a young age that being a woman had its advantages.

"You put your tits on display for those fuckers to stare at so you can spend more time with an asshole who put himself there?" he snarled.

"What I do is none of your fucking business, Brett," I said, my voice turning cold.

"Like hell it's not." He reached out and grabbed my shirt, doing up the buttons.

I slapped his hands away.

Brett's face reddened as I pulled the buttons apart, defiantly lifting my chin.

"Evvie," he growled.

I pushed him. "You don't get to tell me what to do. You don't own me, Brett."

He cupped the back of my neck and pulled me closer. "Yes. I. Do."

I inhaled a gasp and punched his shoulder. "No, you fucking don't. You don't own any part of me."

The tendons in his neck strained against his skin as he glared at me. "Well you fucking own me, Evvie. Every single piece of me. Mind, body and soul. I am fucking yours."

114

Sixteen

I SAT there and gaped at him. He was mine? Like hell he was. Me and every other woman that entered his office. I was just a lay. A good time. He didn't want me permanently. His cold eyes and his mood swings proved it.

His eyes searched my face, waiting for my response.

I shook my head and pushed open the door. "I can't deal with this right now, Brett."

He grabbed my arm, forcing me to look up at him. "Just…" he took a breath. "tell me you feel something for me."

My mouth fell open. Big strong dominating Brett MacLean was asking if *I* felt something for him. Hell had officially frozen over. "Are you teasing me?" I shook my head. This didn't make sense. It was just sex between us. Sex. That was it. I didn't understand—

Warm lips captured mine in a soft but demanding kiss. My eyes fluttered closed as Brett cupped the back of my neck before licking his way into my mouth.

I sucked on his tongue, needing him inside me.

A rumble erupted from his chest as he pushed against me.

I grabbed his shirt, pulling him closer, needing to crawl up his body. If we weren't sitting outside a jail waiting for me to visit my brother, I would have begged him to take me right then.

Confusion coursed through me. I didn't know how Brett felt about me but the kiss was hot, passionate as he devoured my mouth. Our feelings for each other mixed, flowing around us as the kiss became frantic.

Brett released my mouth, trailing light kisses down my jaw. His breathing deep and heavy, scorching my neck. "Tell me you're not attracted to me."

My eyes fluttered closed as his lips caressed my skin. "Of course I'm attracted to you."

"Do you have feelings for me?"

I pulled back and stared intently into his heated gaze. "Brett, I thought this was just sex."

"It was." He rubbed his kiss swollen mouth, a smug smile splaying on his lips when he caught me staring. He pinched my chin. "But the need for you consumes me."

My eyes popped open at his deep words. "What are you saying?"

His gaze lowered to my lips and down.

I followed his gaze and found his hand gripping my inner thigh like I was his. My heart thudded hard. I was nobody's possession, but the way Brett touched me let me know that he would not give up without a fight.

"I'm saying that I want more. With you."

I met his eyes and swallowed. "I'm not one of your whores. You can't use me like you've used them."

His jaw clenched. "I would never fucking use you, lover."

"Is that what you tell all of the other women, too?" I cringed as soon as the words left my lips. They just slipped. I wanted something more too, but I wasn't just a hole he could fuck whenever he got bored.

He pulled away, his back stiffening. "I guess I deserve that."

I sighed and placed a hand on his arm. "Brett, I'm sorry. I'm just shocked."

He shook his head. "And you don't think I am? I've only had feelings for one woman in my life and that turned to shit." He chuckled. "I'm such an idiot."

My stomach twisted. "No, you're not."

His head snapped to mine. "I'm not? I'm telling you how I feel and you assume I'm fucking using you."

"You're cryptic. I don't—"

"I'm falling in love with you, Evvie. There, is that less cryptic for you?"

His words hit me like a slap in the face. In love? With me? It was too soon. Wasn't it? "Why?"

His eyes went cold, deadly as he glared at me. "You're fucking asking me why I'm falling in love with you?"

I swallowed hard. "I just—"

"Go see your brother," he bit out.

***

I STORMED to the doors of the large building, my heels clicking along the sidewalk. My blood boiled and my ears rang. He loved me. I scoffed. Yeah, right. My heart fluttered and I sighed. If he did, it would make the raging emotions that had travelled through my body since the first time we kissed make sense. I was deeply attracted to him but was it love? My stomach flipped. *Mine.*

Brett was also right when it came to using my cleavage to spend more time with a brother who obviously didn't want my help. God, what was I thinking? The shit Ethan did to get himself locked up throughout my life probably should have made me hate him but I couldn't. He was my brother, my best friend besides Kane and I was the only one that could even make an attempt at getting through to him.

I took a breath and pushed through the double doors, heading into the waiting area. A cop sat at a desk behind a window typing away at the computer. He looked up as I approached him, his eyes immediately falling to my cleavage.

A flutter of unease spread through me and I opened my mouth to speak when the hairs on the back of my neck tingled. I turned around and frowned when I saw Brett sitting in a chair against the far wall. His gaze bored into mine, daring me to challenge him.

We continued to stare at each other as I did up the buttons on my shirt.

A smug smile spread on his face and he crossed his arms under his chest. The casual demeanor made my stomach flip.

"Evvie?"

I startled at the deep voice behind me and turned around, looking up into the warm gray eyes of Officer Bronson. "Hi."

He smiled, the lines on his hard older face relaxing. "Here to see your brother?"

I gripped my clutch at my side and nodded. "How's he doing?"

Office Bronson indicated my clutch. "Rules, remember?"

My cheeks heated and I headed to Brett. "Hold this for me, please?"

Brett grabbed the clutch and made a point of brushing his thumb along my hand sending a jolt of electricity straight through my body. "Anything for you, lover," he purred.

I rolled my eyes and ignored the flutter of my heart. *Focus, Evvie.*

I walked back to Officer Bronson as he opened the door. "Boyfriend?"

My gaze snapped to his. "No," I bit out.

The corners of his mouth twitched. "Ethan is pretty pissed that he got caught."

I breathed a sigh of relief at the change in subject. "What the hell did he do?"

"Evvie."

I stopped as we reached the end of the hall. "Please, tell me."

Officer Bronson sighed. "Dealing, again."

My stomach dropped. "What was he dealing this time?"

"Everything."

Of course he was. "How's my dad?"

Officer Bronson opened the door after it buzzed and we walked down another long corridor. "Keeping the peace."

I let out a breath. As we reached the waiting area, my heart sped up. No matter how many times I had been to the jailhouse to see my father and brother, it always made me nervous. Left a bad taste in my mouth.

"Deep breaths, Evvie," Office Bronson coaxed.

I sighed and walked into the large waiting area. Metal tables and chairs lined the vast space as people milled about. Males, young and old in orange jumpsuits visited with family, friends, anyone who would go and see them.

I sat on the cool hard chair at the back of the room and waited, wringing my hands in my lap. I squeezed my eyes shut, taking deep cleansing breaths. I hadn't seen my brother in a year. The last time, I had pleaded with him to stay out of trouble. If not for him, then for me.

Images of the first time he was taken from our childhood home rained full force in my mind. Police vehicle lights flashing red and blue across our yard. Cops raiding our small house and taking my fourteen-year-old brother away.

118

"Evvie."

I looked up into eyes that were big and blue, filled with so much strength that it took my breath away. The hard contours of Ethan's young face relaxed when our gazes met. A year in age between us showcased eyes of an older soul. Why he put himself through the shit he did, I'd never understand.

Ethan smirked. "Aren't you going to give me a hug?"

I rose to my feet but noted the dark purple bruise under his left eye. He hadn't been here for long and already he was fighting. I swallowed past the hard lump in my throat and stepped into his open arms. The rough fabric of the orange jumpsuit scratched at my cheek as I embraced him in a strong hug. "You shaved your head."

He pulled out of my grip and ran a hand over his buzzed head as he sat down. "Makes me look tougher."

I scoffed and sat across from him. "You don't need help with that."

He grinned and rubbed his jaw.

My chest ached at the cold permanent stare of my older brother's deep blue gaze. Tattoos lined his thick neck, travelling down beneath the collar of the standard uniform.

Ethan leaned back in the chair and looked around the room.

"What did you do this time?" I demanded.

His gaze travelled back to mine, twinkling with mischief. "No beating around the bush, huh Ev?"

"No. What happened?"

He leaned forward, placing his elbows on the table. "Don't worry about me, sis."

"Ethan."

He slapped the table. "I don't want you worrying about me. I can take care of my own shit."

"Clearly. You're doing a damn good job at it, too." I glared, feeling the familiar sense of anger bubbling in my belly at the constant fight I had with him. Same fight. Different day.

Ethan's jaw clenched. "Did you come here to give me hell or 'cause you missed me?"

I crossed my arms under my chest and leaned back in the chair. "Both, asshole."

He sat back and looked around the large room. "The last time I was here, I was sitting where you are, visiting Dad."

A lump formed in my throat at his admission. "How is he?"

Ethan met my gaze and shrugged. "He's stuck in this hell hole. How do you think he is?"

I raised an eyebrow. "You don't have to be a dick."

Ethan smirked. "God, I've missed you."

"That's because I'm the only one that won't put up with your shit."

He laughed and crossed his arms under his chest. "Yeah, I guess getting caught was stupid on my part."

I searched his face. He always got caught. It was like he was punishing himself. "Ethan." I rose from my seat and walked around the table, sitting beside him.

He looked away and I followed his gaze. Officer Bronson raised his hands, indicating ten minutes left of our visit.

Ethan looked back at me. "Who's the guy?"

My back stiffened, my cheeks heating. "I don't know what you're talking about."

His eyes twinkled. "Bullshit."

I frowned. "How do you know there's a guy?"

Ethan winked. "You seem more relaxed and that's saying something after the shit Dad and I have put you through."

"It's not just me."

Ethan grabbed my hand. "Everett left the country and Evan doesn't think of anyone but himself."

I shook my head. "That's not true."

"You know it is."

"I…" I never thought about it before. Evan always took care of us while our dad and Ethan…I swallowed. If he spent more time with Ethan like he did Everett and I, maybe we wouldn't be sitting at the jail.

Ethan sighed and scrubbed a hand down his face. "Evan loves you. Just don't let him try and control you like he did me."

No one controlled me. Not up until now at least.

"He treat you good?"

He tried to control me and dominate me, taking ownership of my life… ""Yes."

Ethan nodded. "Good, then I won't have to kill him."

120

I sighed and placed a hand on his arm. "Please be good. I'm begging you."

Ethan's strong jaw tensed. "Don't worry about me."

"It's not just me that worries about you," I cried.

Ethan rose to his feet. "I'll come see you when I get out."

"Ethan."

He turned back to me and winked. "They won't be able to hold me here for long."

***

ONCE REACHING the waiting area, my gaze instantly met Brett's. My tense body relaxed at the sight of him sitting there waiting for me.

I took a step towards him when a large man came into my view. My eyes widened. *"Daddy!"*

Edward Neal grinned a toothy smile as I threw my arms around his hard middle. Being in his late fifties, he shouldn't have been so fit for an older man.

"Hello, sweet pea." My dad ran a hand over my hair and kissed my head.

I released him and blinked past the tears that burned my eyes. "You're out?"

He nodded and cupped my cheek. "I am."

I bit back a squeal and wrapped my arms around his middle. No matter the shit we had been through in our lives, he was my father. I knew he loved us. He did everything. For us.

He chuckled and held me tight against him. "Who's the young man staring our way, Evvie?"

I swallowed a groan, my cheeks heating. God, sometimes I forgot that my father was a retired cop. Once a cop, always a cop. "A friend."

My dad held me at arm's length and stared into my eyes. White stubble covered his strong jaw as his full lips tightened. "He's in love with you. I'd say that's more than a friend."

My mouth fell open. "How…what…" I stumbled over my words, my cheeks heating.

"I'm falling in love with you, Evvie."

My dad smiled and kissed my forehead.

121

"How did you know?"

He looked at Brett over his shoulder.

I followed his gaze.

Brett sat up, his body stiffening waiting to pounce. To protect me.

My heart swelled and I smiled lightly.

My father's breath caught before he turned back to me. "Only your mother could make me look like that. All hot and bothered ready to pounce for her."

$\mathcal{S}$eventeen

"EVVIE?"

I turned to the deep smooth voice of Brett as he came up beside us. My heart fluttered at the warm look of concern in his blue gaze.

My dad stiffened and looked up at him.

My gaze passed between the two and I swallowed as the silent battle of protection over me soared around us.

"Daddy, this is Brett MacLean." I looked up at Brett and placed a hand on his arm. He met my gaze and smiled. "My father, Edward Neal."

Brett held his hand out in front of him. "Sir."

My dad raised an eyebrow, his hard gaze boring into Brett's. He slowly returned the handshake, sizing him up in the process.

"Eddie?" Officer Bronson clapped a hand on my father's shoulder.

"I'll call you soon," my dad told me.

I nodded and gave him one last hug before I watched him follow the cop to the waiting to see Ethan.

My chest ached, anxiety swirling deep in the pit of my belly. A shaky breath escaped my lips as I wrapped my arms around myself. I needed to leave. To get out of there before my body broke. Would my family ever be normal? God, I missed my mom.

"Brett," I said, swallowing past the hard lump in my throat.

"Yes, lover?" Brett cupped the back of my neck, brushing his thumb up and down the side.

My heart swelled, the unease that had settled in my belly, simmering. "Take me home," I whispered.

Brett wrapped his arm around my shoulders and led me outside to his car. He opened the passenger door and I slid into the seat.

I pinched the bridge of my nose, breathing through the oncoming headache that started pounding in my skull.

A warm hand landed on my inner thigh, gripping me in a hold of possession and protection? I didn't need to be protected. I needed the men in my life to stop treating me like I'm fragile. An expected sob escaped my lips. I needed my mom. She would know what to do. She would know how to keep Ethan out of jail.

Brett squeezed my leg reassuringly.

My back stiffened. I didn't need reassurance. I grabbed his hand and pushed it off of me. "Don't."

"Evvie."

I ignored the warning in his voice. "Please, stop...I just...I don't..." I sighed heavily, tears flowing down my cheeks.

I didn't bother wiping them away as they dripped off my chin. I was confused, angry, empty. The fact that a man so dark and possessive was in love with me scared the shit out of me. And not to mention my family. Overbearing and protective of their own. That was the Neal men way and I was sick of it.

I scrubbed a hand down my face.

Brett went to pull away but I grabbed his hand, holding it tight in my lap. I realized then that I needed him. The strength I pulled from him, eased my aching heart and soothed my rattled nerves. "I'm sorry."

He moved his hand to my thigh, holding me. "Shhh...just let me touch you," he whispered.

I looked up at him but he didn't meet my gaze. He kept his eyes on the road. His strong jaw tense, the muscles jumping and twitching every so often.

I sighed and curled my legs under me, leaning my head against the seat.

My eyes grew heavy and I let them close, reveling in the warm body beside me.

We drove in silence, the sounds of the city soaring around us. Cars honked, sirens blaring in the distance but the only thing I could focus on was the beating of my heart.

"Lover."

I smiled at the deep husky voice in my ear. My eyes slowly opened to find Brett's face mere inches from mine. A slight smile tugged at the corner of his full lips before he looked away.

I followed his gaze and gasped. The mid-day sun shone over a group of trees that surrounded a small lake. It was simply breath taking.

"Where are we?" I asked, sitting up.

"My sister calls it The Cove, but I don't think it has an official name," Brett answered, brushing a finger down my arm.

I smiled and continued to stare out at the stunning view. "Every time I leave the jail, I get this empty feeling inside of me. I feel helpless and it pisses me off when I'm told not to worry."

Brett linked his fingers in mine, rubbing his thumb over the back of my hand. "It pisses me off when I lose control."

My head whipped to his. I already knew that, having faced the wrath of the aftermath of his no control. "You weren't mad when we got drunk last night and both of us lost control."

His gazed darkened. "That's because I wanted to be there with you. Losing control as one was exhilarating."

My heart thudded hard at the erotic undertone of his words. "I can't compete with the other women in your life," I mumbled.

Brett searched my face, staring into my eyes intently. "There's only one other woman in my life and that's my sister."

"What about Claire?"

Brett's hand tightened in mine. "Claire was a mistake."

I scoffed. "I think you should tell her that."

He scowled. "Lover, I don't want to ruin this moment by talking about that woman."

"Fine." We would have to talk about her eventually, especially if we made our relationship official.

I pulled myself from his grip and left the vehicle. The cool afternoon air flowed around me, kissing my skin as I took a couple of steps towards the small body of water.

The sound of a door closing echoed around me making my heart jump.

A thought came to me. Needing to forget the day I had. Needing to just live in the moment. To feel alive.

I took a breath and looked at Brett over my shoulder.

He leaned against the car casually, watching me. Every time he looked at me with his deep blue captivating depths, my stomach fluttered.

Not taking my gaze from his, I kicked off my heels and untucked my shirt.

His eyes followed my movements as I started unbuttoning my blouse. "Have you ever been skinny dipping?"

Brett raised an eyebrow and crossed his arms under his chest. "No."

"Neither have I," I said, pulling off my shirt. I didn't know what was coming over me. I knew that for once in my life, I was going to be in control. Last night, we got drunk. Neither of us was in control once we finished that bottle of tequila, but waking up beside the sexiest man I have ever seen made the hang over worth it.

I threw the shirt on the ground and turned around while unzipping the back of my skirt. I shimmied it down my hips and made a point of bending over. I smiled when Brett inhaled a groan.

I rose to my full height when the hairs on my body tingled. "What are you doing, lover?"

I jumped at the hot whisper in my ear. "I'm breaking the rules. I want to do something I've never done before."

Brett ran his hands down my arms igniting a tingle that raced down my back. "It seems to me like you've been doing a lot that you haven't done before."

My body heated as the memories of our times together rained full force into my mind. "Since my brother has been in and out of jail since I was a kid, I've played by the rules. I didn't want to be like him. He's a good guy but just makes the wrong choices. Just once, I want to do something that I'm not supposed to do." I stepped out of his grasp and unclasped the back of my bra.

"Like what?" Brett asked, walking in front of me.

I let the bra fall beside me and looked up at him. My breathing deepened, desire curling inside of me. My nipples pebbled under the cool air, begging for his rough caress.

He brushed his thumbs along the peaks.

Jolts of electricity raced to my groin at the soft movement.

His nostrils flared as a breath escaped my lips. "I love the way your nipples harden under my touch."

I kept my hands at my sides, fighting back the urge to jump in his arms and devour him completely. I tilted my head and licked my lips. "I love the feel of your hands on my body."

He smirked and lowered his head to kiss me when I stepped out of his grip.

I felt him watch me as I pulled off the panties, leaving me standing naked before him.

"I hope you can swim fast, lover."

I looked at him over my shoulder and raised an eyebrow as I waded into the water. A shiver ran up my body spreading goose bumps on my skin.

"Why's that?" I asked, going knee deep in the refreshing water.

A wicked grin spread on his face as he ripped open his shirt. Buttons flew around him, landing on the ground.

My core clenched at the sight and I stood there, wide eyed as I watched him strip.

"Because once I catch you and take you how I want you, I'm never letting you go." He took a step towards me, closing the distance between us.

My breath caught and I squealed as he stalked towards me.

Diving under the water, I heard a splash and rose to the surface. Brett was nowhere to be found. I swam a couple of feet and looked around but still couldn't see him.

He should have caught me by now.

"Brett?" I called out but the only response I got was chirping from the birds nearby. Knowing he wouldn't have left me since the car was still here, he was probably hiding, waiting until I least expect it and then make his move.

The pounding of my heart eased as my body relaxed from the stresses of the day. I continued floating on the water when a hard body wrapped around me.

I gasped, struggling to get out of his grip, swallowing some water in the meantime.

A deep chuckle sounded in my ear as Brett held me against him, bringing us to shore.

My heart raced, adrenaline rushing through me as I attempted to push out of his strong hold.

"Trying to escape are we, lover?" he breathed in my ear.

"Now why would I do that?" I asked, prying his fingers off of me.

He lifted me off of my feet once we reached the shore and he pushed me face first onto the cool grass. "You enjoy the chase."

I panted and crawled away when he pulled my ankles out from under me. My blood soared, pumping through my body as he pinned me beneath him. My core throbbed, needing him inside of me. "Brett?"

He ran his nose up the side of my neck, fisting my hair in his hand. "Yes, lover?"

I gripped the grass and arched my hips. "I need you to fuck me."

He moaned and bit my shoulder. "Do you now?"

I lifted my ass, rubbing myself over his rock hard cock. "Yes. Right now."

Brett lifted my knee to my chest, spreading me before him. "I am so hard for you."

"Please," I begged, never needing him so bad in the short time we started sleeping together.

"Tell me," he demanded.

"I need you to make me feel good." I gasped as he sank into me, filling me to the hilt. "Oh God."

He stopped, letting me get used to the size of his girth. My body wrapped around him, stretching to fit him.

"I'm going to fuck you rough, lover and you're going to think of just me."

I moaned when he slowly started thrusting in and out of me. "Faster."

"Patience my little vixen." He kissed my neck. "Spread your legs wide for me."

I did as he said and whimpered as he drove into me hard, his swollen length hitting my g-spot.

"God, your body was made to be fucked by me," he groaned, pushing into me as deep as he could go.

I cried out, a tingle spreading through me at the deep impact as he thrust into my throbbing pussy.

"Fuck, Evvie," Brett breathed.

I arched my hips as his pelvis hit my ass. "Yes, harder."

128

He moaned and nipped the skin below my ear. "Lover, you like being fucked by my thick cock?"

His erotic words washed over me, heating me from within as he drove his long length into me. The pace was rough, frantic, delicious. Like he was desperate for me. Two bodies moving as one.

"Come. I need to feel your pleasure as you let go."

I moaned, pushing back against him as I tilted my hips. The movements became hard, deeper as I felt him to my womb. Past the barrier of comfortable. To a place only he could reach. He hit that spot just right as I opened myself to him. Baring all as he stripped me completely.

"Come for me, Evvie."

I shook, quaking around him but I held back. Wanting to join him in that high of ecstasy. "Brett."

He wrapped a hand around my neck and gripped my hip with the other. Owning me. Possessing me.

I broke. My body released on a spasm of bliss as I screamed and clenched around him.

He grunted and shook, pouring into me with such strong ferocity, I could feel his semen running down my inner thighs.

His hips sped up, elongating the explosion that had erupted inside of me. The feral way he took me, marked me as his, let me know that he was mine. And I was his.

Eighteen

THERE WAS no way that I could deny the possession erupting between us. After our swim and the rough way Brett took me, my body felt heavy and sore, but relaxed. Satisfied.

Several weeks had passed since our skinny dipping adventure at The Cove. We met often, either at my place or his but I still have never seen his bedroom. My body bloomed when I realized we never made it that far once we were in his apartment.

After seeing Ethan, Evan had called me a couple of days later. He let me know that he would be out of jail soon and that he wasn't dealing again.

I didn't know how to handle the problems with my family. I also didn't know if Brett could deal with the several tempers from my brothers and father.

Finding out that my father was released from jail but didn't even attempt to contact me, hurt. I wasn't sure when he got out. No one would tell me. They wanted to protect me.

"I didn't want you to worry about me, sweet pea."

"Come over tomorrow."

We never went to see my father. He called me, making some lame ass excuse about needing more time.

It tore my heart in two when I got that phone call. I broke in Brett's arms. Crying against him as he rubbed my back. He was the only constant thing in my life and even then, I didn't know how permanent that was. He didn't mention that he was falling in love with me again and I didn't either.

I huffed and wiped down the counter, rubbing the cloth over the same spot more than once.

"Ev, you keep rubbing the counter like that, you're gonna turn it on."

I turned to Tatiana standing in front of me, holding her tray. "Drink order?"

She raised a pierced eyebrow.

I noted that it was new. The metal barbell shone in the glow of the dim room. "Order?"

130

"Who's got your panties in a twist, girlfriend?" she smiled, licking her dark red lips.

"Tatiana." I rolled my eyes.

She chuckled. "I need a rum and coke and a martini, dry."

I nodded and started mixing up the drinks.

"If you ever need a shoulder, Ev, I'm here."

A laugh escaped me at the sexual innuendo in her voice. I looked at her over my shoulder. "Thank you."

Tatiana shrugged and winked. "Anytime, babe."

I placed the drinks on the tray and gripped the counter.

She smiled and walked away, sashaying her hips.

I giggled and shook my head when the hairs on my body prickled. Brett was close by. We didn't put an official title on our relationship, if you could even call it that, but I was attuned to him on a level that left me breathless. The attraction between us was strong, controlling. Intense.

"Lover."

I smiled and turned to Brett standing beside me.

His blue gaze warmed as he closed the distance between us. His hot breath caressed my neck, soothing the uneasiness that had set up residence in my belly since speaking with my father.

"What's wrong?" he asked, wrapping a hand around my wrist.

"Nothing."

His grip tightened. "Don't lie to me."

I frowned, meeting his hard gaze. "I'm not."

His jaw tensed.

I pulled out of his grip and continued wiping down the counter. I could feel him watching me but he didn't do anything. He just stood there and waited.

We had spent as much time together as possible. But it was still sex. A lot of sex. We hardly talked and I knew nothing about but the man that I was sleeping with. Going into this, I just wanted to feel alive. I was always safe. Never dating someone my family didn't approve of. Now with Brett, I didn't care what they thought. But I still wanted more.

"Evvie, talk to me," he said softly.

My back stiffened.

"Tell me you feel something for me."

131

The words rained in my head. Of course I felt something for him but his lack of an attempt at making our relationship official bothered me.

"Hey Ev. Boss."

I turned to the sound of Jake's smooth voice and smiled. "Jake, can you take over?"

He nodded. His warm brown eyes flicking between Brett and me.

A breath I didn't realize that I was holding left me on a whoosh as I walked by Brett. I didn't need to look behind me to know that he was following me. My body buzzed, my heart thumping hard. What would I tell him when we reached his office? *More.*

With a shaky hand, I opened the office door and walked into the cool room.

The sound of a lock clicking into place set my blood on overdrive.

My eyes scanned the small room before they landed on the black leather couch. Our first kiss pushed its way into my thoughts, igniting my blood on fire.

Once reaching the small bar, I poured a shot of tequila, slammed it back and turned to Brett.

He watched me with dark scrutiny as he leaned against the wall.

My gaze followed his hand as it rubbed the scruff of his strong jaw. The burn of the alcohol warmed my body like a lover's touch.

"Is there an issue, lover?" he asked, crossing his arms under his chest. The deep burgundy shirt stretched across his shoulders.

The first four buttons were undone, making my mouth water. My lips tingled, wanting to kiss and nibble his thick neck.

"Evvie?"

My eyes snapped to his.

He smirked and brushed a finger along his full bottom lip.

My core clenched, my stomach flipping.

Our gazes locked at he took a step towards me.

"Stop."

He raised an eyebrow, pausing in his steps. "Something wrong?"

132

"Yes. No. I just…" I huffed and backed up to the wall as he closed the distance between us.

The black dress pants fit his lower body like they were made for him. The muscles of his powerful thighs filled them out as he stalked towards me.

My body hummed as images of his body between my legs rained into my mind.

The air crackled between us as he placed a hand on the wall beside my head. He brushed a finger down my cheek sending a hot shiver racing down my spine.

I pushed out of his grasp and paced back and forth, taking deep breaths to control my raging hormones. "I can't talk to you when you touch me."

"Lover."

I took a deep breath and turned to him. "These past couple of weeks have been amazing."

His eyes darkened, taking me in. "I agree," he purred.

I fought back the urge to run into his arms and stood my ground. "But…" I looked away and continued pacing the small office.

Brett didn't press. Didn't ask me anything while I stomped across the small office. He waited knowing eventually I would spill. That was one thing I loved…my eyes widened. Oh shit. I *was* falling in love with him. My heart beat hard as I swallowed a gasp.

It explained everything. The need that gripped the core of my being every time I was near him. The way he invaded my thoughts. God, it all made sense. But was it too soon? I didn't know how to tell him how I felt. I didn't want to scare him off and ruin possibly the best couple weeks of my life.

At that moment, I did the only sensible thing I could think of. I ran.

Nineteen

I HEADED out of Brett's office. We had only been sleeping together for a couple of weeks but I knew that I loved him. I knew that I needed him and that scared the shit out me. What if something happened to our relationship? What if I lost him like my dad lost my mom? I couldn't go through that. I wasn't strong enough.

"Lover," Brett barked.

My back stiffened as I continued walking down the hall.

"Evvie, don't you dare walk away from me," he said, his voice hardening.

I took a breath and ignored him, reaching the end of the corridor. I stopped and waited. For what I wasn't sure.

The deep bass of the dance music washed over me as I watched the crowd move to the beat. A haze covered the vast room from the smoke machine, glowing from the dim red lights.

The tiny hairs on my body rose and I knew Brett was inching towards me with every sure step.

"Don't walk away from this," he pleaded.

My heart thumped hard. *I love you.* The words froze on my tongue. It was too soon. Too fast.

"Evvie, from the moment I first saw you, I've been attracted you. Something passed between us and I know you felt it."

He was right. I did it feel it. It was strong. Raw.

"I fell in love with you after our first night together. The way you looked at me while I was pleasing you made me realize that I wanted more."

My breath caught, feeling him take a step closer to me but still keeping his hands to himself.

"And you're fucking hot as a hell, lover," he said, brushing a finger down my arm.

I laughed but the nervous butterflies still flew around in my belly. I took a breath and let it out in a slow exhale. "I haven't had many relationships. My family scared them away I guess."

"Your family doesn't scare me."

I turned to him and met his gaze. "You don't know who my father is, do you?"

Brett frowned. "I don't care who he is, lover. This is between you and me."

I sighed and chewed my bottom lip.

He grabbed my hand and kissed my knuckles. "Come talk to me."

My heart fluttered. Every time we've been alone, there hasn't been a lot of talking. At all. "I can't."

His brows furrowed, his jaw clenching as his hold on me tightened. "Evvie."

"It's not that I don't want to talk but being alone with you will end up with me wrapped around you."

Brett smirked and kissed my forehead, letting his lips linger before he took a step back. He crossed his arms under his chest and leaned against the wall. "I promise to keep my hands to myself as long as you promise to talk."

I searched his face and nodded. I paced in front of him, searching for the proper words. "My dad loved my mom. Even though I was young when she died, I can remember it so clearly."

A lump formed in my throat but I kept going. Never needing to talk so bad in my life.

"When she—" I swallowed. "Died, I saw a part of my father die with her. All of us were affected but my dad was destroyed. It was like his soul shattered. My brother, Ethan is the youngest boy. He and my mom were close." The tears flowed freely down my cheeks at that point and I wiped them away. My body felt lighter as the words left my lips.

"Ethan rebelled. I remember the police saying he should be in juvie but my dad would have none of that. Didn't want to separate his kids." I stopped pacing and leaned against the wall opposite Brett.

Sliding down the wall, I sat on the floor and looked up as he sat beside me. I pulled my knees to my chest and hugged them tight. "I'm not strong enough to go through what my dad did."

Brett cupped the back of my neck, rubbing his thumb up and down the side. "Your dad wouldn't want you to give up your happiness."

"I know," I mumbled and picked at a fuzz on my pants.

"Your dad loved your mom."

"More than life itself. But…" I looked up at him. "I'm scared." Those two words leaving my mouth set my aching heart at ease. The unexpected emptiness inside of me that I never realized was there until now, mended. It was a slow start but talking to Brett helped. Because of him, the pain from losing my mom after all of these years began to melt away.

His eyes warmed. "Evvie, I've never had a relationship. The one that came close, ended when the ex came back."

I sighed and ran my hands down my thighs. My heart stuttered at the black pants I now wore thanks to a possessive lover. Was I in over my head?

"Lover, look at me."

I slowly met his gaze, my stomach flipping at the warm look of adoration in them. A hint of dark lust roared to the surface, setting my body on overdrive.

He pinched my chin and placed a soft kiss on my mouth. "I'm glad it's over." His lips moved down my jaw. "I wouldn't be here with you if it wasn't."

My heart thumped hard. "I guess things happen for a reason," I mumbled.

Brett's jaw clenched before he rose to his feet. He held out his hand, his deep sapphire eyes boring into mine. "Come with me."

I let him pull me to my feet and guide me to his office. My heart sped up. Being alone with him would not allow the words to leave—

A warm mouth captured mine in a tender but passionate kiss.

Brett's hands ran down my body. They were soft, gentle. Not rough and intense like usual. Before I could open to him, he pulled away and kissed my nose.

He brought me to the couch and pulled me into his lap. "I knew from the first moment you kissed me, that it was going to be more. I even tried fighting it."

I turned to him.

He met my gaze, the corners of his lips tugging into a small smile at his admission.

136

"I can't go through what my dad did."

He grabbed my hand and kissed my knuckles. "You can't stop yourself from being happy, lover. It's not fair to you."

Tears burned my eyes. Watching my father deteriorate into a shattered, alcohol-driven mess made me hesitate.

I pushed out of his lap. "I should go back to work."

His hold on my waist tightened. "No."

"Brett," I said, trying to pry him off of me.

"Stop fighting it," he whispered in my ear.

"I'm not ready." I wanted to tell him how I felt. But I couldn't. A man like Brett MacLean would hurt me.

"Evvie."

I shoved out of his grip and rose to my feet. I loved him. But what if I lost Brett?

"You can't live life on 'what if's,' lover."

I jumped and spun around, not realizing I had spoken out loud.

He took a step towards me, his blue eyes warm and inviting. "You're not the only one that's scared, Evvie."

I frowned. Knowing I wouldn't get any more of an explanation from him, I let out a deep breath. "I don't know how to deal with these feelings I have for you," I said as he closed the distance between us.

"What do you feel?" he asked, cupping my nape.

"I…" I gripped his shirt, trailing my other hand down his strong chest. My fingers tingled, needing the feel of his skin against mine. "The first time I looked at you, I felt something. Even though I thought you were an asshole, I was attracted to you."

He chuckled and brushed a finger down the length of my jaw. "I felt it too. That magnetic pull that drew me to you. At that point, I knew that I had to have you."

"Is that why you approached me with your proposition?" I smiled, remembering the shock of him telling me that he wanted to fuck me.

"That and I was desperate to get between those milky white thighs of yours," he said, his voice lowering.

My heart sped up.

"I was determined to make you mine, lover. At first, I wanted to just fuck you, but now, it's so much more." He gripped my chin, holding me tight like he thought I would run away again.

I felt it too. From the first moment I kissed him. I couldn't deny it any longer. The need that gripped my core. "Brett," I whispered.

He kissed my forehead and then my nose before placing a tender peck on my lips. All the feelings poured into that small touch. I needed more. My body would show him how I felt when the right words wouldn't form on my tongue.

I wrapped my hands around his neck, deepening the kiss.

He ran his hands down my body and cupped my ass, lifting me.

I licked between his lips, igniting a groan from him when he laid me on the couch.

Our breathing picked up when the kiss became intense, hot as he devoured my mouth.

His pelvis pushed against mine and the feel of his erection pressing against my center made my skin hum. I could feel him everywhere. I tilted my hips, rubbing myself over him, moaning at the delicious contact.

He wrapped a hand around my throat and trailed light kisses down my jaw. "Fuck Evvie, I love kissing you."

I licked my swollen mouth and ran my fingers through the hair at his nape. "Make love to me."

"Tell me how you feel," he said, nipping the soft skin under my ear.

I frowned. "Are you bribing me?"

He lifted his head and stared intently into my eyes, gripping my jaw. "I know you feel something for me. Just tell me."

"I did tell you."

His gaze darkened. "You didn't tell me everything."

I huffed and pushed him. "I don't know what you want me to say."

Brett's eyes hardened. "Tell me you don't love me. Tell me you don't want more."

"Of course I want more," I snapped as I sat up. "But I'm not competing with all of your whores."

138

He snarled and pushed me back onto the couch, pinning me beneath him. "There is no fucking competition. None at all. I want you and only you. What the hell do I have to do to make you see that?"

I struggled against him but his hold on me only tightened.

"Lover," his voice softened. "Everyone has a past. I want my future to be you."

My heart flipped but a deep part of me warned our future wouldn't be all sunshine and rainbows.

"Why?"

He frowned. "Why what?"

I took a breath, bracing myself for his reaction. "Why do you love me?"

His jaw clenched, the muscles twitching under the skin. "You're questioning how I feel about you?"

I swallowed. "Well, we haven't made our relationship official."

"Do you love me?" he demanded.

My blood rang in my ears but the three words froze on my tongue.

"Answer me," he said, his voice firm.

My heart thumped hard at the intense fire in his eyes.

"Evvie."

"Fine," I snapped.

He sat back on his hunches and braced his hands on his thighs. His eyes twinkled with amusement, searching my face. "I'm waiting."

I huffed. "I am in love with you. Alright? Happy now, asshole?"

A smug grin formed on his face. "Say it."

I rolled my eyes and grabbed the back of his neck. "I love you."

He crushed his lips to mine. "Again."

"I love you," I breathed against his mouth. Once the words left my lips, a weight lifted off of my shoulders. I loved him. He loved me. Fuck everything else, for now.

***

AFTER A light swat on the ass and a hard kiss to the lips, Brett kicked me out of his office to get some work done.

I had asked him again to make love to me but he said he wanted to wait until we were at his place so he could show me exactly how he felt in his bed. Which would be a first for us both since he'd never had a woman in his bedroom before.

"Hey gorgeous, I need a vodka martini, please."

I turned to Tatiana and smiled. "Coming right up, babe."

Her pierced brow raised. "You feeling alright?"

"Of course. Why?"

She searched my face before looking behind her. "He the reason?"

I shrugged. "I have no idea what you're talking about," I said, my heart fluttering.

She nodded. "Uh-huh. Right."

I smiled, my eyes glancing around the room.

Brett stood at one of the private booths, chatting with an older couple. He looked over his shoulder, our gazes colliding. His eyes flashed with love and an undertone of passion.

The hairs on my neck tingled and my stomach flipped.

"My girl's in love."

I looked back at Tatiana, my cheeks heating. Smiling to myself, I placed the drink on her tray.

My body hummed and before I even looked up, I knew that Brett was approaching me. Not wanting to be too obvious, I grabbed a cloth and started wiping down the counter.

"Lover, look at me."

I swallowed hard at the deep voice by my ear and met Brett's heated stare.

He winked and before I knew what was happening or could even protest, he captured my mouth in a rough kiss.

I vaguely heard cheering around us and Tatiana's "It's about fucking time" but all I could focus on was the warm lips pressed against mine. He cupped my cheek and licked his way into my mouth, deepening the kiss.

A moan erupted from the back of my throat and if we were alone, I would have crawled up his hard body. Devouring every inch of him.

He chuckled and released my mouth.

140

"What was that for?" I panted.

He smirked. "Making it official." He trailed kisses down my jaw to my ear. "And letting every man here know that you are mine."

My heart thudded. "Well then every woman here will know that *you're* mine."

He grinned and placed a soft kiss on my mouth. "Good. Now get back to work, lover."

I laughed and watched him walk away.

"Ev."

I turned to Tatiana as she came up beside me.

"I think that was the fucking hottest thing that I have ever seen."

I smiled. I couldn't help myself. The grin probably split my face but I was happy.

Twenty

"IT FEELS weird being here without you," I said into the phone as I stepped inside Brett's apartment.

"Whether I'm there or not, my home is yours, lover," Brett responded.

My heart fluttered and I shut the door behind me. After our very public kiss, the rest of the night flew by. Brett was supposed to leave with me but things had come up at the club that he had to handle.

"I would have waited for you in your office." I headed down the short alcove that lead into the vast expanse of his apartment.

Brett chuckled. "That would have been too distracting."

I smiled and headed into the living room. Blueprints lined the hallway table as I passed by it. "And why is that, lover boy?"

"You know why."

I kicked off my shoes and walked down a long hallway that led to the bedrooms. "Tell me."

"We're playing this game now, are we?"

My body heated. "Never."

"I enjoy knowing that you're in my apartment, lover," he purred.

Desire curled in my belly as his deep voice washed over my skin.

"What are you doing now?"

"Looking for your bedroom."

"Second door on the right," he said, a hint of amusement in his voice.

I reached the door and opened it, stepping into the dark room before turning on the light. "How long are you going…holy shit." My eyes widened when they landed on the large four poster bed that leaned against the far wall.

"What?"

Black linen covered the king sized mattress with several fluffy pillows against the head of the bed.

"Evvie?"

"Your bed is huge," I exclaimed.

Brett laughed.

My heart thudded as I imagined lying on top of the bed with him between my thighs—

"What are you doing now?" he asked.

I cleared my throat, walking around the bed and ran my hand over the cool black comforter. "I'm feeling up your bed," I joked.

"Hmm...now there's an image."

I moved to crawl onto the bed when an engine sounded. I frowned. "Where are you?"

There was a pause. "Around."

"Brett, where—"

"Don't worry about it."

I huffed and sat on the edge of the bed, the mattress sinking under my weight. I laid back and sighed. "Fine. I should go. I'll see you when you get here."

"Lover, you're not getting rid of me that easily."

My heart thudded, wondering if there was more to that statement then he was letting on.

"Evvie?"

"Yes?" My eyes fluttered closed as I snuggled into the softness of his bed.

"Strip."

My eyes popped open. "Excuse me?"

"Take off your clothes. I want you naked in my bed, ready for me."

Deciding to play his little game, I took a breath and placed my cell on the bed. Hitting the speakerphone button, I gripped the edge of my shirt. "How long are you going to be?" I asked, pulling off my top.

"Long enough. You bare for me, lover?"

I smiled and threw the last bit of clothing on the floor, leaving me standing naked in his bedroom. "Yes."

"Pull back the covers."

I did as he said and pulled the comforter to the foot of the bed.

"Done?"

"Yes."

"Good girl. Now lay on the bed."

I crawled onto the bed, lying on my back. The soft cotton caressed my skin, sending light tingles over my body.

"Close your eyes."

"Brett," I said, hesitating.

"Close those beautiful eyes or else I'll tie you to my bed and blindfold you."

My stomach flipped, a small gasp leaving my lips at that image.

A deep chuckle sounded through the phone. "Would you like that? You strapped down, spread open for me to do whatever I want?"

Oh God.

"Would you like that, Evvie?"

"I like anything you do to me, Brett," I whispered.

"I know. But as much as I would love to see you bound and open for me, that will never happen."

"Oh." I frowned as my stomach clenched unexpectedly. "Why not?"

"Because I'm selfish. I like the feel of your hands on my body. Your nails scratching down my back as I fuck that beautiful pussy."

My heart beat hard, the tiny hairs on my skin tingling at his words. "God, I love the way you talk."

"Good. Now close your eyes."

My eyes fluttered closed as I laid in the middle of his big bed.

"Spread your legs."

Doing as he said, I took a breath and waited in baited anticipation.

"Picture me kissing your toes, to your ankles, to your calf."

I imagined his warm lips on my skin, spreading light touches over my body.

"Now I'm licking up your inner thigh and I place a soft kiss on the freckle at the crease."

I moaned, my breathing picking up at the erotic images his words put into my head. Liquid heat spread from my core through my body, heating my skin.

"Want me to continue, lover?"

144

"I need you here. Right now," I pleaded.

A soft click sounded around the room making my eyes pop open. Brett leaned against the door, his eyes dark with lust and desire as they roamed down my body.

A wicked glint flashed in his gaze when he walked to the black cushioned chair in the corner of the room.

"Brett, what are you doing?" I asked, surprised that he didn't join me on the bed.

He smirked and rubbed his chin before loosening the tie around his neck. The veins in his thick forearms strained against the movement, his strong fingers unbuttoning the first couple of buttons of his shirt.

I sat up, leaning on my elbows and raised an eyebrow.

"Get off the bed."

I rose from the bed and took a step towards him when he raised his hand and pointed at the floor.

A smug smile spread on his face. "On your knees. I'm going to make you beg for my cock."

My stomach flipped at the hard demand and with shaky legs, I lowered to my knees.

I watched as he unbuckled his belt and reached inside his pants before pulling out the rigid length. My pussy pulsed and clenched, needing him inside me. I licked my lips, tensing at not being able to touch him just yet.

His large hand wrapped around the thick veiny muscle, slowly stroking from base to tip. "You like watching me?"

I nodded, words lost on my tongue. It was highly erotic the way he fit so perfectly in his large hand as he pleased himself. It was simply beautiful.

His body strained, the muscles in his jaw tightening as his hand picked up speed. The tip turned a dark shade of pink, like he was holding back on his release.

Taking a breath, I inched my hand up my inner thigh before grazing my fingers over my mound.

His eyes followed my movements. Drawing from my new-found bravery, I pushed a finger through my soaked folds.

His breath hitched at the same time as I moaned while we both pleased our bodies.

"Finger your pussy," he husked.

I spread my knees wider, leaning back against the bed and inserted a finger into my sex. The walls of my core clenched around me as I moved my hips back and forth.

"Fuck, lover," Brett said, squeezing his cock hard.

I licked my lips and moaned, grazing my finger of my clit. A jolt of electricity shot through my body.

"Come for me."

My eyes widened. Not even hesitating, I pushed the hard nub and cried out. Flicking my finger back and forth, a tingle spread through my body.

"That's it. Stroke your clit. I want to watch you come against your hand."

I moaned at his words of encouragement and gasped as an explosion of desire erupted through me. My eyes fluttered closed, his name leaving my lips as I came hard around my fingers.

Suddenly, I was lifted into the air and bent over the edge of the bed as a rough hand smoothed down my naked back. My feet dangled, not touching the floor as Brett held me down.

My heart pumped hard, my skin humming from the remnants of my orgasm.

"Beg," he demanded.

I looked over my shoulder and watched him continue to stroke himself. Our gazes collided and I smirked, waiting.

"Lover," he breathed, his hand moving fast over his cock. A moment later, he shook and growled, warm liquid shooting from his body.

I moaned and arched under him, feeling his release coat my ass and tailbone.

"Shit." His hand slowed, a shiver trembling through his body.

"Brett?"

His passion-filled eyes met mine.

"Now I'm begging."

***

MY BODY stirred awake the next morning, sore and stiff in all the right places. I rolled over, expecting to find a warm body beside me but found the space empty instead.

I got off the bed, pulled on Brett's white t-shirt and a pair of his boxers when I heard voices in the living room.

I opened the door and peaked out into the hallway. My stomach twisted at the sound of a woman's voice.

"Claire, you can't be here."

My heart sunk. No, not that woman. She was here. In my boyfriend's apartment. A territorial edge fluttered through my body, my hackles raising over her being here.

"She won't even know, Brett. Come on, baby. Have a taste of what you've been missing these past couple of weeks."

"Get your fucking hands off of me."

Bile rose to my throat. She was touching him. Her hands were on a body that was meant for me and me only. Mine.

"Claire, stop," Brett demanded.

"Brett, I know you've missed me. Can that little whore please you like I can?"

Fury erupted through my body but I was frozen. I couldn't move as I listened.

"She's not a fucking whore. Now get out of my apartment."

"Where is she? In your room?"

I heard heels clicking on the tiled floor, heading my way.

My first thought was to run, to hide but there was no way that I was going to let her win. It's what she wanted. I would claw off her face before I let her get a hold of him again.

"You need to leave. Right the fuck now," Brett snarled.

"Oh yeah, Brett. Push me. You know I like it rough. Does your little slut please your dark sadistic desires, baby?"

I frowned. What the hell was she talking about? And I was getting fucking sick and tired of the name calling. I neared the end of the hall and braced myself for what I would walk in on but all I saw was her with her back to me.

Her vibrant red hair hung down to her waist and she was almost as tall as Brett with her high heels. My stomach clenched, unease soaring through me. They looked perfect together.

Brett met my gaze, his blue eyes warming and filling with apology.

Claire turned to me and raised a perfectly arched brow.

I smiled sweetly and crossed my arms under my chest. "Call me a slut or a whore again and I'll drive that perfect face into my knee."

Her jaw clenched and she looked back at Brett. "You sure have yourself a real lady, Brett."

I laughed. "More than I can say for you. At least I'm not desperate enough to show up at my ex-lover's apartment." I took a step towards her. "Did you beg him? Get on your knees and grovel? Is that how you got him to sleep with you?"

"You're a bitch."

I sneered. "Oh girl. You haven't seen anything yet. Now get the fuck out before I get mean."

She looked between Brett and I. Taking a step towards me, her blue eyes were dark with rage.

I tilted my chin, standing my ground.

"I will be back…" she smirked. "Slut."

I glared. "I look forward to it."

She walked past me, shoving me in the shoulder before leaving the apartment.

A breath left me on a whoosh when the door slammed shut behind her. My heart raced, my blood pounding in my ears. I knew she would be back. It was only a matter of when.

Brett sat on the couch and scrubbed a hand down his face.

At that point, I really took him in. He wore blue jeans that were ripped at the knees and a plain white t-shirt. He dressed casual but dominated so much superiority, it left me breathless.

My heart ached. A part of me wanted to be mad at him for letting Claire into his apartment but then another part felt as though he had no choice.

I walked over to him and sat at his feet, leaning my head against his knee.

He seemed surprised by my actions and wrapped his arms around my shoulders. "I'm so fucking sorry, lover."

My heart thumped at the vulnerability that passed between us. The level of trust that we had for each other dwindled as each day past. It was like we weren't meant to be together.

"Evvie, I—"

"I'm scared, Brett," I blurted.

148

He pushed me forward and sat behind me on the floor. Wrapping his body around me, he held me against him. "I love you and only you. Please know that," he whispered into my ear.

I turned in his arms and leaned my head against his chest. I knew he loved me and I loved him. But I felt like something was pulling us apart. Keeping us from truly being happy. And I had a feeling that it would only be a matter of time before I would find out just how deep his dark sadistic side went.

Twenty-One

AFTER SHE-Bitch-From-Hell left, we spent the rest of the morning in bed until it was time to get ready for work. But things still felt off. Brett was on edge and it made it hard to talk to him. I didn't like seeing him upset but I didn't know what to do to make it better. I also didn't like his constant mood swings.

We got to the club and Brett retreated to his office in silence. Everyone knew that we were together, he had made that very clear so I have to admit, it kind of stung.

"Hey, what do I have to do to get some fucking service around here?"

My breath hitched and I stopped wiping the counter, turning to the deep voice behind me. I squealed with delight at seeing Ethan sitting at the bar. "Ethan!" I said, walking around the counter.

A cheesy grin spread on his face as he met me halfway.

I threw my arms around his neck and giggled as he spun me around before setting me back on my feet. "When did you get out?"

"Yesterday." He looked around the room. "You like working here?"

"I do," I said, raising an eyebrow.

His gaze met mine. "I see you're wearing a different uniform."

"How would…" I frowned. "You talked to Evan."

Ethan winked. "I also hear that your boyfriend is the owner."

My heart fluttered. "He is."

"How old is he?"

"Twenty-seven. Why?" I asked, placing my hands on my hips.

"Little young to own all of this, isn't he?" he said, sitting on a stool.

"No. God, you're worse than Evan."

J.M. Walker

Ethan smirked and rubbed his jaw before looking past me. His eyes narrowed and he rose to his full height. "Who the hell is that?"

I followed his gaze and found Brett heading our way. I swallowed hard at the cold look Brett was giving me.

"Who is that, Evvie?"

"My boyfriend," I mumbled.

"Fuck, sis, you sure know how to pick 'em." Ethan took a step past me.

I grabbed his arm. "Ethan."

He shoved out of my grip. "I don't like how he's looking at you."

I looked back at Brett and realized his cold stare wasn't directed at me. My heart raced, my stomach twisting at what I knew was to come.

Ethan got in Brett's face, tendons protruding from his thick neck as the rage of the Neal temper took over.

Brett smirked and crossed his arms under his chest like he was waiting.

Ethan pointed at me and Brett met my gaze. His eyes warmed but the coldness from a moment ago still lingered.

I took a step towards them when Ethan pushed Brett.

Brett sneered and punched him across the jaw.

I gasped and rushed to their side. Where the hell was Kane?

Just as Ethan took a step back and grabbed his jaw, I took that as my chance. I pushed my way between them and shoved Ethan.

"Both of you, stop," I demanded.

"Evvie, get the fuck out of my way," Ethan growled.

"You need to watch your tone with her," Brett said. His voice was calm, in control but I could see the tendons in his neck tensing.

"Guys, stop." I placed a hand on Brett's chest, holding him back.

At that moment, Kane stepped up beside us, breathing heavy, his cheeks flushed.

I frowned as Tatiana walked by and adjusted her skirt. She looked at me over her shoulder and winked.

Well that's new. "Take him home, please," I told Kane.

"Evvie, this fucker started it," Ethan said, motioning to Brett.

"I don't care who started it. You just got out of jail. Do you want to go back for fighting, jackass?" I spun on my heel and stared at up at Brett. "Office. Now."

A twinkle of mischief flashed in his eyes before he cupped the back of my neck. Pulling me towards him, he placed a hard kiss on my lips. "You're mine, lover."

"That is my brother, Brett."

He looked up past my head and back down at me. "Shit."

"Yeah, time to start kissing my ass 'cause I'm so fucking pissed right now."

He pinched my chin. "I enjoy kissing your ass."

I huffed and pushed out of his grip. "Office."

He turned and walked towards his office.

"Evvie," Ethan said.

I looked up as he and Kane came up on either side of me.

"I will not apologize for fucking trying to protect you." Ethan's jaw clenched, his brows furrowing with concern.

I sighed and handed him my keys. "You can stay at my apartment but I'm still mad at you."

Heading to Brett's office, I took a deep breath as I neared it. Deep bass thumped from the small room as I reached the door.

I jumped when it was shoved open and with a rough hold, I was pulled inside.

Brett pushed me up against the wall and brushed his nose along the side of my neck. "I'm so sorry. So fucking sorry," he whispered, wrapping an arm around my middle.

My stomach fluttered at the intense heat coming from his body. "You hit my brother, Brett. What the hell were you thinking?" I asked, shoving out of his grip.

"Evvie." He went to reach for my hand but I brushed past him and sat on the couch.

"I didn't know he was your brother," he said. He closed the distance between us and stepped between my legs.

I looked up at him as he hovered over me, placing his hands on either side of my head on the couch. "And that would make it okay if he wasn't?"

His eyes narrowed. "I didn't say that."

152

"Well what are you saying then?"

Brett gripped my jaw, our lips mere inches apart. As many times as he had kissed me, I would never get used to the feel of his mouth on mine. "I'm fucking saying that I don't like it when any man touches you. I don't care who the hell it is."

I pushed out of his hold but his hand only tightened. My body heated with adrenaline as I fought against him.

He pushed my head back against the couch and brushed his mouth along mine. The contact, although soft, sent jolts of electricity straight to my groin.

My lips parted on a breath as I grabbed onto his wrist. "You can't stop every man from touching me."

His eyes darkened. "Maybe not. But I will make it my mission to fucking try."

"You don't trust me?"

He frowned. "Of course I trust you." His lips brushed down my jaw to my ear, his hot breath scorching my skin. "I don't trust other men."

"If you trust me, like you say you do, then you have nothing to worry about," I said, pushing out of his hold.

He grabbed my wrists and held them above my head. "I can't control it. The feelings I have for you, Evvie…" He breathed against my neck. He lifted his head, his heated gaze boring into mine.

"Do you love me?" I whispered.

His eyes searched my face. "What I feel for you is deeper than love. It's an all-consuming need. It's like you have a firm grip on my heart and one twist, it would shatter into a million pieces. *You* have that control, Evvie."

I swallowed hard at his admission. "I don't—"

"I'm sorry." He let go of my wrists and knelt at my feet before wrapping his arms around my waist. He placed his head in my lap and let out a deep sigh.

"For what?" I asked, curling my fingers in the short hair at his nape.

He looked up at me and pulled me into his lap. With a gentle touch, he trailed his finger down the length of my jaw and over my bottom lip.

My heart thudded, racing hard against my ribs. "Brett?"

153

"For loving you too much," he whispered.

A lump formed in my throat. We had only been together for a couple of weeks but the love that surrounded us was controlling, powerful as it took over our thoughts and actions. Was it possible to love someone too much?

"I…" I sighed and gripped his shirt in my hands before wrapping my arms around his neck. I didn't know what to say. But I did know that we would move past this and find our happiness again.

I inhaled, the scent of musk and man invading my nostrils. My favorite smell.

"I've already been left for another man. I won't go through that shit again."

I lifted my head, shock tearing through me and cupped his face.

A sense of insecurity flashed in his eyes as he looked away.

I placed a soft kiss on his lips, forcing him to meet my gaze. "I won't leave you for anyone. You are it for me."

His hand moved to the back of my neck, the vulnerability in his eyes no longer there. "I like the sound of that, lover."

I gasped as he tugged my head back, the dominating Brett I had come to love, taking control. His eyes flashed with a hunger that was ferocious and desperate. Desire curled in my belly at his heated stare.

A smug smile formed on his face and with one hand, he had my pants undone and off faster than I ever thought was possible.

I gave him the control and watched as he undid his belt. Licking my lips, I spread my legs and waited.

Brett rose to his knees and still holding my hair in his hand, he pulled out his rigid length with the other.

I moved my panties to the side, not having enough time to take them off. My body ached for him.

He smirked and thrust into me so hard, my breath was knocked out of me. He didn't wait for me to get used to the size of him. He was desperate for me.

The feeling of his pants rubbing against my center, knowing that he needed me too much to take off his clothes, sent a thrill down my spine.

We continued to stare at each other. No kissing. No hands touching. Just our most intimate parts meeting as one.

I could feel him swell inside of me as he pumped into me at a frantic pace.

Beads of sweat coated his brow, the muscles in his neck straining from his movements. God, he was beautiful. The control he had over his body and how he used it for both our pleasure made me hungry for him.

He grunted, pushing into me as far as possible.

I gasped as an explosion was set off inside of my core, spreading ecstasy over my body. His name left my lips on a whimper and I moaned as I felt him release into me.

He came so hard, I could feel him fill me with his semen. His hips stopped moving and I straddled his lap, keeping him inside of me. At that moment, I placed a hard kiss on his mouth before licking my way between his lips.

A groan erupted from the back of his throat as he wrapped his arms around me, tightening his hold. No words were said. They didn't need to be. At this point, we spoke through our bodies.

I cupped the back of his neck, deepening the kiss when a knock sounded on the door.

We broke apart and Brett sighed heavily.

"What?" he barked.

"Sorry boss, Mathis is here to see you," Kane said, his voice muffled by the closed door.

"Fuck him," Brett snapped.

"Be nice," I said, placing a soft kiss on his mouth. I rose from his lap and pulled on my pants.

Brett frowned and looked up at me before righting himself. "We're not done talking."

I leaned down and kissed his cheek. "We can talk later." I headed to the door and let Kane in.

"How's it going?" he asked, leaning against the wall.

I smiled softly. "Better." I met Brett's gaze as he came up beside me. The dark look of possession took over as he captured my mouth in a hard kiss.

He looked up at Kane. "Tell him he can go to hell."

I grabbed Brett's arm. "Maybe it's important."

"He said he needs to discuss some business dealings with you. Something you care to share with me, boss?" Kane asked, his jaw clenching.

Brett scrubbed a hand down his face and placed an arm around my shoulders. "Nothing I haven't told you already.

I looked at Kane. "Tell him to give Brett five minutes."

Brett's head whipped to mine, his eyes narrowing but I ignored him.

Kane nodded once and left.

Brett grabbed my arm and slammed me up against the wall. "I don't like being undermined, Evvie."

I frowned and shoved out of his grip. "I was not undermining you."

"No?" His jaw clenched, his mouth set in a firm line as he wrapped a hand around my throat.

My heart thudded at the dark look of fury deep in his blue gaze. "Brett."

"Don't make decisions for me again, you fucking hear me?" he snarled.

My blood boiled and I pushed him. "I was trying to help."

"I don't need your help. I need you to get back to work and do your fucking job," he said, taking a step back.

My mouth dropped, my stomach twisting. "What the hell is your problem, asshole? I'm not one of your whores that you can control and boss around." Where was the sweet Brett from a moment ago?

Brett pulled on his jacket and closed the distance between us before placing his hands against the wall on either side of my head. "You're not my whore, but you do love it when I control you, lover."

"Control me in bed. Not threaten me with your hand around my neck," I snapped.

"This is my club. Since you walked into my life, this is the only thing that I have control over."

"But you just said—"

He placed a soft but demanding kiss on my mouth. "I control your body. That's it. What I feel for you? It's all you." His hand cupped the back of my neck, tilting my head to him. "You're the reason I can't sleep at night. You're the reason I feel

156

this need to consume you when really, it's you that consumes me."

Consumed by his love. It was beautiful, erotic and intense as hell but as deep as the feelings went, I wasn't sure if it would be enough for him. We didn't trust other people when really, I wasn't sure if we even trusted each other.

Twenty-Two

BRETT'S JAW clenched as he practically dragged me to see what the hell Mathis wanted. He told me since I wanted him to talk to the guy so badly, that I could join him. Asshole.

Tension wrapped around us as we neared the end of the hallway when Kane met up with us. He clapped a hand on the back of Brett's neck and leaned down, whispering something into his ear.

Brett nodded, his shoulders relaxing and the tight hold he had on my hand loosened. His eyes flicked to mine, warm and dark. No anger. It settled my nerves. "I know. Thanks, my man."

Kane smiled. "Mathis is in the same booth as last time."

Once we reached the private booth, I slid onto the bench with Brett following in behind me. The scent of sweet spicy cigar smoke wafted into my nostrils, setting my heart racing. It would be a smell that I would never forget as long as Mathis was around.

Brett placed an arm on the back of the seat behind my head, rubbing a thumb up and down the side of my neck.

"Well, it seems you two have become closer since the last time I've seen you," Mathis pointed out.

Brett harrumphed.

I met Mathis' gaze, taking in the air of superiority surrounding him. He reminded me so much of Brett, it was uncanny. They both dominated. They walked into a room and it was like time stopped.

Mathis' tanned skin glowed in the dim red lighting, his black hair slicked back into a short pony tail. He was very good looking even though he was a domineering ass. I bit back a smile. Almost like the man sitting beside me.

Mathis' dark eyes twinkled when he caught me staring.

My cheeks heated and I looked away, inching closer to Brett.

Mathis smirked and looked at Brett. "Have you thought of my offer?"

Brett tensed beside me. "The answer is still no, motherfu—"

"Be nice," I said.

Brett met my gaze, a flash of anger swirling behind his deep blue eyes but I stood my ground. I wasn't going to have him make a fool of himself just because he was mad at me.

His jaw clenched and unclenched before he turned back to Mathis and waited.

Mathis looked between us and smirked, sitting back against the bench. He reached into his jacket pocket and pulled out a stack of folded paper. He slid it across the table to Brett and tapped it. "That's a contract explaining exactly what I want. Read it thoroughly before you say no. Again." He slid out of the booth and walked to the bar.

I almost giggled as Jake dropped a glass when he saw the large man approaching him. Looks like I wasn't the only one who thought the dark brooding European was attractive.

"Lover."

I met Brett's gaze.

His brows furrowed. "You checking him out?"

I rolled my eyes. "Really? You have a huge decision to make and you're worried about who I'm checking out?"

He leaned down to my ear. "The only man you should be checking out is me, lover."

I turned my head to his. We sat and stared at each other for what seemed like an eternity. He was worried about me checking out other men when every night for the past couple of weeks, I've been with him. My stomach clenched, the realization hitting me full force. He didn't trust me. At all.

"Evvie?"

"You should read over the contract," I croaked. A lump formed in my throat and I swallowed past it. I would not cry. Not here.

Brett pinched my chin. "Talk to me."

I huffed and pulled my head out of his grasp. "I'm fine."

"You will talk to me and tell me what's bothering you, lover," he breathed against my neck.

"Yeah? Just like you do the same, Brett?" I countered and crossed my arms under my chest.

His eyes bored into mine before turning back to the contract in his hand. He sighed and scrubbed a hand down his face. Inner turmoil flashed on his handsome features. "I don't know what the hell to do."

I could tell that bothered him. He was right. He was always in control. Especially of his club and things changing without him knowing it, pissed him off.

"What does the contract say?" I asked, ignoring the nagging thoughts of what was really bothering us.

"Just that I need to make him money. If I don't, I have to pay it back. But I'll have full control of the club."

I grabbed his free hand and linked our fingers together, praying that small gesture would show him that I was his and only his. I could deal with his possessiveness and domineering ways but not when he didn't trust me.

He didn't say anything as I curled my feet under me and leaned my head against his shoulder. His eyes moved across the page, reading, deciding on what was best for him.

"I have to make the club a hundred grand in six months," he mumbled.

My eyes widened. "Is that even possible?"

"Yes."

I looked around the vast room. No wonder Brett lived in one of the richest parts of the city. "Are you tempted?"

"Very." He sighed. "He would be giving me free reign of his club. I could do whatever I wanted to help pick up business."

"Where is the club?"

He frowned. "New York."

My stomach sunk. "How long would you be there?"

Brett looked towards the bar catching the attention of Mathis. He headed back our way.

"What are you going to tell him?" I asked.

Brett ran his thumb along my bottom lip before placing a tender kiss on my mouth. "I'm going to do what is best for me."

I smiled lightly. "Always in control."

His eyes darkened. "You know it, lover."

My stomach flipped and his deep blue eyes captivated me, drawing me in as the minutes ticked by.

A throat cleared and Brett glared in Mathis' direction.

Mathis smirked and rubbed the dark scruff on his jaw. "So, did we come to a decision?"

160

Brett tapped the contract. "I need to speak with my lawyer first and ask some questions before I answer."

Mathis nodded. "Fair enough. What are your questions?" he asked, pulling a gold container out of his pocket.

"What's the catch?"

"There is none," Mathis said, his voice calm, even.

Brett's face tightened, his brows drawing together. "Yeah. Right."

"You make me money, I make you money." Mathis lit a cigar and inhaled, the embers glowing before he exhaled small puffs of smoke. "It's a win-win all around." The sweet spicy scent of the cigar wafted into my nostrils, burning its way into my senses.

"Why me?"

Mathis shrugged. "Don't trust me, Brett?"

"No."

Mathis smirked. "Good."

Brett rolled his eyes and let out a heavy sigh. "It's in New York?"

"Yes. I have clubs all over North America but for some reason, the club in New York isn't doing too well," Mathis stated.

"Give me a couple of days to think about it," Brett said, putting the contract in his suit jacket.

Mathis smiled and looked at me before turning back to Brett. "You're a lucky man, Brett MacLean. I hope you know that."

I gaped at him as he left the privacy of the booth.

Brett watched him leave the large room. "I do," he whispered.

My heart fluttered. "Brett?"

"I'll see you at your place, Evvie," he mumbled and headed back to his office.

I sat there, alone and confused. I didn't know what was wrong with us. Did we really not trust each other? Or was there more to it than that? Brett was fine with me when we were alone but once we weren't, it was like a switch went off inside of him that left him jealous and possessive or worse. Maybe something was wrong with me that I put up with it.

Twenty-Three

THE NEXT morning, I stirred awake and rolled over to find a warm sleeping body beside me. I smiled.

I vaguely remembered Brett joining me during the night. A flutter of disappointment settled in my belly that he didn't wake me up like he usually does.

Was this it? Were things taking a turn for the worse already and we had only just started dating? I wasn't sure, but I needed him to trust me. There was no one else for me. He was it. He filled the void that had settled in my heart since my mom died. I hadn't told him that. Maybe if I did, it would help.

My eyes roamed down his naked form, the white sheet resting on hips. His strong back rose and fell with each breath. God, he was beautiful.

I leaned over and kissed his shoulder, trailing hot wet pecks to his nape. Covering his body with mine, I ran my hands down his strong arms that were under the pillow. His muscles jumped under my touch. I inhaled his scent. Musk and man. It made my mouth water and my pussy clench with desire for him.

I curled our fingers together and rested my head on his upper back.

His eyes were closed. He looked peaceful, at ease while he slept. The dark scruff of his five o'clock shadow covered his jaw and my tongue itched to lick it.

Placing a soft kiss on the back of his neck, I let my teeth graze the sensitive skin.

A shudder rolled through him and he flipped me onto my back, pinning me beneath him.

I gasped, his hands wrapping around my wrists above my head, holding me in place. My gaze travelled down his body to the erection between his thighs.

I licked my lips and wrapped my legs around his hips, tilting my pelvis.

He smirked and sank into me, filling me to the hilt.

I moaned and my sex clenched around him.

162

The movements were erotic, delicious as he made love to me. His mouth covered mine in a hard bruising kiss before he licked his way between my lips.

I panted, restrained by his hard body as he gave slow even strokes. I dug my heels into his ass, pulling him deeper that ignited a growl from the back of his throat.

He released my mouth, a wicked smile forming on his handsome face when he turned me onto my stomach.

My heart raced when he covered my body with his. His hot breath scorched my skin as he ran his nose up the side of my neck.

With a rough hand, he wrapped it around my throat and slammed back into my waiting heat.

I whimpered, spreading myself for him, giving him access to what our bodies craved.

He grabbed my wrists, holding them behind my back with one hand and tightened his grip on my throat. He tilted my head and kissed my forehead before pumping into me at a delicious rate.

I moaned, my body buzzing with adrenaline at being completely and utterly restrained by him. I couldn't move and I had no desire to.

Muffled voices sounded from behind my door and I bit back my cries of ecstasy.

His hand moved to my mouth as his hips sped up.

Holy shit, his body was on fire. The heat travelled through us like hot flames and I couldn't take it anymore. I broke.

I screamed around his hand, not caring in the least if anyone heard me. I shook and trembled beneath him as he pushed my hips off the bed.

He grunted, slamming hard into me each time.

A snarl erupted from his chest as he pushed into me as deep as possible before he covered my body.

His release filled me. It was so hard, I could feel him pulsing inside of me as his warmth coated my center.

Brett let go of my wrists, rubbing his hands down my arms as he held me. "I love you," he whispered. "I don't deserve you. I'm an asshole and I'm sorry for being a dick last night."

"I feel like you don't trust me," I mumbled.

He sighed heavily and kissed my neck. "The thought of losing you to someone else scares the shit out of me."

My eyes widened. Shock tore through me at what he said but I didn't respond, needing him to continue.

"I trust you. I do. I…fuck."

I frowned. "Brett?"

"I know we've only been dating for a couple of weeks but like I said before, I fell for you hard. The urge I have to claim you and mark you as mine every time a man comes near you is powerful. I can't control it, lover," he breathed against my shoulder. "Right now, I like knowing my come is inside of you."

My pussy clenched at his words. The walls of my core squeezed him as his rigid cock lengthened inside of me. He pushed into me making a gasp escape my lips.

"You're mine, lover," he said, slowly pumping in and out of me. "And I want you to know, that no matter what happens, moments like this make it all worth it."

***

I WALKED to the kitchen in dire need of coffee. My thigh muscles burned, my core clenching with every step. I could feel Brett inside of me even though he was no longer there. It was like he was permanently etched into my body, marking his territory, making me his. Knowing he would like that made me smile.

After the multiple orgasms and sweet words, I felt lighter. Whole.

We both had our issues to work through but the love we had, although new and fresh, was strong and intense. It took control as our bodies continued to meld together as one.

Being alone, just the two of us, we were happy. But once we weren't, shit unravelled and I was damn determined to fix that.

I sighed, taking a sip of the much needed caffeine. The hairs on the back of my neck tingled and I smiled into my cup.

A warm body came up behind me and soft lips placed a kiss on my neck. "Hmm…you smell like me," he said, inhaling deep.

My body stirred at the husk of Brett's voice. I placed the cup on the counter and turned in his arms, wrapping my hands around his neck.

His eyes flashed with hunger. "I enjoyed the attempt at control you took this morning, lover. Even though it didn't last long," he purred, running a finger down my arm.

I laughed. The sense of losing control, even for just a minute with him, was exhilarating and left me needing more.

"I never wished you a good morning, so mornin', Evvie." He kissed my forehead and grabbed a cup of coffee for himself.

I shook myself and headed into the living room. Birds chirped in the back ground as I sat on the couch and waited for Brett to join me.

"Where's Kane?"

I looked up as Brett sat beside me and placed his arm across my lap. I shrugged. "I know he sometimes goes to visit his grandma or he could be out for a run."

It was the weekend so he could have gone over to a woman's house...I frowned. "Is Kane sleeping with Tatiana?"

Brett looked at me, his eyebrow raised. "I don't know. Why?"

"Just curious."

"Would it bother you if they were?"

"No."

He pinched my chin and placed a soft kiss on my mouth. "Be happy for him."

I smiled. I was. Confused but I was happy. I liked T. Even though I thought she was into women but if they were happy, then that was all that mattered to me.

"You're beautiful."

My cheeks heated at Brett's compliment and I leaned in to kiss him when footsteps sounded down the hall way.

I sighed and took a sip of my cup when Brett snarled.

I followed his gaze. My stomach sunk when my eyes landed on Claire. In my apartment. With Ethan standing behind her. "What the hell is she doing here?"

Claire sneered, her ruby red lips plump and full of gloss. "Well don't you two look cozy?"

"What's going on?" Ethan asked, frowning.

I rose to my feet and pointed at her. "Get the fuck out of my apartment."

"Evvie." Shock coated Ethan's voice but I ignored him. I would explain later. Right now I needed the she-bitch from hell to leave my home.

"Get out. Now," I yelled.

A heavy hand landed on my shoulder, squeezing, holding me back from jumping at the woman who I swore wanted to destroy my relationship.

"You need to control your woman," Claire stated matter-of-factly.

"I think you should leave." Brett's voice was calm, collected.

"Aww, come on, Brett," she purred. "Didn't you miss me?"

Bile rose to my throat.

"Leave. Now," Brett's voice boomed through the small apartment.

"Fine, I'll leave but I just have to ask." She looked at me. "How do I taste?"

I dove at her when arms wrapped around my middle. A string of curse words left my lips that would make my mother roll over in her grave. "Get out. Now!"

She laughed and headed towards the door. "Oh and Brett, did you tell your little pet that you slept with me right before you fucked her?"

My mouth fell open, my blood boiling through my body. "Get. The. Fuck. Out."

She licked her lips. "With pleasure."

***

"EVVIE, I am so fucking sorry. I didn't think."

I looked up at my brother and frowned. "That's because you always think with your dick."

Ethan's jaw clenched. "I've been in jail—"

"So you fuck the first thing that approaches you?" I snapped.

"That's not—"

"How did you even meet her in the first place?" I asked.

166

Ethan huffed and rose to his feet. "She was waiting outside the club. She came onto me."

"Did she say who she was?"

"No," he frowned. "Why would she?"

I rolled my eyes. "Of course not. Let's just sleep with the first woman we see in a week."

"I said I was fucking sorry, Evvie. It's not like you've never had a one night stand," Ethan said looking between Brett and I.

My back stiffened. "That is not the same thing."

"Uh-huh. Right."

I shook my head. "She must have known you were my brother."

"How the hell would she have known that?"

"Because she's fucking psycho!" I cried.

"Evvie," Brett whispered in my ear and rubbed a hand over my upper back.

I jumped up from the couch. "No. And you," I pointed at Brett. "How could you?"

Brett's eyes narrowed. "Evvie," he said, his voice filled with warning.

"What? You get on my case about other men but I can't when it comes to Claire?" I asked, placing my hands on my hips.

"We weren't together, Evvie."

"God, I know. It's just…" I shivered. The thought of her touching Brett made me sick. I flopped back onto the couch and placed my head in my hands. "Ethan, I'm sorry." I let out a deep sigh. "It's not your fault and I shouldn't jump down your throat."

Ethan knelt before me and gave me a hard hug. "If I would have known, even though I don't like Brett, I wouldn't have slept with her."

I looked into his big blue eyes. "I know."

"I'm going to leave. Give you guys some time alone."

I nodded and waited for him to leave the small apartment before turning to my boyfriend. "Do you still have feelings for her?"

Brett searched my face, his jaw clenching and unclenching. "No."

"Did you ever?"

"She was around when I got bored."

167

"You didn't answer the question," I pointed out.

"She was familiar." He grabbed my hand, squeezing it tight. "With you, it's always something new. I can't get used to the sex with you or even just being with you, because it's different each time. That's what I want. What I need."

"What did Claire mean about your deep dark desires?" I blurted. I took a breath and waited for him to close up on me.

"I don't know how to explain that," he mumbled, shoving his other hand through his hair.

Anxiety swirled in my belly. Was he a sadist? Did he like pain? Threesome's maybe? I had no idea why he was concerned to tell me what it was. It's not like I wouldn't do anything he was interested in, but threesomes? No thanks.

"You can tell me, Brett." And that was the truth. Who was I to judge?

He sighed. "I like it rough. As you know already. I like being in control. It turns me on having your body doing whatever I want."

I knew that already too and I enjoyed every minute, every hour of it. "You don't see me complaining."

His deep blue eyes searched my face. "I enjoy administering pain for pleasure. The feel of your skin warm underneath my palm gets my blood pumping."

I swallowed, my body heating at his words. "I've liked what you've done so far."

A smug smile formed on his face. "You have, haven't you?"

I nodded, words lost on my tongue.

He looked away, his gaze darkening like he was remembering something. "My mom used to beat me."

A gasp escaped my lips at his admission. "Brett."

"Not my step mom but my real mom. She died a couple of years ago." He turned back to me. "No one knows this, Evvie. Not even my sister. It happened when I was really young but has stuck with me ever since. That's why my dad left her."

I had no idea. My heart broke for him. "Did…" I swallowed.

"It was nothing sexual if that's what you're wondering. Just mental and physical." He chuckled. "God, that was so fucking long ago."

168

"I'm so sorry," I whispered. He was just a boy when it happened. What kind of mother did that? I wanted to ask more but the fact that Brett opened up about it in the first place was enough. For now.

"Lover?"

I met his gaze, swallowing past the hard lump that had formed in my throat. "Yeah?"

His eyes warmed. "I love you. I hope you know that. I've never been into looking into the future and shit but I meant what I said before. *You* are my future."

A sob escaped my lips and the tears rolled freely down my cheeks of their own accord. I couldn't control them.

Brett sighed and wrapped his arms around my shoulders as I broke against him. "My Evvie. So heartfelt."

I snuggled against him and cried. My body shook, breaking for the little boy that was hurt by someone who was supposed to love him. Protect him. Be there for him but instead, hurt him in one of the worst ways possible.

"Hey, it's over. I'm better. Don't cry for me, lover," he crooned against my neck.

I tried to stop the shakes but the cries of agony for him kept wracking through my body. My childhood wasn't the greatest but I knew that both of my parents loved me. My mom spanked me once when I was a little girl over stealing candy from a store and that was the last time. She felt too guilty to do it again and she cried with me.

"I love you. I love you so much," I sobbed.

Brett pulled me onto his lap and cradled me against him. "Shhh." He kissed my tears away and cupped my face in both hands.

I looked deep into his eyes, fighting back another sob.

His eyes were soft, gentle even as they took me in. "No one has ever cried for me before."

"I'm—"

Warm lips captured my mouth in a tender kiss. "I think I fell in love with you all over again, Evvie."

Twenty-Four

THREE WEEKS later, I walked into Brett's apartment and threw the keys on the table against the wall. Since my break down and the confession about Brett's past, we've become closer, more intimate. Emotionally naked.

We didn't talk about his childhood again. Ethan had become a permanent fixture in my apartment so finally, Brett and he started getting along. They would joke, argue, just like any of our other brothers. It brought back memories of my childhood and I reveled in it. Needed it. I missed my family.

Since having the day shift at the club, it was nice leaving when it was still light out. After Brett gave me a key a week ago, rumors were flying around the club that we were moving in together or that I was pregnant. Both were ridiculous but the thought of having Brett's baby made my blood soar. Just thinking about something growing inside of me that was ours and that would link us together forever made a giggle escape my lips. "Way too soon for that, Evvie," I said to myself.

I sighed, shook my head and walked into the living room. I noticed a pile of mail on the table that Brett must have thrown on it before heading to work that afternoon. A large manila envelope that had my name spread across it caught my eye. Did Brett not see this? I frowned. Why would someone send me mail at his place?

I opened the large package and pulled out several pictures. My heart raced when I realized they were photos of two people. I spread out the photos on the table before me and gasped.

The pictures stared up at me. Laughing in my face as I gripped the edge of the couch tight in my hands. Naked bodies. Limbs twisting in a passionate display of ecstasy. My boyfriend and his ex…whore.

I picked the pictures up, bile rising to my throat.

My stomach twisted as I let the pictures fall out of my hands before they landed on the floor. I took deep cleansing breaths, needing to control the racing of my heart before it exploded from my chest.

170

I loved Brett. We've been doing so well since the last time we saw Claire but now, this would make things worse.

I looked for a date on the photos but found none. God, she was desperate. Trying to make my life fucking hell.

I took a breath and rose to my feet, wiping the tears from under my eyes. No more. She would not win. Brett and I had our issues but we would work through them. We had to.

The sound of the door unlocking and opening erupted through the vast apartment. I sat there frozen as Brett walked into the living room.

He threw his keys on the counter before meeting my gaze. The small smile on his face hardened as his eyes turned cold. "What's wrong?"

I swallowed and pointed to the floor.

His gaze followed my movement, a frown splaying on his handsome face before his eyes met mine. "What are you going to do?"

His question threw me off guard. I had expected him to deny it. Tell me it was all lies or even photo shopped.

"Are you going to deny it?" I asked even though I knew the answer already.

His eyes darkened. "Why would I?"

"I was hoping they were fake," I whispered.

"Do they look fake?"

My stomach clenched. "You don't have to be a condescending asshole. Care to explain these to me?"

He shrugged and headed down the hall. "I think they're pretty self-explanatory," he called out.

I gaped after him. No denial. No begging for my forgiveness. Just pretty much for me to except it and move on. Like hell.

I rose to my feet and stomped after him. "What the hell is your problem? Do you not care that I found these? They were addressed to me, Brett."

He didn't stop. He just continued walking to his office like nothing had happened.

Once reaching the small room, I watched him walk to his desk and sit behind his computer. "Brett."

He slapped the hard wood and narrowed his eyes. "What Evvie? What do you want me to say? Want me to tell you that it's not me in those pictures?"

"I want you to apologize," I cried. "I want you to tell me why your stupid ex sent me these in the first place!"

"How the hell would I know?"

"You're acting like you don't even fucking care. Oh wait." I laughed. "You want both of us, don't you? When you get bored with one, you go to the other, like the fucking asshole you are."

"Watch the tone, Evvie," he demanded, rising to his feet.

"Whatever. I'm out of here." I turned on my heel and headed towards the door.

"Do not fucking leave," he yelled.

I looked at him over my shoulder before heading out into the hall. "Fuck you."

A hard body crashed into mine, slamming me up against the wall. A breath left me on a gasp as I was lifted into the air. "Put me down," I screamed. I fought in his hold as he brought us to his bedroom. I kicked and struggled in his grasp when he threw me onto his bed.

Brett crawled between my legs as I squirmed out of his hold. "Do not fucking leave me."

I moved to the edge of the bed when he pushed me onto my back. My chest rose and fell, adrenaline running through my body at the rough hold. "You should have thought of that before you cheated on me."

His eyes darkened. "I didn't cheat on you," he snarled.

"Then what, Brett? You didn't tell me about the pictures in the first place."

"The pictures were none of your fucking business."

God, I knew that. I was just hurt that they were sent to me. I didn't want to know what he did with other women. "Then tell me why she sent them."

"Because she's a bitch."

I frowned. "You don't seem surprised that she sent them."

He shook his head. "I'm not. Once Claire gets her claws into someone, she never lets go."

I swallowed, my stomach clenching. "Why didn't you tell me this?"

172

"Because I didn't think it would matter. I thought it was over. I told her to move on. Demanded she leave me alone. She broke it off with me but now that she knows you're around..."

"So just because she doesn't want you, no one else can have you?" I scoffed and pushed out of his grip.

He pulled my arms above my head, pinning me down under his hard body. Under normal circumstances it would have turned me on but at this point, it just pissed me off. The control he had over my body and the fact that I couldn't do anything about it, sent fury swimming in the pit of my belly.

"Lover," he said, brushing a hand down my cheek.

"Let go of me." I squirmed under his touch. I wiggled against him but he was too strong. Too big. His hold on me tightened, his grip on my wrists bruising. I stared into the depths of his deep blue gaze. He wasn't letting me go. Ever.

"I love you, Evvie. You and only you. I've fucked up in the past. I don't deserve you but I need you. Those pictures were taken before you. I'm not a cheater," he said softly.

I knew the pictures weren't recent but hearing him say it out loud, made me feel...better. Like a part of me had doubted him. Guilt ate at me. I sighed. "I hate fighting with you."

Brett brushed his nose along my neck. "I hate when you doubt me, lover."

I frowned. "I didn't—"

He looked down at me, his eye brow rose.

I huffed. "Okay. Fine. I did, but wouldn't you in my position?"

"No. I trust you."

I searched his face. He was calm, cool. No other emotions splayed in his eyes except for warmth and love. I couldn't read him and that set my skin on edge. "You trust me? Really? One hundred percent, trust me?"

His eyes narrowed. "Yes."

I wiggled my wrists out of his grip and cupped his face. "Then why did you punch out my brother?"

"Fuck. I told you it was men that I don't trust, not you," he snapped, sitting back on his hunches.

I leaned on my elbows. "If that were the case, Brett, then you would trust that I would stop it. I keep telling you that I love you. That you have nothing to worry about."

"And I tell you the same fucking thing when it comes to Claire."

"What the hell are we doing then?" I blurted and rose to my feet.

Brett scrubbed a hand through his hair and chuckled. "The first time I fall in love and it's fucking toxic."

My mouth fell open to deny it. Tell him he was wrong. Scream that our love was normal but was it really? It took over us. Controlled our actions and I was scared shitless that it would eventually destroy us both.

***

I WOKE during the night, staring at the ceiling. Nightmares of Claire having her hands on Brett crashed into my mind. My mind played tricks on me. Trying to convince me that Brett wanted her and not me. I knew that wasn't the case but the small insecure part of myself reared its ugly head whenever she was involved.

I knew Brett loved me. Maybe it was more than love. Was there even such a thing? I wasn't sure but all I knew was that whatever these feelings were, they were intense, dark. Scary.

I rolled over and found the bed empty beside me. A hard lump formed in my throat. I didn't know what I had expected. Brett worked. Constantly. He was probably in his office, doing stuff for the club. He spent his time in there whenever he got stressed or upset and clearly, we were both feeling off tonight.

I didn't want to leave. I wanted to stay with him forever but we needed time apart. Maybe it would do us good.

After our fight, we made love but it felt distant, like we weren't in sync or our heads weren't really in it. I didn't feel connected to him on that level that I had grown so used to every time we touched. The delicious passion that surrounded us, like we couldn't get enough of each other, wasn't there. Yes, it felt good but it wasn't enough.

I pulled on a t-shirt and shorts and grabbed my overnight bag before quietly leaving Brett's room. I closed the door behind me and walked down the dark hallway noticing a light coming through the bottom of his office door. My heart raced with each step. If he caught me leaving, he would be pissed.

Slipping on my flats, I turned and looked at the vast room of his apartment. My stomach fluttered. This place had been a part of me for weeks. I sighed and placed a hand on the door knob just as the hairs on the back of my neck tingled. Shit.

"Where the hell are you going, Evvie?"

My back bristled at the harsh tone in Brett's deep voice. I slowly turned to him and leaned against the door. His black tie was loose around his neck, the buttons of the white dress shirt undone at the top. The vee of the cotton delved deep into a hard chest that I had my hands on just hours before. God, he was beautiful.

"Evvie, answer me," he demanded.

My core pulsed at his command and I shook myself. "I'm going home," I mumbled.

His eye brow rose. "At three o'clock in the morning?"

Crap. I let out a frustrated sigh and with a shaky hand, ran it through my hair. I needed to get away. To run but his dark stare held me captive. It backed me into the corner as I waited.

"What are you running from this time, lover?" he asked, taking a step towards me.

I frowned. "I'm not running."

"Do not fucking lie to me. I know you well enough to know that whenever you get upset, you run. You always fucking run, Evvie."

The air around us crackled, like a magnetic force was pulling us together. It was so strong, I had to hold myself back from throwing my body into his arms. He did this to me. He made it so I couldn't concentrate. I loved him. With all of my heart but he made me lose myself.

"Talk to me," he said softly.

I dropped my bag and walked into the living room, pacing back and forth. "I feel like there's something off between us," I admitted without meeting his gaze.

"Go on."

I took a breath and continued. "After our fight last night, things felt different. It wasn't...raw, passionate." I stopped in my tracks and looked at him. "Desperate," I whispered.

His gaze darkened. "I could feel you slipping away from me," he said, closing the distance between us. He cupped my cheek, running his thumb over my bottom lip. "I know a part of you doesn't trust me."

I shook my head and opened my mouth to deny it when warm lips covered mine. It was a tender kiss. The softest he's ever given me and it broke my heart. Tears burned my eyes and I forced them back, swallowing past the hard lump in my throat.

He lifted his head, a soft smile splaying on his handsome face. "I want to work through this but we can't if you keep running away."

"I'm not—"

His hand wrapped around my throat, tilting my head back.

I gasped, my body heating at the rough hold. The tender sweet moment passed as a roar of lust filled his dark gaze.

"I know we have our issues. I know we both have shit to work through when it comes to trust but I'm really fucking done with you lying to me," he said, his voice firm. His jaw clenched as he forced me to take a step back. "Now, you want raw? Passion? You want me to show you how fucking desperate I am for you and only you?"

I swallowed and grabbed onto his hand that still had my head in a firm hold. "Brett," was all I could get out. My body ached for him. Needing him inside of me at that very moment. This is what I was used to. What I wanted from him. Making love was one thing but what was it without the connection? I needed him to control me. Show me exactly what he wanted from me.

"Tell me," he growled, pushing me up against the patio door.

My heart fluttered, memories of our first time reigning full force in my mind. He was passionate then but now, weeks later, he consumed me.

He brushed his nose up the side of my neck and inhaled. "Tell. Me."

My eyes fluttered closed. "I need you."

176

"Where?" he asked, nipping my ear lobe.

"Inside me," I croaked out.

"Why?" He ground his hips against mine, his growing erection pressing into my lower stomach.

I licked my dry lips. "Because you make me feel good."

"What do you want me to do, lover?" he husked, circling his pelvis.

"I…" I bit back a moan as he sucked on my bottom lip.

"Tell me."

"Fuck me," I breathed.

"How?"

Oh God. "Brett, I need you hard. I need you to control me."

"You like it when I control your body, lover?" he purred, breathing slow and deep.

Words froze on my tongue as he pinned me against the wall.

"You enjoy the way I control how your pussy drips, how it aches and throbs, begging for my dick." He leaned down, placing kisses along my jaw line.

I arched against him and gasped when the kisses turned to bites. The delicious pain turned into pleasure as electric jolts shot straight to my groin.

"Hmm…I can still smell me on you," he whispered against my neck.

This is the Brett I wanted.

"What else do you want from me, lover?" he asked, cupping my ass in a firm, almost painful grip.

I grabbed onto the waistband of his black pants and pulled him tighter against me. Never getting close enough. "I need the real you. The raw, possessive lover that I had the first night."

He lifted his head and stared down at me. "Oh Evvie." A wicked grin flashed on his face.

I licked my dry lips. "What?"

"I'm way more possessive now since falling in love with you."

"Then show me. Give me you. The real you," I demanded.

His brows furrowed. "I have been."

I shook my head. "You didn't last night."

"Neither did you."

"That's because I thought you cheated on me," I blurted.

He let go of me and took a step back, his eyes darkening with fury. "How many times do I have to say that the pictures were taken before you?" he asked, his tone calm and even.

My heart beat hard. God, what the hell was wrong with me? "Brett, I'm sorry. I just—"

He spun on me. "No. You don't fucking trust me. Just admit it, Evvie."

"I...I didn't say that."

"You don't have to. I can see it in your eyes." He shook his head. "God, I'm such a fucking moron."

I took a step towards him. "You don't trust me either," I whispered.

His head whipped around to mine, his cheeks flush with rage. "I told you. I don't trust other men. I know how they think. They don't care if the woman is single or not but you, you don't trust me. Me, Evvie. Do you know how much that fucking kills me?"

A lump formed in my throat at the hurt in his voice. I had no idea but it wasn't him that I didn't trust. "I don't trust Claire."

"Do not fucking bring her into this," he yelled.

My back stiffened. "It's true. I don't trust her but I do trust you. I know you love me. I know you would never cheat on me."

"Then I'm going to ask the same question you did last night. What the fuck are we doing then?" he snapped, his nostrils flaring.

My chest rose and fell, my heart thumping against my ribs. We stood there and stared at each other. As time passed, the anger and tension grew thick, strong as unsaid words of pleading flew around us.

My chest was tight, anxiety swimming around in my belly. I needed to leave.

I looked away and walked by Brett when he grabbed my arm and spun me to him. My hands landed on his chest as his mouth crashed to mine in a hard bruising kiss.

My lips parted of their own accord, letting him in to devour and control my mouth.

All too soon, he let me go, panting and trembling before him.

The air shifted around us, snapping with unadulterated lust.

178

I took a step back, my lips tingling from the rough kiss. My body ached, needing him on a level that left me shaking.

Brett's nostrils flared and he leaned his head from side to side, the sounds of the tendons in his neck cracking. "Lover?"

I swallowed hard at the deep husk of his voice. "Yes?"

A wicked smile spread on his face. "If you're going to leave, do it now."

I backed up against the wall, my heart thumping hard. This would be intense. Raw. Real. What I needed from him. A nagging part of me was telling me something wasn't right, that this wouldn't end well but I shook it off. Ignoring the voice deep inside of me.

He started unbuckling his belt and pulled it out of the loops with a snap.

My core pulsed at the sound echoing around us.

"Once I catch you and lover, I will catch you, I'm gonna split that pussy wide with my thick cock." He took a step towards me. "I'm going to fuck you rough, giving you me, just like you asked."

A hot shiver ran down my back as I sidestepped around the couch, keeping my gaze locked with his.

He raised an eyebrow. "Evvie?"

I licked my lips. "Yeah?"

He smirked, his strong fingers unbuttoning his shirt. "Run. *Now.*"

Twenty-five

I MADE a mad dash down the hall when a heavy body crashed into mine, slamming me up against the wall. I never had a chance.

My head was pulled back making me gasp.

Brett wrapped his hand around my throat, breathing against my neck as he pressed his hard lower body into mine.

My core clenched, desire unfurling deep in the pit of my belly. My body throbbed, aching for him as he ground his hips against my ass.

I reached behind me and cupped his erection, squeezing hard.

A growl escaped his lips as he bucked in my hand and pushed me back up against the wall.

He ran a hand up my hip, grinding his pelvis into me.

I panted, my heart racing at the feel of his hard body surrounding me. My core clenched, liquid heat seeping between my thighs.

A zipper lowered, sending my heart pounding on overdrive. I tilted my hips, waiting, ready for him.

Brett moved my shorts to the side and plunged into me so hard, my body lifted into the air.

I swallowed a gasp. His swollen cock filled me, pulsing inside of me as he pushed to the point of uncomfortable. He lifted me higher into the air, the pain turning into a delicious roar as he held me suspended.

"You wanted raw. Real. *Me*," he growled before lowering my feet to the floor.

I nodded, slapping my hands against the wall as he slowly pulled out of me. "Please."

He gripped my hips, his thumbs moving to the folds of my pussy. He spread me open as he thrust into me hard. "Feel me fuck your hot pussy."

"I feel you everywhere." I whimpered, my body shaking during each rough impact.

He pushed his cock deep, filling me before he pulled out completely and took a step back.

My sex pulsed, throbbing as if he was still inside me. I looked over my shoulder and watched him wrap a hand around his length. His white shirt was unbuttoned revealing the chiseled torso of his hard body. A treasure trail of brown hair delved deep between his powerful thighs that made my mouth water.

"Take off your shorts and bend over." His gaze met mine. "I want to see how wet your cunt is."

I took a breath, and did what I was told, placing a hand on the wall. I jumped as a finger ran over my core, reaching the tight opening in my rear. A moan escaped my lips as Brett rubbed the puckered area.

He licked his thumb and pushed it through the barrier before slamming his cock into my pussy at the same time. He was deep and I felt him everywhere as he used my body for pleasure.

The area between my cheeks burned with delicious pain as he pumped into me.

He pushed his thumb deeper, matching the rough movements of his length.

I whimpered, shaking around him as a tingle spread through my body.

"Come on my dick, lover. Give me your orgasm," he demanded.

The hard deep strokes of his length mixed with the pumps of his thumb made an explosion of ecstasy burst from the pit of my being. I screamed, pulsing and shaking around him as he sped up his hips.

"That's it. Let me hear how good I make you feel," he husked, gripping my hips. He pushed into me hard, lifting me onto the balls of my feet.

I slapped the wall and gasped. I could feel him to my womb. Deep in my core. My body stretched for his size, squeezing him in a vise-like grip as he fucked me hard.

Brett gripped my hips, digging his fingers into my flesh like he couldn't get enough.

I could feel his cock swell inside of me.

"Come, lover. I want you with me," he husked tightening his hold on me as he continued to pump into my waiting heat.

181

My skin hummed. "Faster."

"Fuck. Me," he growled. His fingers squeezed.

Hot pain erupted through my body that set off an unexpected explosion deep inside of me. The orgasm was so hard, my legs shook, giving out beneath me.

Brett wrapped an arm around my middle, catching me before I fell. His hot breath was on my neck, heating my skin as he bit my shoulder.

Another wave of ecstasy rolled through me. I moaned his name as he pumped into me one last time. He came hard on a growl, filling me with his warmth. Knowing my body was making him feel that good set off another explosion deep inside of me.

Brett released me and lifted me over his shoulder.

I squealed as he brought me to his bedroom, his hand caressing my ass before giving a hard swat. A sharp pain spread through my body, heating my skin. A small moan escaped my lips when he dropped me onto the bed and crawled between my knees.

He gripped my hips and pulled me under him. "I love you. I will fight for you. When I stop fighting, that's when you should be worried, Evvie."

***

A FEW nights later, I was home watching movies with Ethan and Kane when Brett walked into my apartment. He looked forlorn, his expression blank as he headed down the hall.

I looked between Ethan and Kane and shrugged before rising to my feet.

"What the hell is his problem?" Ethan mumbled.

"Evvie."

I met Kane's gaze.

His eyes softened, his jaw tense. "Careful."

I frowned, confusion coursing through me and nodded. I met Brett in my bedroom, catching him pacing across the room. Closing the door behind me, I leaned against it and waited.

He slipped his hands into his pockets, his posture going stiff. He fidgeted, looking uneasy as he walked back and forth across my room.

"Brett?" I asked, bracing myself for his reaction.

His blue gaze met mine before he closed the distance between us and crashed his mouth to mine. The kiss was hard, bruising as he shoved his tongue between my lips.

My hands wrapped around his neck, pulling him tight against me.

He released me, leaning his forehead against mine, small bursts of air leaving his full lips.

"What's wrong?" I asked, my heart racing hard.

"It's my fault. My fucking fault," he mumbled.

I frowned. "What's your fault?"

He shook his head. "I am so fucking sorry."

My stomach clenched. "Why are you sorry?"

He grabbed my hands and kissed my knuckles before placing a soft peck on my mouth. "Just know that I'm sorry."

"Talk to me."

"I love you. I will always love you. I love every piece of you. You are the best fucking thing that's ever happened to me."

A lump formed in my throat at the desperation in his voice. "Why does this sound like goodbye?"

His mouth was set in a grim line as he cupped my face, staring intently into my eyes like he was memorizing me.

I grasped his wrists. "You're scaring me. What happened?"

He took a breath before placing a hard kiss on my mouth. "I'm breaking up with you."

I gasped. "Excuse me?"

He let go of me and reached for the doorknob but I stepped in front of it. There was no way I was letting him go without some sort of explanation.

"Move," he said, his voice firm.

"No. What the hell is going on, Brett?" I demanded, gripping his shirt.

He looked away. "I think we should see other people."

I shook my head. I couldn't believe what I was hearing. "Why? I love you. You love me. Why would we see other people?"

He let out a heavy breath and pinned me with his hard cold stare. "I cheated on you. Those pictures? They were recent. I fucked Claire while being with you." His voice was monotone, like his words were scripted.

What the hell? "I don't believe you."

In a quick move, he slammed me up against the door and leaned into my face. "I don't want to be with you."

My stomach rolled with fury. "You're a fucking liar. Why are you doing this? What happened? We can work through—"

"No," Brett yelled, punching a fist against the wall beside my head. "Forget about me. Move on. I'm not worth it."

"Yes you are! You are worth it. I need you," I cried, pushing him. "You said you would fight for me. Are we not worth fighting for anymore?"

His jaw clenched. "No."

My mouth fell open. I took a couple of deep cleansing breaths. Maybe something happened but we could work through this. We were strong. Our relationship was still new but I knew we could handle anything. "What happened?"

"I decided I'm not ready for a relationship." He took a step back and walked to my dresser, fingering a photo of the two of us in a small picture frame. I had a huge grin on my face and Brett was kissing my cheek. After having a little too much wine, I took a picture of us. Memories of the rest of that night reigned full force in my mind. We were happy. Or I thought we were.

I didn't know what was going on or what had happened since I saw him last night. He had been busy with work so all I could do was text him but he seemed fine. None of it made any sense.

"Brett, you are ready. We're both ready. We're ready for us," I said, walking up behind him. I placed my hand on his back when he spun on me and grabbed my wrist.

"No," he snarled. "I am not fucking ready. If you know what's good for you, you'll forget me, Evvie. Forget everything."

He moved to walk past me when I stepped in front of him. "If you're not going to fight, then I will." I pushed him back against my dresser. "I love you. I've always loved you. Yes, we

184

have our issues but no relationship is perfect, Brett. I don't know why you're lying but I need you."

"I'm not fucking lying. Get it through your head, Evvie. I cheated on you. I don't want to be with you. I'm not a one woman man."

A painful tightness erupted in my throat as I swallowed. "We were fine last night. What happened?"

He chuckled. "You obviously don't know me that well."

"You're a coward."

He glared at me, his eyes going cold. "I'm not a fucking coward," he said through gritted teeth.

"No? You're using any excuse to get out of our relationship but you're not telling me why."

His gaze searched my face before he let out a heavy sigh.

"I just don't understand," I whispered.

"You don't have to." He pushed past me.

I grabbed his arm, desperate to make him see reason. I don't care what he said. He did not cheat on me.

He stopped in his tracks and looked down at my hand gripping his arm before meeting my gaze. "Let go of me."

I swallowed hard at the harshness in his voice but stood my ground. "No. I'm not giving up on us."

"Evvie," he said in warning.

"I don't know what happened but I'm here for you. We can work through this togeth—"

He pulled me against him and crashed his mouth to mine before pushing me against my dresser. Items crashed to the floor as he ground his hips into mine.

I cupped the back of his neck, pulling him against me and wrapped my legs around his waist. My core throbbed, aching for him when my brain was telling me it was wrong. Wasn't the right time but I ignored that little voice and let him have his control of me.

The sound of his zipper lowering, sent a chill down my spine. He pulled off my pants and before I could even process what his next move was, he was deep inside of me, fucking me against my dresser.

I whimpered, my fingers digging into his shoulders as he filled me.

He devoured my mouth and pulled my head back, plunging his tongue deeper between my lips.

My heels dug into his ass, taking him as far as my body would allow, igniting a rumble from his chest.

Brett brought my knees up to my chest and thrust into me hard, still keeping our mouths locked. Our tongues entwined, danced, fought for ownership even though I knew that this was goodbye. I knew in the back of my mind that we were using each other one last time for pleasure but I couldn't stop it. I didn't want to.

The erotic words he usually had for me were silent as he pumped into me at a frantic pace.

His thick cock hit that special spot that was meant just for him and I cried out, a wave of ecstasy exploding deep from within.

He swallowed my cries, pushing into me hard before his dick twitched inside of me. He came hard, filling me.

All too soon he released me, leaving me naked from the waist down on top of my dresser.

I watched him right his pants, not meeting my gaze.

"Forget me, Evvie," he whispered.

Tears welled in my eyes. "Never."

His jaw tightened as he headed for my door. "You will."

In a quick reflex, I picked up something off of my dresser and threw it at the door just as he closed it. Glass shattered to pieces and a sob escaped my lips when I realized that I had thrown the picture of us.

Questions bounced around in my mind, my chest constricting. I couldn't breathe. A sob escaped my lips as I crashed to the floor. Even though we were both doing the using, shame and guilt tore through me.

He had only been gone a couple of minutes and already it felt like a piece of me had left with him.

Twenty Six

MY EYES were dry, no longer shedding the tears that had consumed me when Brett left my bedroom a couple of hours before. Voices carried through my small apartment as I lay awake, staring at the ceiling. I had cried myself to sleep only to wake every so often from nightmares of our fight.

A shiver ran down my back as I replayed the fight over and over in my mind. What did I do wrong? Could I have done something different to make Brett stay?

I texted him, even called him but got no response. None of it made sense. He fought for me in the beginning. Begging me to tell him how I felt about him and now that our feelings are laid out for both to see, he leaves me?

A tightness erupted deep inside of me and I huffed, turning over onto my stomach. I punched the pillow and let out a heavy sigh. The scent of musk and man invaded my nostrils making my body heat. My chest tightened, my vision blurring.

I rose from the bed and grabbed a pair of pajamas before heading to the bathroom. Once leaving my room, the voices of Kane and Ethan stopped me in my tracks.

"I warned her about him," Kane said, his voice sounding gruff.

Oh God. I prayed this wouldn't ruin the friendship between Kane and Brett.

"My sister is known for making shitty decisions when it comes to men," Ethan mumbled.

I scowled. No I wasn't. Yes, I had met some crappy guys through my dating years but not enough to become "known for it".

"I don't know what the hell happened but I know Brett loves her," Kane responded.

"Didn't seem that way tonight with all of the yelling."

"They weren't yelling for long," Kane stated.

"Dude, that's my fucking sister, asshole," Ethan said, his voice filled with disgust.

My cheeks heated. They heard us. I shook my head. Whatever. It's not like it would happen again anyways. A lump formed in my throat and I placed a hand on the doorknob

"Sorry, man." Kane chuckled.

"This better not ruin her or I will fucking kill him. I don't care if it puts me back in jail. If my sister doesn't get over this because of that asshole, the last thing he sees will be me."

An icy shiver ran down my spine at Ethan's words. I shut myself in the bathroom and took a shower. The hot water caressed my skin, easing some of the ache in my bones. I frowned and sank to the floor, wrapping my arms around my knees. Only one person could ease the full ache since meeting him weeks before.

Tears rolled down my cheeks as my heart felt heavy. I swallowed past the hard lump in my throat, trying to ease the shakes, but I no longer had control. I cried. Missing Brett. He had forced his way into my life and now he was gone. Wanted nothing to do with me. If I would have had a better explanation, I would be able to deal with it but why would he lie about cheating on me? Something had happened to force him to break up with me and even if we didn't end up back together, I was damned determined to find out what it was.

***

A WEEK later, after the club had closed for the night, I was putting bottles away. The hairs on the back of my neck stood on end and I knew that Brett was watching me. He always watched me. Maybe to see if I was okay. I didn't know but I knew that I wasn't okay. I needed him.

All week he didn't call me, text me or even talk to me at work. I was tempted to quit and get a different job but I couldn't.

Rumors flew around the staff that he already had a new plaything. It pissed me off but I ignored them.

"Hey girl, you okay?"

I startled and looked up at Tatiana. Her warm caramel skin glowed in the dim red lighting and her piercing gaze softened. I nodded.

She placed a hand on my shoulder. "If you need anything, I'm here for you."

I bit back a sob as tears burned my eyes. "I know," I whispered.

"I don't know what happened but I know he loves you."

"Apparently that's not enough," I mumbled.

"I know, honey."

I shook myself and put on a smile. "Whatever. I'm over it."

Her lips tightened and she pulled me into a hug. The scent of vanilla invaded my nostrils and I sighed returning the embrace.

"God, T. It hurts. It hurts so fucking much," I sobbed.

"I know." She squeezed me tight before holding me at arm's length. "Something good will come from this."

I scoffed. "Yeah. Right."

Tatiana smiled and looked over her shoulder.

I followed her gaze, instantly finding Brett. He was leaning against the wall, his arms crossed under his chest. My heart flipped at the casual but dominating pose.

"Take care of yourself, Ev," T said, giving my shoulder a gentle squeeze before leaving the club.

I sighed. Alone. With Brett. Memories of the last time we were alone at the club together made my heart stutter. I shook myself.

A vibration erupted through my body and I frowned. I reached into my pocket for my phone and saw Ethan's name flashing on the small screen.

I swiped my thumb across it. "Hello?"

"Hey sis," he mumbled.

"What's wrong?" It was nearly three A.M. Why was he calling so late?

"Dad's in the hospital."

My stomach sunk and I gasped. "What? Why?"

"I don't know anything yet."

He gave me the details of where he was and I quickly wrote them down before hanging up the phone. Oh God, please let our father be okay.

"Evvie, what's wrong?"

189

I jumped at the deep voice in my ear and looked up at Brett. "Nothing."

His eyes narrowed and he grabbed the piece of paper from my hand.

I huffed, ignoring the scent of musk and man that invaded my nostrils.

His gaze met mine. "I'll take you."

I scoffed. "I don't fucking think so."

"Evvie."

"No!"

His eye brow rose.

"You've wanted nothing to do with me for a week and now all of a sudden you do?"

His lips flattened. "I'm trying to help."

"Please," I said, rolling my eyes and grabbed my bag off the counter before storming down the hall.

"Evvie. Stop."

I stuck my hand up and gave him the middle finger.

"I'm not having you out in the city at this hour by yourself," he said, his voice hard.

I swallowed, ignoring the little voice inside of my head telling me not to argue. "Well I'm not going anywhere with you, asshole."

Once we reached outside, he grabbed my arm, stopping me. "I'm driving you."

My pulse sped as we stood there staring at each other.

Brett let me go and closed up the club. He walked by me. "Get in the car, Evvie."

My body tensed. I wanted to yell and scream at him. Beg him to have me back but the words froze on my tongue. I would not give him the satisfaction of having control over my feelings. I huffed and stomped to the passenger side of the red sports car. My heart pounded against my ribs the closer we got to it. This was the first time we were alone since he broke up with me. I couldn't do this. I couldn't be this close to him and not be allowed to touch him. I reached into my pocket and dialed the cab company. "Hi, yes can I get a cab—"

The phone was snatched out of my hand.

I spun on Brett and pushed him. "Give me my phone."

190

J.M. Walker

He stuck the cell in his suit jacket, his face passive like he was over this game. "No."

"Give me my damn phone, Brett." I pushed him again and reached for his jacket.

He grabbed my hands, holding them against him. "I am driving you to the fucking hospital."

"Why? Why do you care what happens in my life?" I asked, shoving out of his grip.

"Why wouldn't I care?" he bit out.

"You didn't care a week ago when you came into my apartment, broke up with me, fucked me and then left. Is that all you've wanted? After all of these weeks? I was some hole for you to fuck when you got bored, Brett?" The verbal-vomit poured from my lips. All of the pent up frustration and confusion over the last week finally left me. This was my chance to tell him exactly how I felt and I couldn't control it.

"Watch it, Evvie," he snarled and forced me to take a step back.

"Or else what? God," I shook my head. "I'm so fucking stupid."

A strong hand wrapped around my throat, forcing my head back. The grip on my jaw tightened, holding me in place as Brett pinned me between his hard body and the side of his car. "I don't like those words coming from your lips, lover."

"I'm not your lover anymore. So you don't get to fucking call me that," I said mockingly.

His jaw clenched and he leaned down, his mouth mere inches from mine. "Under normal circumstances, I would put that dirty mouth to good use."

My body heated but I ignored it. "Yeah well, when had our relationship ever been normal? Now let me go."

He stared intently into my eyes, holding my stare captive. "I miss you," he whispered.

My back stiffened. "You should have thought of that before breaking up with me."

"I told you—"

"You didn't tell me a damn thing. I don't know why you lied to me. I don't know why you broke up with me. I don't know anything."

Brett released me and opened the passenger door. "Get in."

"Are you trying to make me hate you?"

His deep blue eyes met mine, pain and sadness flashing behind his cold stare. "Get. In."

"'Cause it's working," I mumbled and slid into the car. Holding my head in my hands, I let out an exasperated sigh.

The sound of the door closing, shutting us into the car together, made my heart thump.

I knew he loved me but I also knew that there was a deeper part of him. Maybe I couldn't fill that need. "Why did you break up with me? Honestly. Did I not satisfy you?"

His gaze met mine. "Satisfy me? God, Evvie, you were the best thing that fucking happened to me."

"Then why are we not together, Brett?" I cried in frustration.

"I cheated on you."

A laugh escaped my lips. "You can say that as many times as you want but I know you didn't cheat on me."

"How do you know that? I use women. Fuck them and leave them and I don't care who I hurt in the end."

"You came back to me. Slept with me once and then—"

Brett looked ahead, his body tense. "I was drunk. You hit on me so I fucked you. I never turn down a piece of ass."

Before I could think twice, I slapped him. The sound of skin meeting skin echoed through the air, my palm tingling from the rough impact.

He turned infuriated eyes on me.

I lifted my chin, not backing down. "That's for lying to me."

His jaw tightened. "Evvie," he said in warning.

"Look me in the eyes and tell me you didn't enjoy these past couple of weeks. Tell me you don't love me."

He didn't meet my gaze or give me a response.

God, what was going on? None of this made any sense at all. "The more we keep doing this, the more I'm falling out of love with you," I whispered and wiped away the one lonely tear that had rolled down my cheek.

Brett's breath hitched but he didn't say anything.

***

"YOU DIDN'T have to come up with me," I said, glancing at Brett as we walked down the long white hallway of the large hospital. I crossed my arms under my chest when he reached for my hand. I backed away, not needing his touch.

Pain flashed in his eyes but was soon replaced by a coldness that made my heart thump.

I let out a heavy sigh, pulling a sense of strength from deep inside myself.

He shoved his hands in his pockets. "Your dad will get through this, Evvie."

I looked up at him. "You don't know that."

"No, I don't," he mumbled.

My steps sped up, anxiety flowing in the pit of my core. Lemon cleaner invaded my nostrils, burning my throat when I swallowed as we walked down the long hallway. I hated hospitals.

"You can leave. You drove me here like you said, so go home."

"I'm not leaving."

I stopped at grabbed his arm. "Just leave. Please. You have no right to be here."

He shrugged. "Maybe not."

"God, you piss me off!"

The corners of his lips twitched and he took a step towards me. "I'm here for you. I'll always be here for you. You may hate me. You may not even fucking love me anymore but you can't be here by yourself."

I frowned. "My brothers are here."

"That means nothing to me."

"Brett, just leave already." I huffed.

"Call me selfish. Whatever. I don't fucking care but I need to see for myself that you're okay before I leave."

"I'm not okay," I blurted. Tears burned my eyes. My chin trembled, my shoulders tight at the thought of my father not making it.

He took a tentative step towards me and slowly wrapped his arms around my shoulders. When I didn't pull away, he embraced me in a warm hug.

My emotions battled against the other as he held me tight. After everything we had been through and even though we weren't getting along, he was there for me. He was with me when I needed him most and I will always be grateful to him for that.

"What the hell is *he* doing here?"

I bristled at the harsh tone of Evan's voice and met his cold stare head on. I wasn't in the mood for his shit or anyone else's for that matter. "He's here for me so drop it, Evan."

Evan got in Brett's face, forcing us apart. "I'll hit you again, asshole."

"I don't think this is the right time for that, Evan. There are more important things to deal with first." Brett's voice was calm, collected as his gaze bored into Evan's.

My older brother backed down, a huff leaving his lips as he spun around and headed back down the hall.

I sighed as tears stung my eyes and brushed them away. Needing to find out what happened with my dad, I went in search of my jackass brother when Ethan came out of a room.

He smiled down at me and pulled me into an embrace.

"What's going on?" I asked, hugging him tight.

"Heart attack."

I gasped, my eyes widening. "How?"

Ethan looked away, his jaw clenching.

"This fucker got in an argument with him, that's how," Evan snapped coming up beside us.

"Excuse me?" I asked, gaping at my brother's.

Ethan's eyes narrowed as he took a step towards Evan. "That's not fucking true and you know it, asshole."

"Stop. Please." I placed a hand on both of their chests, keeping them separated. "Someone tell me what happened."

"They got in a fight over why he was in jail and how stupid he was for getting caught. Dad said that he taught him better," Evan said, keeping his eyes locked on Ethan.

"He did teach me better but I was sloppy. It's my fucking fault I got caught. No one else's. Mine," Ethan growled.

194

I didn't know exactly what Ethan did to get thrown in jail but I knew that they wouldn't tell me. I didn't care about that. I just wanted my family whole again. I wanted everyone to get along even if it meant bashing some heads together.

"I just want to know what's going on with dad," I stated, pushing Evan back.

"Your father is resting."

The three of us turned to a deep voice. A tall man sporting a white coat walked up to us, his green eyes softening.

He held out his hand to me first, his mouth lifting into a warm smile. "I'm Dr. Charles."

"Evvie," I said, returning his handshake.

Introductions were said between him and my brothers but I couldn't help the tumble of anxiety in my belly.

"How's our father doing?" Evan asked, his mouth set in a grim line.

"He's stabilized. We'll keep him here under observation for the next couple of days," Dr. Charles answered.

A breath left me on a whoosh. "Can we see him?"

"Of course," the doctor smiled. "I'll be back in a bit to check on him."

"You guys go in first," I told Ethan and Evan. Something held me back as I watched them walk into the room that held our father.

I wanted to see him. I wanted to make sure that he was truly okay but my body froze in place.

The hairs on the back of my neck tingled and my shoulders relaxed when a warm hand cupped the back of my neck.

"Are you okay?" Brett asked, rubbing his thumb up and down the side of my throat.

Was I okay? A part of me felt lost, like I had no control.

"I've been there, Evvie," he whispered.

I looked up at him, not realizing once again that I had spoken out loud.

His blue eyes were distant, like he was remembering a terrible pain. Losing both of his parents at the same time must have been awful. I couldn't imagine and then to have his real mother out there, doing God knows what, made my stomach cringe.

I wrapped my arms around him, squeezing him with everything in me. A lump formed in my throat as he returned my embrace. We may not have been together but he being there gave me strength.

"Will you come see my dad with me?" I asked, looking up at him.

He nodded and kept a firm grip on my hand leading me into the room where my father slept.

When we walked past the curtain, I gasped. Anxiety swirled in my body at the sight of tubes and wires covering my dad. He was still, his skin ashen as he rested.

I wanted out of there. My heart started beating fast against my ribs, pounding hard in my ears.

Rough calloused hands cupped my face forcing me to look into Brett's deep blue gaze. "Look at me, Evvie."

My breathing picked up and I squeezed my eyes shut. I couldn't control the raging urge to run. To bolt. To escape my problems. Daddy.

A sob left my lips, my heart threatening to explode.

"Damn it, Evvie. Look. At. Me," Brett said, his voice firm.

My eyes popped open and I focused on him.

"Listen to the sound of my voice. Breathe with me, Evvie." He took a breath.

I followed his actions and took several cleansing breaths of my own, easing the impending panic attack.

His handsome face relaxed and he pulled me into an embrace.

"Please don't leave me." I couldn't deal with this on my own. My brothers being there was one thing but having Brett nearby helped more.

"I'm not leaving," Brett said and kissed my hair. He wasn't leaving at the moment but he would after. I had no doubt about it.

He released me and pulled me around the curtain that surrounded my father. Ethan and Evan were sitting in chairs by his bed. I could feel their eyes on Brett. But I didn't care. I was only able to focus on the large man lying before me, sleeping so still in the hospital bed.

My dad, big bad Eddie Neal looked at peace. Like he was ready to go at any moment and if he did, he would be fine with it. But I wasn't fine with it. I needed him. He was the only man in my life that never intentionally hurt me. Yes, he going to jail hurt but that wasn't intentional. He didn't mean to cause me that pain.

Brett lied to me. Told me he cheated on me when he didn't. What the hell was I doing? Why was I putting myself through this torture? For love? The sex?

A sob escaped my lips as I fell to my knees. I grabbed my dad's hand, holding it tight in mine. My chest constricted, my throat tightening as I cried.

"Fuck," Ethan mumbled, his voice thick.

Shuffling sounded around me and I looked up to find myself alone with my father.

"Brett?" I called out, my voice small.

"I'm here, Evvie," Brett said, coming around the corner of the curtain holding a chair. He placed it behind me and sat, pulling me into his lap. He pushed us close to the bed, wrapped his arms around my middle as I held my dad's hand.

"You don't have to stay."

"I'm here for you." Brett rubbed small circles on my back, gently massaging his fingers into my muscles.

"Why?"

His eyes narrowed. "You asked me to come in here with you."

I huffed and turned back around. This wasn't the time or the place. My father needed positive energy flowing around him. Not my messed up relationship with my...with Brett.

"I don't know what we'll do if things take a turn for the worse," I whispered.

"You all are strong. You'll make it through this. Your dad is a fighter from what I hear."

A small laugh escaped my lips. "That's an understatement. I remember seeing him take down four cops because they handcuffed him in front of me." I smiled at the memory.

"God, Evvie. What you've been through."

I turned to Brett, keeping my hand in my dad's. "Don't judge him. My dad is a good man. He loves us. He just made some stupid choices and he had to pay for them."

Brett cupped my cheek. "I don't judge but I do worry when it comes to you."

My stomach quivered. "Why?"

He frowned. "Why do you keep asking that?"

"Never mind. This isn't the right time anyways," I mumbled. I brought my dad's hand up to my lips and kissed his knuckles, praying that my strength would pour into him. He needed to survive this. He had so much left to live for.

"Hey sis."

I looked up as Ethan walked back into the small area. I rose from my spot on Brett's lap and wrapped my arms around Ethan, giving him the hug that I knew he wouldn't get from anyone else.

His big body tensed before he returned the embrace, crumbling against me. "It's all my fucking fault."

A sob escaped my lips. "No. It's not."

"Evvie, I caused the heart attack."

I pulled away and stared up at him. "You listen to me. You did not cause this. You hear me?" I asked, my voice firm.

He shook his head, looking anywhere but at me. "You weren't there. It was fucking brutal, Ev."

"You guys have fought before."

"This was different. If he doesn't wake up from this…" His breath caught, his eyes glossing over.

A hard lump formed in my throat and I squeezed him, wrapping my arms around his hard waist. Guilt radiated off of him as I hugged him. I didn't know what to do. I didn't know what to say to make this all better

For the first moment in my life, I felt a tug, a pull at my soul to pray. I wasn't a spiritual person or even religious. My mom grew up in the church but stopped going when she met my father but at this moment, I was desperate. I would do anything to help ease the ache in my family's lives, so I prayed. For what I wasn't sure.

A deep guttural groan sounded from the bed.

A sigh of relief left my lips as I met the blue eyes of my father. His sapphire gaze, although tired and strained, bored into mine.

Thank you.

Twenty-Seven

BRETT AND I left Ethan alone with my father. As much as I wanted to talk to him, I knew that Ethan needed him more. The guilt that was eating at him needed to be eased before he could move on.

"Are you alright?" Brett asked me as we made our way to the waiting room.

"I guess." I flopped down in a chair and leaned my head against the wall, my emotions weighing me down.

Brett took off his jacket and placed it in his lap, bunching it into a pillow. "Rest."

I shook my head. "I can't sleep."

His deep gaze met mine. "Even if you don't sleep, it'll help make you feel better."

"Yeah right." But I took his word for it and leaned against him, resting my head in his lap.

His heavy arm curled around my waist while his other hand brushed my hair off my forehead. "I love you," he whispered.

A lump formed in my throat. *I love you, too.*

I wanted him to explain what happened. I wanted everything back to the way it used to be. I wanted him. The real, raw Brett MacLean.

I rolled onto my back and squeezed my eyes shut, tears rolling down my cheeks. I didn't want him to see me cry. I didn't want to expose the pain he had caused. All of the emotions since Brett had broken up with me and now everything with my father, crashed into me. It was suffocating as the sorrow gripped my core.

I sat up and leaned my head in my hands. I couldn't do this.

"Evvie," Brett whispered, wrapping his arms around my middle.

"Stop. Please. God, it hurts too much," I sobbed.

"I'm so fucking sorry. For everything. For me. For us. For your dad. I'm sorry."

200

I looked up at him over my shoulder and wiped my cheeks free of my tears. "I can't do this. I can't be near you and not touch you."

"I'm touching you right now," Brett said, swallowing hard.

My stomach hardened as nausea set in. I knew what I had to do. "I'm quitting the club. I can't be there. I can't be around you."

"Evvie, please. Please stay."

I shook my head and looked away, my heart breaking at the hurt in his voice. Yeah, well he hurt me too. But then why did I feel so damn guilty? "I'll stay until you find a replacement but after that, I'm gone. I'm moving on." I met his gaze. "I'm forgetting you."

He winced and he pulled away, releasing me completely.

A cold shiver ran down my spine as I watched him shut down in front of me.

His eyes turned icy, his jaw tense as he rose to his feet. "I wish your dad well." And with that he left. Again.

***

TWO WEEKS later, there was still no replacement at the club so I was forced to stay. I could just leave but that wasn't in my nature and I wouldn't do that to Jake or Tatiana. As much as I was pissed at Brett, I wouldn't take it out on my friends.

Paying little attention to the things around me, I willed myself to be happy. To move on. It's the reason I was quitting. It was too hard and I wasn't able to get my job done knowing he was around.

"Hey Ev, can you stock up Brett's bar?"

My back stiffened at the mention of his name and I turned to Jake, pasting a small smile on my face. "Sure," I said, my voice small.

Jake's eyes saddened as he handed me three bottles of rum. "I can do it if it's an issue."

I shook my head. "No. It's fine. Really." I had to face him sooner or later.

I turned and headed for the office that had changed my life. Memories of our first kiss forced their way into my mind. Brett's dominating control over my body as he kissed the hell out of me. God, would I ever get over him? Not if I stay here.

Once reaching his office, I lightly knocked on the door but got no reply. Brett had probably left early like he had been doing for the past couple of nights.

I took a breath and opened the door, walking into the office when I saw it. Them.

Claire had Brett pressed up against the wall, rubbing her lower half over his.

My stomach sunk, my heart raced as I stood there, staring at the both of them as she ground her hips into him. "Kiss me, Brett. I know you want me. You're not with that little whore anymore so what will it hurt?"

Brett pushed her back and snarled. "I don't want you."

"But you need me, handsome," she crooned, licking up the side of his neck.

They didn't notice me. Brett was too busy trying to pry her hands off of him.

"No, I fucking don't."

"You're stuck with me for life and I'll do anything to make you mine."

My vision clouded, a sob escaping my lips. Brett released her. His eyes widened when they landed on me.

Claire smirked and ran a hand down his chest. "As much as I don't like you, you're more than welcome to join us."

Bile rose to my throat and I shook my head in disgust.

Brett shoved out of her grip. "Get out," he told her before meeting my gaze.

Her face reddened. "I don't fucking think so. We were just getting started." She reached for him again.

"And now it's ended. Get. Out," Brett snarled, not taking his eyes from me.

"Bitch," Claire mumbled. "I'll be back Brett. You can't fucking get rid of me that easily."

"I don't care. Threaten me all you want. Just get the fuck out," he yelled.

Her eyes widened before she glared at him and gave him the middle finger. She stopped in front of me. Her eyes were clouded, glassy as she tried to focus on me. "He will be mine

202

again." She shouldered past me in a huff and slammed the door shut behind her.

My heart jumped and a breath left me on a whoosh. Why was I still there? I should leave. I needed to leave. To get out of there and never look back. I needed to forget him. He was the only man that could destroy me. Take away something that is mine. My heart.

"Evvie," he whispered, tentatively taking another step towards me.

I looked up into warm blue eyes that captivated me from the very beginning. His dark stubble lined his jaw, begging for the touch of my fingers. My gaze travelled down his body. His clothes were wrinkled and images of Claire rubbing herself against him made my stomach twist with fury. My vision clouded and the next thing I knew, I slapped him. "I hate you. I hate you for what you've done to me. I hate you for changing me." I punched his chest as a hard sob escaped my lips. "I hate you for making me fall in love with you." I continued punching him, my arm muscles burning.

He didn't stop me. He let me hit him as I cried out my anger.

"I love you," he said softly.

"No!" I screamed. "If you loved me, you would be with me!"

He reached for my hands but let them fall to his sides instead. His shoulders slumped and he didn't say anything. He had no response and that pissed me off even more. "I'm sorry you walked in on that."

"Why? Why would you go back to her?"

"I didn't," he mumbled.

I pushed him, punching him in the shoulder. "You could have had me if you only explained. God, I've thrown myself at you like an obsessed tween. I've begged, pleaded for you to tell me what's going on. So don't you tell me that you can't have me 'cause you haven't even tried."

"I'm so sorry. So fucking sorry for everything I put you through, Evvie," he said, his voice thick.

I covered my face and wiped the tears from under my eyes. "Do you know how I felt walking in on you and Claire?"

He looked away.

"No? 'Cause I'm going to tell you. I felt like you shoved your hand into my chest, grabbed my heart and pulled it out. You told me that I have that control. You also told that me that you were mine. 'Mind, body and soul, I'm yours, Evvie.' Do you remember that?" I asked, grabbing onto his arm.

He shoved out my grip but wouldn't meet my gaze.

"Do you?" I pressed.

Brett spun on me, forcing me to take a step back. "Yes, I fucking remember. I remember everything. About you. About us. Every breath, every sound, every fucking smell, I remember it."

Tears stung my eyes. "Tell me why you broke up with me then. The real reason."

"No."

I took a step in front of him and pushed him. "Tell me. I at least deserve that much," I demanded.

"I can't have you because I got her fucking pregnant," he yelled.

My mouth fell open at Brett's admission. Nausea settled in my belly, threatening to escape. My stomach burned. "You…you…" Oh God. She had a piece of him, forever. A piece that I wanted some day. We never talked about having children. Way too soon for that but I liked to think that it was a possibility.

Brett took a step back and pinched the bridge of his nose before meeting my stare. "I didn't cheat on you. I would never cheat on you. I'm so fucking sorry that I said that. I didn't know what else to do so I lied."

"Why didn't you just tell me?" I asked, still not quite believing what was happening. As much as it hurt, I would get over it. I would be there for him.

"I couldn't handle it if you broke up with me over my own stupidity, so as much as it killed me, I broke up with you instead," he said, scrubbing his hand down his face.

"You don't know me at all, do you?"

His eyes narrowed. "What the hell does that mean?"

I shook my head. "Do you think that little of me that you couldn't come to me with something like this? You slept with her before me. I would know that it wasn't because you cheated on me. I loved…love…" I huffed. "I trusted you."

204

"Did you? Did you really trust me, Evvie? I don't think so."

"Did you…did you use a condom?" I knew it wasn't any of my business but I needed to know if everything Brett had told me during the weeks we were together was the truth or not. I needed to know that we shared at least something. A first for us both that we had never given another person. My stomach clenched. Neither of us had been in love before and now that we were, we couldn't be together.

He took a step towards me and pinched my chin, tilting my head. "Yes. You are the only woman I've slept with where I didn't. The only woman I've actually felt."

I swallowed hard. "I wish you would have told me."

"I was scared. I'm not ready to be a father. I'm still learning how to take care of myself," he mumbled. With a shaky hand, he scrubbed it down his face.

My heart broke for him even though I was still mad. I had never seen him lose it. Never seen a side of him where he let people truly in until me. Even then, I wasn't sure if he was giving me the real Brett. "So now she has a grip on you forever."

Brett's jaw tightened and he pulled away, pacing back and forth.

"I feel like there's something else that you're not telling me," I whispered, leaning against the door. I crossed my arms under my chest but couldn't stay still. My nerves were shot.

He shook his head. "I'm done."

I nodded and pushed off the bar. With a heavy heart, I stopped once I reached the door to his office. "I think we could have worked through our trust issues." I looked at him over my shoulder, my vision blurring.

He sat on the couch, a glass tumbler of golden liquid swirling inside of it in his hand. "Would you want to raise someone else's baby?"

"If it meant being with you…" I took a breath, the tears rolling free down my cheeks.

Twenty-Eight

MY FATHER had to stay in the hospital for a couple of weeks thanks to him not listening to the doctors' orders about eating healthy. My brother's snuck him in fast food unbeknownst to me or else I would have put a stop to that.

With everything that had been going on, I forgot to call my brother, Everett. Not looking forward to the reaming out I would get, I let Evan call him instead. Ethan had called him as soon as our father was taken to the hospital but no one had called him since. He was not happy when I saw him at our dad's place the day he was discharged from the hospital.

"I can't believe none of you fucking called me to let me know that he's alright," Everett snarled. He roughly pushed his black-rimmed glasses up the bridge of his nose and glared at us.

We all sat at the small table in our old family home while we attempted to catch Everett up on everything. He may have been skinny and shy but he had the harsh Neal temper that the rest of us had.

"We're sorry," was all I could get out before Everett rose to his feet and stormed out of the kitchen and down the hall to our dad's room. A door slammed shut making my heart jump and I let out a shaky breath.

"God, I've never seen him so pissed," Ethan mumbled, his eyes widening in awe.

"He has every right," Evan said, clapping a hand on the back of his neck. Evan looked at me. "How are you doing?"

I knew he was asking about Brett. I hadn't seen him since the night I walked in on him and Claire. My stomach cringed at seeing her all over him, practically fucking him with her clothes on. After I left his office, he didn't chase me down, didn't beg me to stay with him and he'd been avoiding me ever since.

I shrugged. "I'm fine."

"Have you talked to Brett?" Evan asked.

"Why do you care?" I snapped.

"Really? You're going there?" Ethan said to Evan before shoving out of his grip and met my gaze. "We need you happy again. Do what you gotta do but I'm sick of seeing you this way."

"I don't know what you're talking about," I said, my voice monotone. When really, I felt like a zombie. Like the world could blow up in my face and I wouldn't care. All because one man wouldn't talk to me. Wouldn't fight for me. God, I couldn't stand this feeling of losing myself. All because of Brett MacLean. He had a firm grip on my soul. He possessed me but didn't want me. I couldn't stand it but I didn't let anyone else know this.

"You're a fucking liar," Evan took a step towards me and towered over my chair. "We need our sister back."

My jaw clenched and I crossed my arms under my chest. "I'm fine."

"Evvie, I may have been in and out of jail for most of my life but I'm not fucking stupid," Ethan said, his back stiff.

"Evvie," Evan stood behind me and placed his hands on my shoulders. "We don't like seeing you like this. If I could find him, I would fucking kill him for the shit he's putting you through."

"Not if I get to him first."

All of us turned to the deep gravelly sound of our dad as he stood in the doorway of the kitchen. He nodded at Evan and Ethan. "Let me talk to her."

Evan kissed my head and Ethan lightly squeezed my hand before they both exited it the small white kitchen.

My dad pulled a chair out from under the table and sat in front of me before grabbing both of my hands. "Tell me everything."

"You don't want to hear—"

"Evvie."

I swallowed at his stern voice and sighed, letting the words flow from my lips. I told him everything that had happened over the past couple of weeks. How Brett demanded my love. Knew me better than I knew myself even though it was such a short amount of time that we had been together. I also mentioned how Brett had brought me to the hospital to see him.

I met my dad's cold gaze. "I'm sorry."

He frowned. "Why the hell are you sorry?"

"For making more poor choices."

He sighed and wrapped his thick arms around my shoulders, holding me.

The scent of spicy cologne invaded my nostrils, sending a wash of peace over me.

"Are you worried that I'd be disappointed in you for going out with an asshole?" he asked, holding me at arm's length.

I nodded, biting back an onslaught of fresh tears.

"Sweet pea, I could never be mad at you, especially not over something like that." He chuckled. "I have to tell you. Brett reminds me a lot of me when I was his age."

My eyes widened. "Really?"

He nodded, his eyes going distant like he was remembering. It seemed like a lifetime ago since he was happy. Truly and honestly happy. He was way too young to lose someone. "Brett clearly made some shitty choices. Letting that Claire woman control who he loves makes me wish that she was a man so I could punch her fucking teeth in."

I gasped. "Daddy."

He grinned. "Well it's true. I don't like seeing my baby girl hurt. Yes, I agree that Brett was an ass but something tells me that there's more to it than the whole pregnancy thing."

"I've tried talking to him. He won't tell me anything."

My dad cupped my cheeks in his big hands. "Patience. I know you want everything to happen right now. You want a perfect relationship but I hate to break it to you, no relationship is perfect. You have to work at it. Make it fit for the both of you and after all this shit, everyone who tried to ruin you, that tried to destroy you, will be the losers in the end. And you know why, Evvie?"

I shook my head.

He smiled, his blue eyes warming. "Because you'll have each other and that makes every damn problem worth it."

Tears burned my eyes. "What if he doesn't want me anymore?"

"Sweet pea, that man loves you like no other. It's deep. Powerful. All consuming. I know it because I've been there. You do that to him. I may have only met him once but I know he loves you. Now you just have to ask yourself, is the love you feel

208

for each other worth it? Whatever the answer is, I will support you and be there for you to the end."

***

THAT SATURDAY night, I walked into the club to hand in my uniform and stopped in my tracks. Jake was behind the counter with another bartender. Someone I didn't recognize. The tall woman was slender, sun kissed skin and long dark hair that was pulled back into a tight pony tail. The tiny uniform fit her curves perfectly making me feel self-conscious about my white t-shirt and black pants.

I walked up to the bar and smiled when Jake noticed me.

He looked between the other woman and me and gave a small wave.

"Hi Jake," I said, stepping up to the counter.

"I didn't think you'd be back," he said, pulling me in for a hug.

"Just handing in my uniform." I was also a sucker for punishment.

"Hi, I'm Janice," the tall woman said, holding out her hand.

I returned the hand shake.

"I'm sorry, Ev. Janice is the new bartender," he said softly, his eyes glossing over.

I nodded, pasting on a smile. "No problem," I croaked. "It's been fun working with you, Jake."

He wrapped his arms around me and gave me a strong squeeze. "Stay in touch. No one can make martinis like you."

I laughed and patted his back. We exchanged numbers. We both knew that I wouldn't be back after that night.

"Girl, I cannot believe you fucking quit and didn't even tell me."

Shit. I turned to Tatiana coming up behind me.

She scowled and threw her arms around my shoulders. "Why? Why are you leaving me to fend for myself?"

I rolled my eyes at her dramatics. "You know why, T."

She huffed and looked over her shoulder.

I followed her gaze, my heart skipping a beat when I saw Brett leaning against the wall in his signature pose. Arms crossed

209

under his chest, fingers rubbing his jaw. The casual display of empowerment that left me wanting.

"I don't care what he says, he's gonna fucking miss you and I'll be here to clean up the pieces."

***

AFTER LEAVING the club, I headed downtown to a small coffee shop not wanting to make my way home just yet. My heart felt heavy. I already missed my co-workers and friends at the club. I hadn't worked there for long but they were like family.

"Have the night off, beautiful?"

My heart gave a start at the deep voice and I turned to find Mathis looming over me. "No. I quit."

"Too bad. I was getting used to seeing your beautiful face there. Mind if I sit?"

I shook my head and leaned back against the cushioned seat, tucking my feet under me.

"So how are you doing, Evvie?"

I rolled my eyes. "I know you didn't come here to make small talk, Mathis, so what do you want?"

He smiled, his gray eyes twinkling. "Perceptive. Your boyfriend agreed to go to New York and manage my club."

"He's not my boyfriend."

Mathis scratched his jaw, the corners of his mouth turning up.

I huffed. "Looks like you got what you wanted after all."

"Not everything."

My cheeks burned at his hidden innuendo. Not on your life, asshole.

"He still loves you, you know."

I scoffed. "If you're here to ruin my evening—"

"I know he fucked my sister-in-law and I know what she did."

I frowned. "What she did?"

Mathis pulled out his gold cigar case and placed it on the counter in front of him. "I can't say that I'm happy about my business partner having relations with a family member. Even

210

though she's not blood," he mumbled. "But that's out of my control. Regarding what she did, you need to talk to Brett about that."

I shook my head. "I don't understand. She's pregnant. That's not something that's just her doing. It's Brett's fault as well."

Mathis nodded. "I don't like my sister-in-law. Never have. Never will."

"Why are you telling me this?"

"I like you, Evvie and not just because I want to sleep with you. I know that will never happen anyway."

I gaped at him. "Well I appreciate your honesty," I muttered.

"But you are a good woman, Evvie Neal. Brett is a lucky guy."

"Tell him that," I said, picking up my coffee cup. I inhaled the dark sweet aroma and rolled my head from side to side. God, I could go for a good massage right now. The muscles in my neck tightened, shooting a pain down my spine. I let out a sigh. "When does he go to New York?"

"Wednesday."

My heart tightened. That was only four days away. "For how long?"

Mathis' gaze warmed. "However long is needed."

I searched his face. "What do you really want, Mathis? Besides getting in my pants."

He smiled but it didn't reach his eyes. "I want him happy. I want his head in the game. If I lose money, I won't be fucking happy."

"Is that a threat?"

He threw his head back and laughed. "No darling. But it can be. I'm not that bad of a guy. Just don't fuck with my money."

"Whether it's legal or not, right? Doesn't matter. Money's money."

"Is that what your daddy taught you?"

I looked away.

"Tell your father I said hi."

My eyes widened. "How—?"

"Be happy, beautiful. Misery doesn't look good on you."
And with that Mathis left the coffee shop.

I gaped after him, confusion coursing through me. He knew
my father? I shook my head. Doesn't really surprise me with the
shit my dad's been in.

***

I STARTLED awake as a bang on the door erupted through my
small apartment. I laid there on my couch momentarily stunned
as the sounds crashed into my head.

"Evvie."

My back bristled at the deep smooth voice that came from
behind the door and I took a minute to let it wash over me,
caressing my skin. It had felt like weeks since Brett had said my
name or even talked to me, for that matter.

"I know you're in there. Open up."

I rubbed the grit out of my eyes and rose to my feet. My
gaze glanced at the clock on the DVD player. 4:00 A.M. It was
fucking 4 o'clock in the morning and he wanted to talk now?

I trudged to the door and turned on the hallway light,
noticing a note on the table from Kane. I smiled to myself when
he wrote that he wasn't going to be home, knowing he was with
Tatiana.

I took a breath and opened the door, keeping the chain lock
in place. "What do you want?"

"To talk."

"Do you know what time it is, Brett?" I asked, fighting back
the urge to let my gaze travel down his suit clad body. God, he
was beautiful.

"Let me in, lover," Brett demanded.

"No." I attempted to close the door when his foot stopped
me. "Brett."

"Let. Me. In."

"Are you going to tell me what's going on? The real reason
why you broke up with me in the first place?"

His eyes narrowed.

I huffed. "Didn't think so."

212

"If you don't let me in, I'll fucking break down this door," he snarled.

"You wouldn't."

"Try me."

My body bloomed. Ah yes, now there was the Brett I had come to know but it was too late. "Fuck you."

He chuckled. "We've done that already, lover and look where it got us."

"That's not my fault."

"It's not my fault either. God." He shook his head. "Evvie, just let me in."

I looked up at him and glared. "Why the hell should I?"

"I want to talk."

I huffed and took a step back, releasing my hold on the door. "Move your foot."

He did as I said and I closed the door, unlocking the chain and walked to the living room.

A sense of defeat washed over me as the hairs on my body tingled. Did he want to fuck me one last time? Get me out of his system? Treat me like one of his whores? God, I was so stupid to think he actually—

A heavy hand grabbed mine and pulled me against a hard body.

I gasped, my hands landing on Brett's chiseled chest.

His heated gaze looked down at my lips as his mouth inched closer to mine and then the unexpected happened. Something I never thought I'd see, ever, coming from Brett MacLean. He fell to his knees.

Twenty-Nine

I COULDN'T believe it. Brett on his knees. Wrapping his arms around my waist. The man was going to beg and I couldn't keep my jaw from dropping.

"I'm so fucking sorry for everything. Please forgive me," he mumbled against my stomach.

"Brett." I tried pushing out of his grasp but it only tightened. "Let me go."

"No. I'm never letting you go."

He wasn't making any sense. One minute he wanted me, the next he wanted nothing to do with me and then he lied to me. Now he wanted me again?

"Brett, I can't do this," I said, my vision blurring. I pried out of his grip and took a step back.

His shoulders slumped as he looked up at me. His full lips were set in a firm line, the muscles in his jaw clenching. "I can't sleep, I can't eat, I can't even fucking work. I love you. I *need* you."

I shook my head and walked over to my couch, flopping down on it. Holding my head in my hands, my heart raced against my ribs.

"Evvie." Brett wrapped his hands around my wrists, kneeling at my feet. "I have so much to say but I don't know where to begin."

"I don't want to hear it."

"I need to tell you—"

"No!" My head snapped up. "I can't have you tell me you love me and then leave me. I won't go through that again."

"I don't want to leave you. I want to be here, with you, if you'll have me," he said, stroking my wrist.

I frowned. "I don't understand. Why now? Why after all of this time, Brett?"

He sat back on his haunches and wrapped a hand around my ankle, caressing his thumb back and forth over my foot. "I..." His jaw tightened as he struggled to find the right words. His deep blue gaze met mine. "Claire isn't pregnant."

My eyes widened.

"She had a miscarriage but honestly, I don't even know if it was mine. I guess I'll never know," he said, staring down at his hand on my ankle.

My mouth went dry and although I was relieved, my heart felt heavy for him. I knew he didn't want Claire to be in his life forever but it had been a couple of weeks so he must have been getting used to the idea.

"Is she okay?"

Brett met my gaze, his eyes warming. "As far as I know, yes. It was a week ago and I haven't seen her since."

I chewed my bottom lip, not knowing where to take this conversation. We needed to talk about us but I didn't want to stop him from telling me what had really happened. "Are you okay?"

He let out a heavy sigh. "Yeah."

I waited, a fluttery emptiness soaring through my belly. We sat there for what felt like an eternity when Brett rose to his knees and grabbed my hands. He kissed my knuckles before meeting my gaze, his eyes boring into mine.

"I'm going to beg for your forgiveness. I will make you fall in love with me again and if it's the last thing I fucking do, I *will* make you mine. Again."

As much as I wanted to believe him, I couldn't. Not yet. "You can't just say you're sorry and expect me to forgive you. It doesn't work that way, Brett."

"I know I'm a dick, possessive, controlling...whatever word you want to use and I know that I lied. But the love I feel for you is not a lie, Evvie," Brett said, his voice pained. "I wish you could forgive me now but I know that it takes time. Especially after all the shit I put you through. I don't expect that. I just—"

"Was that the only reason you broke up with me?" I knew the answer. I knew deep down in my belly that there was more to his story.

He grimaced and let out a deep breath. "No."

"I didn't think so. Tell me."

He met my gaze, a hint of amusement in his gaze at my demand. "Claire knows things about me. Threatened to ruin me and my career if I didn't break up with you. I was arguing with her one night when Mathis walked in and overheard everything. He's the reason I'm here. He put an end to her shit."

My heart lifted. "What things?"

"She said she would tell everyone about my dark sadistic ways. Tell people that I force pain on the women I sleep with. She," he swallowed hard, fury flashing in his gaze. "had bruises on her and threatened to report them to the police, telling them it was me that hit her. I didn't. I swear to fucking God I didn't."

"I know. I would never think that of you." I wrapped my arms around his neck, holding him tight against me. Claire. That woman was evil. My pulse pounded in my ears, my vision clouding over the threats that had almost destroyed us.

"I didn't. I would never abuse a woman," he said against my shoulder.

"I know," I whispered.

"I'm so sorry. I should have come to you in the first place. I shouldn't have tried to deal with this on my own." Brett pushed out of my arms and rested his head in my lap.

Running my fingers through the hair at his nape, I sighed. The tension that had built up on my shoulders since Brett had broken up with me, lifted off of me.

"Please forgive me. I'm begging you." He looked up at me. "I want you to be mine again."

"You hurt me, Brett," I said, my voice small.

His jaw clenched. "I know."

"But I'm…" I took a breath. "You can't leave me if you get scared. You need to come to me."

"I know and I will. I fucking promise I will." His eyes twinkled as he rose to his knees. He lowered his mouth to mine and when I thought he was going to kiss me, he hugged me instead.

My stomach clenched but I returned the embrace. The scent of musk and man invaded my nostrils, sending a flutter through my heart.

"I love you. I love you so fucking much."

"I love you too," I whispered against his neck.

"God, I don't deserve you."

I pulled back and cupped his cheeks. "We're in this as one. Together."

216

He nodded and kissed my forehead. "I will do anything to make you happy again. To make you trust me, forgive me, love me again. I will spend the rest of my life making this up to you, lover."

Tears welled in my eyes and I threw my arms around him making him fall back on his ass.

He returned my hug, squeezing me with everything in him. Like he was never going to let me go and I revelled in it.

***

I STIRRED awake feeling light and elated. The few hours I slept were the best I've had in weeks.

After our very long talk that brought us past the dawn of morning, we went to bed. Brett had kept his distance, not pushing me. Just he lying beside me had helped me through the night.

I turned onto my back and met his open stare, my heart flipping.

"Mornin'."

I licked my dry lips and swallowed. "Morning."

"Can I touch you?" he whispered.

Words froze on my tongue at him asking for permission. I nodded, needing the feel of his hands on me.

He reached a hand out from under the covers and brushed a finger down my cheek before running his thumb over my bottom lip.

An electric current travelled through me, but I laid still, needing him to be in control. To take what he knew we both wanted and craved.

A tingle ran down my spine at the soft caress of his finger over my mouth.

"Can I kiss you?" he asked, his voice lowering.

I watched as his tongue peaked out between his lips. The fact he was asking me for permission left me breathless. This was something I had never seen from him before. He was always in control. Took what he wanted, demanding my pleasure.

My heart thumped and all I could do was nod.

He cupped the back of my neck, his mouth inching towards me. He paused, hesitating before brushing his lips along mine.

The kiss was tender and was filled with so much love, tears burned my eyes.

His hot breath caressed my skin making my mouth part. I needed to taste him.

Placing my hand on his shoulder, I pressed my mouth hard against his.

His body relaxed, his mouth opening as our tongues licked and explored each other.

My core clenched with need, desire curling deep within me as the kiss deepened.

Brett rolled onto his back, bringing me with him.

My eyes widened as I straddled his waist. "Brett," I breathed against his mouth.

His hands roamed down my body before moving under my shirt to squeeze my hips. "I'm giving you my control."

My heart skipped a beat and I looked down at him. My fingers brushed his hair off his forehead and placed a soft peck on his kiss swollen lips.

"Make love to me," he whispered, running his hands up my body.

I sat back and pulled my shirt over my head.

Brett's eyes travelled down my naked body, heating my skin under their dark scrutiny.

Moving down the length of him, I knelt between his legs and pulled off his boxers, springing free his thick erection.

My sex clenched at the sight. Hard and swollen, the tip glistening with pre-cum.

I licked my lips and lowered my head, stroking my tongue up the velvety underside of his cock.

It bucked against my mouth, a hiss escaping Brett's lips as I slowly closed my lips around him.

The salty essence coated my tongue, sending my taste buds on overdrive. His hips thrust upwards, pushing him deeper into my mouth.

I moaned and wrapped a hand around the base before releasing him with a pop.

Our gazes' collided, as small bursts of air left his lips.

218

Keeping our eyes locked, I licked the tip and smiled when his breath caught.

"Lover," he groaned, the muscles in his neck straining. Despite his obsessive need for control, I revelled in how much he fought the urge to take it back.

I kissed his hip bone, the muscles hard under my lips. Grazing my teeth over the hard flesh, I nipped his skin gently, smirking when his cock jumped.

But as much as the need for play tried to take over and take things slow, it had been way too long. I straddled his hips, placing my hands on his tight stomach and ran my soaked core up his length.

"Fuck. Me," he growled, clenching his hands into fists at his sides.

A hot shiver ran down my spine as I repeated my movements, over and over again, torturing us both.

"Please. Shit. Evvie." Brett's eyes rolled into the back of his head and I took that as my chance.

Lifting my hips, I gripped his waist and lowered myself onto him. I whimpered, my body stretching to meet his size. He filled me to the hilt as I slowly circled my hips.

"Faster. Please, lover," he groaned.

Hearing him beg changed things. He had given a part of himself that I had never seen before.

My hips sped up. Sweat coated our bodies as I rode his cock, hard and fast, slamming my pelvis against his.

In a quick move, he sat up, swinging his legs over the edge of the bed and cupped my ass.

I gasped and cried out as my body opened to him, taking him deeper.

"Ride me. Fuck my dick like I've taught you," he growled, digging his fingers into my flesh.

He didn't move as I licked between his lips, devouring his mouth. I lifted myself up and down his length, panting at the delicious feeling of him inside me again. My fingers dug into his shoulders, scratching my nails into the hard contours of his back.

"That's it. Control me. Take what you want from me, lover," he demanded.

I circled my hips faster against him and threw my head back.

"God, you're beautiful," he whispered.

I smiled and placed a hard kiss on his mouth, wrapping my body around him. "Come with me."

He grunted and dug his fingers into the flesh of my ass.

I moaned as a sting of pain erupted through me.

A wicked smirk spreading on his face. "My little vixen likes some pain mixed with her pleasure."

I leaned down and licked along his jaw, the stubble scratching my tongue.

Brett tilted his head and leaned back on his elbows.

His breath caught but not enough to my satisfaction. "I think you do too, lover boy."

His chuckle sounded more like a groan.

I took the hint and trailed kisses down his chest, slowing my hips. I swirled my tongue over the taught peak of his nipple, his cock swelling inside of me.

A hiss left his lips on an exhale.

I smirked and gasped when he pulled my head back.

His eyes darkened. "I'm giving you one last chance to finish this. If you don't, I will give you the pain *your* body desires, lover."

He lowered his head to my neck, his teeth running over my skin.

I whimpered, a tingle shooting through my center.

"You like my teeth grazing over your skin. The anticipation flowing through your body wondering if I'm going to bite you or not." His sharp teeth trailed over my collar bone sending a jolt of electricity straight to my clit. "Do you want me to bite you, lover? Want me to give you pain with your pleasure?"

I cried out as his teeth bit into my shoulder, a sharp pain spreading through me. My pussy clenched around him at the unexpected sensation.

"Mmm…I think you like that. Now, fuck me. *Hard*."

Lifting my hips, I did as he said. As much control as he gave me, I knew it wouldn't last long.

I placed my hands on his chest and dropped onto him, a shiver running up my spine at the rough impact.

He groaned as I did it again. A tremor of ecstasy shot through my body. I screamed his name as pure bliss heated me from the inside out.

His cock swelled inside of me, pulsing his release, filling me with his warmth.

I crashed against him, my heart racing.

Brett ran his hands down my back, holding me tight. "I've missed you. So fucking much."

I kissed his chest and looked up at him. "I've missed you."

He smirked. "I can tell."

I laughed and sat up when he flipped me onto my back.

His eyes smoldered as he held my hands above my head and looked down at my body. He licked his lips. "I enjoy seeing my marks on you, lover."

My heart flipped at the deep husk of his voice.

His fingers ran down the middle of my body before wrapping around my throat. Possessing me. Taking the control that I so willingly gave him. He leaned down and licked my bottom lip. He closed his mouth around it and sucked hard.

My core clenched, my skin humming at the rough pull.

He growled. "*Mine.*"

***

"ARE YOU happy?"

I smiled at the concern in Ethan's voice. "Yes," I said, leaning my head back against the couch. The sound of running water erupted through my small apartment. I pulled my feet under me, my body twitching with each movement. I smiled to myself, remembering the hard way Brett used me after he took back the control.

"Are you sure?"

I laughed. "Yes, I'm sure."

He nodded. "So I guess you don't need me to kick his ass then?"

"No." I patted his arm. "We talked. Everything's—"

A hard knock on the door made me jump and I frowned. Ethan looked at me and shrugged.

I walked to the door and opened it. My eyes widened as I mentally smacked myself for not checking the peephole first.

"Why hello, Evvie," Claire purred, licking her gloss injected lips.

My stomach cringed. "What the hell do you want?"

Her green gaze looked behind me.

I turned my head.

Ethan rose from the couch and glared as Brett rounded the corner, running a white towel over his wet hair.

"Perfect timing," Claire whispered.

I frowned and stepped in front of her when she tried to come into my apartment. "I don't fucking think so. You need to leave. Now."

She sneered. "I forgot something here."

Bile rose in my throat. "Ethan, go get whatever she forgot please."

"Fuck my life," Ethan mumbled, his feet shuffling down the hall as he left the living room.

"So, you two cozy again? Getting reacquainted? Did he show you his dark, sadistic desires yet, Evvie?" Claire crooned.

I glared. "I think you should stop before I throw you out."

She rolled her eyes and looked down at me. "Bitch, please."

Ethan stepped up beside us and handed her a plastic bag. "We're done. Leave."

Her eyes narrowed. "Did Brett tell you that he got me pregnant?"

My jaw clenched. "I know every—"

She smirked. "I don't think you do. It's his fucking fault I lost the baby."

"We don't even know if it was his," I said, my voice calm even though my nerves were racing a mile a minute through my body.

"Oh it was his, Evvie. I made sure of it."

My eyes widened and I pushed her, not wanting any more of an explanation. "I have three brothers. I'm not fucking scared to hit a woman, bitch. Get out. Now."

Claire looked over my shoulder. "You're seriously not going to do anything? After all that we shared?"

"Why would I? You're dead to me," Brett said, his voice calm.

A gasp escaped her lips before her eyes went cold, deadly. "Fuck you all." She spun on her heel and left my apartment, slamming the door shut behind her.

A breath left me on a whoosh and I hugged myself.

"Evvie?"

I looked up at Ethan and patted his arm before turning to Brett.

He sat on the couch and placed his head in his hands. The air around him crackled.

Ethan squeezed my shoulder and headed down to the hall toward his room.

I walked over to Brett and sat beside him, placing my hand on shoulder.

His body relaxed under my touch. "I'm so sorry."

I shook my head. "You didn't know she would show up."

He looked up at me and sighed. "No. But I knew she wouldn't give up easily."

"Do you think she'll be back?" I asked, my heart thumping hard.

"At some point, yes."

I sat back and let out a deep sigh. As much as I couldn't stand Claire, a part of me felt sorry for her. Pining over a man who hated her. Did she really love him? Or was it a sense of possession? Maybe she felt a deeper need for him like Brett felt for me.

"Did he show you his dark, sadistic desires yet?"

I curled my fingers in Brett's and held him tight, placing my arm around his shoulders. My fingers lazily grazed his nape.

No matter what cravings he had that I hadn't seen yet, I would accept them. Or at least learn, but so far I embraced everything he threw my way. Willingly.

Thirty

LEANING AGAINST the counter, I waited in anticipation, nervous butterflies flying through my belly.

When Brett rounded the corner, our gazes collided. My body bloomed at the mere sight of him. He pulled off his suit jacket and placed it on the back of the chair before taking a step towards me.

"Cooking for me, lover?" he asked, brushing his knuckles down my cheek.

His question, although casual, was filled with so much lust, all I could do was nod. After being with him for weeks, you'd think I would get used to his demeanor. His commanding ways. The way he oozed with a sex appeal that still left me breathless and wanting.

He smirked, rubbing the pad of his thumb over my bottom lip. "Something wrong?"

I shook my head and turned around, distracting myself by preparing the pasta.

"Mmm...smells good," he husked, his hot breath scorching the side of my neck as he inhaled.

I smiled. "I wanted to surprise you."

Brett took a step back and leaned against the table. "I have a surprise for you, too."

I looked up at him. "Really? What?"

He winked. "Patience my little vixen."

I huffed.

He laughed and sat at the table, taking in the meal.

I joined him and as we ate in silence, we kept stealing little glances at each other. The savory spices of the tomato sauce that Kane had given me the recipe for, washed over my taste buds. God, he was a good cook.

"That, lover, was delicious."

My cheeks heated. "Thank you."

Brett took our empty plates to the sink and came back with two glasses of red wine. He grabbed my hand and pulled me to my feet before placing a hard kiss on my mouth. "You're the first woman that's ever cooked for me."

"Don't get used to it unless you want Kane helping me all of the time," I teased.

He chuckled. "You could make me a peanut butter and jam sandwich and I would love it, Evvie."

I raised an eyebrow as we sat on the couch.

He shrugged. "Too corny?"

"Never."

He smiled and placed his glass on the table before taking mine from my hand. "Do you want your surprise?"

My eyes widened. "Yes. Please."

"In my suit jacket, you'll find your surprise."

I took a breath, my heart thumping hard as I rose to my feet. I grabbed his jacket from the back of the chair and reached into the inner pocket, pulling out an envelope. I opened it and frowned.

Take off your dress and walk to the fireplace.
There you will find your next clue.

I looked at Brett.

He leaned back in the chair and smirked. "You better do what the note says."

My heart thumped. Placing the note down, I kept my gaze locked with his and pulled off my dress, leaving me standing in my bra and panties.

His gaze roamed down my body, heating my skin. "Simply beautiful," he said, crossing an ankle over his opposite knee.

I smiled and headed to the fireplace, noting a white envelope behind a picture frame. I picked it up, anticipation brewing deep in my belly.

Take off your bra.
Then turn around and bend over, slowly pulling down your panties.
I want to see how excited you are for your surprise.
--
Then come to me and get your next clue.

225

Holy hell. My core clenched almost as if he was actually telling me the instructions himself.

Reaching behind my back, I unclipped my bra, letting it fall to my feet and turned around. Taking a deep breath, I hooked my fingers in the waistline of my panties and bent over.

A growl erupted from the couch, giving me the courage that I needed to go on. I pulled down the panties and rose to my full height.

I sauntered to him and knelt at his feet.

His eyes blazed, taking in my naked form. "Want your next clue?"

My stomach flipped at the deep husk of his voice and nodded.

Brett pulled an envelope out of his shirt pocket and handed it to me.

I opened it and gasped. Two plane tickets to Mexico. "You're taking me on a trip?"

He grinned and leaned forward. "I'll be in New York for a couple of weeks but when I get home, we'll be leaving for Mexico."

"For how long?"

"Two weeks, lover."

A squeal escaped my lips and I threw my arms around him.

He laughed. "I take it you like your surprise?"

"Yes. Oh, thank you," I said, squeezing him.

Brett pulled me onto his lap. "Anything for you, lover. I meant what I said about making everything up to you."

I straddled his hips and started unbuttoning his shirt. "Brett—"

"I mean it. I love you." He placed a soft kiss on my lips. "After what we've been through already, we need some time alone. Just you and I. Think you can handle being alone with me for two weeks?"

My body heated. Two weeks. Alone. Together. Oh the things that we could do in that time.

"Lover."

"Hmm?"

226

Brett smirked, his eyes darkening as he ran his hands down my bare back. "What kind of dirty thoughts are going through that beautiful head of yours?"

"The same thoughts that are going through yours."

A wicked smile formed on his face. He cupped the back of my neck. "Lover, the things that you *think* I'm going to do to you are nothing compared to what I'm actually going to do."

My mouth went dry as I stared at him. "Tell me."

He brushed his lips along mine, sending a hot shiver down my spine. "You'll have to wait and see."

"Give me a hint," I breathed.

He trailed kisses down my jaw to my ear. "I suggest you don't pack a lot of clothes."

***

I WATCHED as Brett zipped up his suitcase, my heart heavy that we weren't going to be together for a month. Could I go that long without seeing him? Would it do us good? Maybe it would be better for us. The time apart could make us closer, stronger since it felt like the universe or the people in it were against our relationship. I missed him already and he wasn't even gone yet.

A heavy sigh escaped my lips when a warm mouth captured mine in a hard demanding kiss.

I moaned, breathing deep.

"Know that I love you," Brett whispered.

I wrapped my hands around his neck and brought him down onto the bed with me. "I do. With all of my heart. I do."

"Good," he said, trailing kisses along my jaw.

I curled my fingers through the hair at his nape, reveling in the feel of his hard body against mine.

"God, I'm going to miss you, lover."

Tears burned my eyes. "I miss you already."

Brett lifted his head, his gaze warming. "Even when we're apart, I'm with you." He placed a soft kiss on my lips. "I still can't believe you're mine," he said, softly.

My heart gave a start. "You made it pretty hard not to be."

A smug smile formed on his handsome face as he rubbed his pelvis over my core. "I told you that you would be."

227

My body bloomed when his erection pressed against my center.

"Every day, I'll think of you and every night, I'll dream of you," he said against my neck.

He was only going to be gone for a month but it felt like forever.

Reaching under my dress, he pulled off my panties. A zipper lowering, sent a shiver down my spine.

I spread my legs and gasped when he sank into me.

He brushed his knuckles down my cheek, placing tender kisses on my face as he slowly moved his hips. "I could live deep inside you."

I wrapped my legs around his waist, opening to him.

"I love you, Evvie Neal," he said brushing his mouth along mine. "And I will spend the rest of my life showing you how much."

***

A HEAVY hand gripped my inner thigh, squeezing me harder than usual.

Tears burned my eyes. I couldn't look at him. Brett was leaving today for New York. It was for a month. But it could be longer. We didn't know for how long but it was long enough. Too long if you asked me.

"Lover."

I jumped at the deep voice in my ear. "I don't want you to leave."

Brett sighed as we pulled up to a stop in front of the airport. The driver of the town car that Mathis had sent of us, stepped out and removed Brett's bags from the trunk.

"It'll only be for a couple of weeks."

With a shaky breath, I looked up at him. "Call me. Every night."

He smiled and placed a hard kiss on my mouth. "I will. I promise you that."

I was happy for him. Happy that he was gaining experience and being challenged to do better. Mathis had his shady moments but I was thankful to him for trusting Brett enough with one of his clubs.

"I can come with you," I offered.

Brett cupped my cheeks. "I wouldn't get any work done."

My body heated and I shrugged. "And that would be a problem because…"

He laughed. "My little vixen. I might just get desperate enough to fly you up there myself."

"Hmm…maybe I should make you desperate," I said, wrapping my hands around his neck.

His eyes smoldered. "God, I love you."

I grinned and crashed my lips to his, licking into his mouth.

He groaned and ran his hands up my back but all too soon, he pulled away.

Our chests rose and fell with ragged breath. It was going to be a long month.

Brett trailed kisses down my jaw. "I will make it so you dream of me every night."

"I already do," I whispered.

A wicked smile spread on his face before he leaned down and nipped my ear lobe.

My core clenched and I bit back a gasp.

"Lover, you will be an aching, panting mess by the time I get home," he husked.

My body bloomed. "How?"

He winked. "You'll see." He kissed my nose and opened the door. "I have to go."

My stomach twisted but I nodded. We stole as many kisses as we could in the short amount of time that we had.

I watched with a heavy heart as he disappeared into the airport. The time away from him would be torture but maybe being apart would be good for us.

After all of the shit we've been through, it was our turn to be happy and I would fight anyone that tried to change that.

Epilogue

Brett

I love her. More than life itself.

It's a love so powerful, it consumes me. Invades my thoughts, controls my actions. It possesses me.

From the first touch, the first kiss, Evvie Neal has been mine. She didn't know it then and now, three months later, here we are, in love. Deep and raw emotional love.

She tells me she feels the same. Shows me more instead. They are just words but every time she says them, those three little words rock me to the core. Brings me to my knees.

She is the only woman ever to get me to submit. To open up. To reveal myself. A part of me I've kept hidden since I was a child.

She is the one. Mine.

I—

My phone rang, startling me from my thoughts. I pressed the speaker and leaned back against the headboard of the bed. "Hello lover."

"I need you," Evvie husked. No *hello*. No *how are you doing?* Just a raw demand that left me hard and throbbing.

My body stirred. It was 3:00 AM. "Can't sleep?"

"No," she breathed. "I keep dreaming about you."

Hmm…interesting. "What were we doing in your dreams, lover?" I asked, putting my notepad on the side table.

"You were touching me."

My fingers tingled and I closed my eyes, imagining her smooth pale skin under the caress of my hands. "Where?"

"All over."

I smiled. "Be more specific."

"Brett."

"Tell me."

"I…" she hesitated. "I miss you."

"I miss you, too." It had been one week since I've seen her. One week, three hours and forty five minutes since I've touched my Evvie. My lover. *Mine.*

"I wish you were here with me," she said, sadness coating her voice.

"I'll be home soon and then you get me all to yourself for two weeks," I reminded her. "Now, you clearly called for something."

She sighed. "I wanted to hear your voice."

I chuckled. "You want something more than that, lover."

"Is your computer on?"

I frowned. "Yes."

The phone clicked and the sound of a dial tone invaded my ears. I was about to call her back when my laptop dinged.

Pulling it closer to me, the screen blinked with the video chat app. I smiled and answered.

"Hi, lover boy."

A grin spread across my face. Her sleepy gaze landed on me making my body heat. "Good morning, lover."

She giggled and pushed the computer back. "I have a surprise for you."

"Do you now?"

Evvie ripped off the black cotton sheets, revealing her smooth naked body.

My eyes widened, my cock lengthening to the point of painful at the beautiful sight. "Holy shit."

She licked her lips and trailed a hand down the middle of her body, stopping before reaching her bare mound. "Like I said, I need you."

"What are you doing?" I asked, biting back a groan.

"I'm imagining your hands on me. Making me feel good," she purred. "Touch yourself for me. I want to watch."

Leaning my head from side to side, the tendons in my neck cracked. This would be good. "Lover, you have no idea what you're getting yourself into."

"Brett, please."

Hearing her beg almost made me come right then. I cleared my throat and pulled off my boxer's. "Are you ready?"

She nodded, a grin spreading on her face.

I wrapped a hand around the base of my cock sending a shiver down my spine. "Stroke yourself. Fuck that tasty pussy with your fingers."

She moaned and did as I said. She pushed her finger inside her and stroked her clit with her other hand.

My hand moved up and down my dick, squeezing hard as I watched her pleasure herself, imagining her fingers were my own.

Her eyes fluttered closed, a breathless gasp escaping her lips.

"Eyes on me, lover."

Her gaze met mine. "Show me."

I pushed the laptop further down the bed until her eyes widened.

"You're so hard."

"For you, lover."

"Brett." Her hips lifted off the bed after each stroke of her finger. "I need you so bad."

She was close and I wanted to give her the release she needed. "Come for me."

Her fingers sped up while I fisted my cock.

"Oh Brett." Her body shook. A shiver ran down her body, her toes curling as she screamed my name.

A groan escaped my lips, my balls tightening as a tremor shot down my spine. I came hard, releasing onto my hand and stomach. It wasn't enough but it would have to do.

She panted, removing her fingers from her center.

"Lick your fingers, lover. Taste your orgasm," I husked.

Evvie smirked and stuck her fingers in her mouth, moaning as her tongue licked them clean.

God, that was enough to get me hard again.

She sighed. "Thank you."

"Thanks for the impromptu quickie, lover." I cleaned myself up and pulled on my boxers.

She giggled. "One week without you is way too long."

"Way too fucking long," I agreed.

"Brett?"

"Hmm?" I asked, my eyelids getting heavy.

Evvie curled into a ball and brought her laptop closer. "I love you."

My heart swelled. "I love you."

A cheesy grin spread on her face. "I love you more."

My body heated. "I love you deep."

A Note From the Author

Thank you to everyone who supported and stood by me. Also for being with me on the beginning of the intense journey of Brett and Evvie's relationship.
I hope you've enjoyed their story as much as I've enjoyed writing it.
Will there be another novel? Yes. Can't have a book without a sequel right? ;)

***

Turn the page for a snip it into Revealed by You (Torn #2), the continuation in Evvie and Brett's story.

Possessed by You

Revealed by You

Chapter 1

Four weeks, three days and eight hours had passed since I've seen my boyfriend. My lover, my best friend.

The day he left for New York felt like a lifetime ago and I couldn't wait to see him again. For him to come home. We weren't living together yet but I spent every day at his apartment, needing to be close to him in same way.

Although video chats were a new thing for us, it wasn't the same. I missed his touch, his hot breath against my skin, him telling me what he wanted and how he wanted it, the dark possessive air about him as he claimed me. Even though he was dark and brooding, demanding and controlling, I gave in willingly.

Working with Mathis Verlinden, a powerful billionaire that had his hand in everyone's pocket whether it be legal or not, was good for him. He gave him free rein of his club, *Club Rouge*, and as long as money was made, everyone was happy.

My phone rang, interrupting my thoughts as I leaned against the black town car and waited. The airport was bustling with people, heading to or from places but there was no sign of Brett MacLean anywhere.

I frowned when I saw that my oldest brother was calling me. "Hello Evan."

He chuckled. "Always so happy to hear from me."

"I am. Just not when I know a lecture is coming on." He was worse than our father. Having three brothers and a father and being the baby of the family, being myself was not always easy growing up.

"Now why would you ever think that I would lecture you?"

I rolled my eyes. "Seriously?"

"Have you talked to dad?"

My back stiffened. "No. Why?"

"He's going through some changes. Really odd stuff. Like he's going through man-o-pause or some shit."

I frowned. "He's been through a lot, Ev. A change in life is bound to happen sooner than later."

"Just call him or even better, go see him. I know he would love to spend some time with you."

"You still staying at his place?" I asked, my stomach clenched at the guilt I felt for not seeing our father in a while.

"No but I visit often."

"Thanks for making me feel way better, jackass."

Evan laughed. "Anytime, sis."

I shocked my head as he hung up and made a mental note to go visit our dad. After his heart attack a couple of weeks ago, I should really have been over more often.

I sighed. I wasn't going to let it bother me. Today was a happy day. Brett was coming home.

Butterflies flew around in my belly and I had to wipe my sweaty palms every so often on my thighs. God, I couldn't keep still. We talked every night and video chatted as much as we could but I needed more. I always needed more. His touch, his kisses, him telling and showing me how much he loved me.

The sun glowed in the distance on the unusually warm afternoon. I looked down at myself. Was I dressed okay? The white spring dress was long enough to leave some to the imagination but hugged my curves perfectly. Only having the cotton fabric on me and nothing else, sent a thrill down my spine knowing Brett would approve.

A heavy sigh escaped my lips and I bent over, putting my blonde curly hair up in a messy bun. The hairs on the back of my neck tingled making my stomach flip.

I slowly rose to my full height and found Brett standing a few feet away from me. His suitcase in hand, aviator sunglasses on his handsome face and four buttons on his white dress shirt unbuttoned. My body heated, my heart thumping hard against my rib cage at the mere sight of him. God, he was beautiful. Possessive and dominating, dark and sensual. Sex rolled off of him like a cool morning fog.

He pulled off his glasses, his blue eyes locking with mine. A smug smile formed on his hard chiseled face. A dark line of scruff covered his jaw and I couldn't wait to lick every inch of him.

My body bloomed, needing his hands on me after so long but I was frozen. Captivated by his deep blue stare as he stalked towards me.

He handed the driver his bags and closed the distance between us. He cupped the back of my neck, brushing his thumb over my bottom lip. "Hi *my* Evvie."

Hearing him claim me by just his words, made my insides quiver. "Hi," I breathed. My heart gave a thump. I swore my insides just turned to mush.

He smirked and leaned down to my ear. "I missed you." His lips brushed down the length of my jaw. "I've missed your smell. Lavender. Vanilla. Me."

My heart thumped hard, pounding in my ears as he held me restrained just by his hand and mouth. I couldn't move even if I wanted to.

His fingers brushed down my cheek before capturing my mouth in a hard demanding kiss.

My lips instantly parted, taking his tongue deep inside me. The feel of his warm lips against mine after all of these weeks ignited something I hadn't felt in a while. A wanton need spread through me. I gripped his shirt, pulling him against me. *More.*

A soft groan erupted from the back of his throat as the kiss deepened. Pushing me up against the side of the town car, his hold on the back of my neck tightened.

I moaned, sucking and pulling at his tongue.

He chuckled and released my mouth, trailing kisses down to my ear. "I've missed you so much, lover," he whispered.

"Hmm…I've missed you," I said, leaning my head to the side.

"I can't wait to do nasty dirty things to that hot little body of yours," he growled in my ear, inhaling deep.

I bit my lower lip to keep from panting and brushed a hand down his hard chiseled chest.

His teeth grazed up the side of my neck. "I can't wait to get you alone."

Possessed by You

About the Author

When J.M. isn't working her Monday-Friday 9-5 job, she's spending her time reading, writing and with the love of her life. She's an all-around Canadian girl. Born and raised in a small city.

If you don't see J.M. writing, you'll find her with her nose in a book. Whether it's her words or someone else's, she's drawn to it.

J.M. loves stories with Alpha broken males and that need to be ripped apart and put back together again. Men that fall to their knees over a wink or a giggle from their females.

Two things you will never find J.M. without; her cell phone and lip gloss. If she has both of those items, you have a happy girl.

Since starting her writing adventure in 2013, J.M. has met many people, real life, online, in her head and she loves every single one of them. Without the support from others, none of this would be possible and she's grateful for all that has been given to her.

Possessed by You

Other books by me:

Shattered Series (Erotic Romance with suspense elements):
Break Me
Always Me
Remember Me
See Me (coming soon)

Torn Trilogy (Erotic Romance):
Possessed by You
Revealed by You
Perfected by You

A Heart Story (New Adult)
In the Heart of Forever

***

Co-Authoring with Dawn Robertson
A Vegas Girls Tale (Erotic Romance):
Uncomplicated
Pursuit (coming soon)

Possessed by You

244

Find me:

Please don't hesitate in contacting me. I love to hear from everyone.

Facebook: https://www.facebook.com/jm.walker.author
Twitter: https://twitter.com/jmwlkr
Blog: http://www.authorjmwalker.com

Possessed by You

Turn the page for a sneak peek into a book that's due out in Spring 2014 from one of my new favorite authors.

Also, check out Hers, Finding Willow and Kink the Halls by Dawn Robertson. Be sure to drop her a hello.

Possessed by You

This Girl Stripped
Coming Spring 2014
From Author Dawn Robertson

The music blared in my ear as the lights damn near blinded me. My heels were far too fucking high, and the club was packed. Why did I ever think this was a good idea? *Oh, that's right! I am fucking broke.*

I keep telling myself I can do this. I try to ignore the cat calls surrounding the stages. One drunk in the corner whistles before throwing back a shot. Another man shouts at me to take my clothes off. Twenty four years old and instead of being a college graduate or settling down, I am taking my clothes off for money.

This morning the owner of the small motel I have been living in for three months gave me until the morning to come up with three hundred dollars or I would find myself homeless in Daytona Beach. Far from any friends or family. I *could* call my sister, Star. But that would mean admitting failure and that would *never* fucking happen. *I am just way too proud for that.*

I am snapped out of my thoughts when some scumbag with a matted beard grabs my leg.

"No fuckin' touching!" my voice fails me. Instead of the authoritative tone I was aiming for, I sound like the scared little girl I really am. I seductively dance back toward the pole in the center of the stage while I start to untie the barely there triangles of pink fabric covering my tits. I have never been shy about being naked, but everything about this screams *run for your fucking life, Paisley!*

"Yeah baby! Shake that ass!" The rowdy men get louder, and I take my thong covered ass to the front of the stage again. The Buckcherry song, Crazy Bitch is nearing the end and I wanted to get as many singles stuffed in my crotch before I walk out that door.

I drop down onto my knees, and thrust my pussy into the faces of three men sitting center stage. My hands slide over my bare breasts, and make their way for the tiny piece of fabric keeping me from being entirely naked. I rub my hand repeatedly over my cunt giving them the show of their lives.

When I open my eyes, I meet the most piercing set of blue eyes I have ever seen. His jaw is square. His hair is long and brown, pulled back into a lose ponytail at his nape. There is a long scar that runs under his eye, and when our eyes meet, he flashes me the most beautiful smile. I forget I am on stage in front of hundreds of perverts, and focus on him alone.

He is the man that will make my every nightmare come to life. I just don't know it yet.

Author Dawn Robertson:
http://eroticadawn.com
http://facebook.com/authordawnrobertson
http://twitter.com/eroticadawn
http://goodreads.com/Dawnrobertson

Made in United States
Orlando, FL
15 February 2023